UNEXPECTED

BAILEY B.

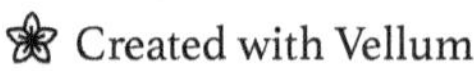 Created with Vellum

Maggie Mills, my best friend since freshman year, hip bumps me then leans against the cold metal lockers that line B-hallway of Ridgewater High School. Her lips pull down into a frown, disapproving dark eyes narrowed into slits. "You're staring again."

I force a smile and close my locker door, forgetting the chemistry notes I opened it for. I leave the spiral bound paper inside, tucked between my English Lit book and my Pre-Calc folder. Grabbing them now will affirm Maggie's suspicion that I was indeed staring at Liam Heiter and press play on her broken record of disapprobation. "Was not."

Maggie turns her head to me, ruby red lips pressed into a thin line. She's quiet, watching me scrutinize the expression that's clear as day on her face. Whatever she's about to say, I'm not gonna like it. "Did you hear? Liam asked Corah to prom. Seems like things are getting serious between them."

I choke on air that lodges itself in my throat but twist the sound into a meager laugh. Liam Heiter—my other best friend, the one I've known since diaper days—doesn't do serious. After a month, two tops, he breaks things off because those girls can't offer him what I can. Family. History. Love without strings.

I twist the cap off of my water and take a sip to settle my nerves. Corah Raymond is no different than any other girl who has tried to settle Liam down. She's the flavor of the moment, whereas what Liam and I have goes beyond words. Our relationship has built every year we've been together, blossoming from a booming friendship into an all-consuming fire.

"There's only one way to find out if the rumors are true." I toss my water bottle at Maggie and pull my phone out of my back pocket.

I talk a good game, pretending that watching Liam with every girl who bats her eyes in his direction doesn't bother me when, really, it does. Even knowing he and I are endgame, the few weeks his arms wrap around anyone else is nothing shy of hell. I live for the moments he's single, when we can be together.

"Lee." I beam at the nickname I've used since before I could form real words. The nickname no one else is allowed to utter. I hold my phone up, pretending to record our conversation for the school paper I don't actually write for. I take pictures that never get used, but the extracurricular looked good on my college applications. "Comment for the paper?"

Liam lifts one corner of his lips into a lopsided grin. My heart flutters as his emerald eyes lock onto my boring browns. High school has been his playground because, not only does his personality demand attention, his good looks attract it.

While Liam grew into a walking god of a man the past few years, I, unfortunately, stayed the same lanky beanpole I've been since middle school.

My boobs came in and filled a smaller than average bra in the seventh grade, but they forgot they were supposed to keep growing; my butt has just enough cushion not to hurt the chair; and my shoulder-length hair hasn't figured out that when I spend forty-five minutes straightening, blow-drying, and sticking every product known to man in it, it's supposed to stay pretty. I blame the Florida heat for that last one.

Most days I look like a pubescent boy who stuck his finger in a light socket. At least, that's what the popular girls tell me. The same popular girls who are currently glaring, wordlessly reminding me that I am not worthy of breathing the same air as them.

"Only for you," he declares. *Always for me.*

"Elaine," Corah purrs with a chastising smile.

I hate her. I hate her perfect hair and toned body. I hate how Liam's muscles flex beneath the sleeve of his shirt when he pulls her close. Most of all, I hate that she's at his side while I'm three feet away trying to remind her, and me, that I am important.

"Football season is over. What could the paper possibly need to know about my Lee Lee?" Corah pinches Liam's chin between her fingers and pulls his lips to hers. The kiss, while quick, is strategic. A show of power on her part. I may be reminding Corah that l was here first, but she's not going to let me forget that, for the time being, he's all hers.

My stomach twists inside itself. I usually avoid Liam when he's got a girlfriend, keeping our interactions to lunch and the confines of my bedroom. Watching him with someone else is too painful. And yet, here I am. *Keep it together, Lainey.* "Rumor has it, you two are going to prom together. Tell me how that happened."

Liam pulls back from Corah's embrace and narrows his ember eyes on me. He knows this conversation won't make it into the paper. This is for me. Sure, I could have texted to ask my burning questions, but I want to hear the truth straight from the horse's mouth. Most importantly, I want to hear that Maggie is wrong.

"I asked. She said yes."

"Don't be modest, Lee Lee." Corah giggles. She leans into him and presses her perfectly manicured fingers against his chest. Corah may be dense, but she is not stupid. She intentionally digs her knife deeper into my wounds, pouring salt with each detail I've yet to hear. "If the people want to know, let's tell them."

Corah pauses, waiting for Liam to spill the beans. When he doesn't, she is more than happy to do it for him. "It was last Saturday. Lee Lee picked me up for our night on the town like he always does, but I immediately knew something was off. He was too quiet in the car and he would barely hold my hand. When he pulled into Riverside, my gut twisted because everyone knows that is his breakup spot."

I stare at Liam, my eyebrows nearly kissing my hairline. Riverside Park is our special place and has been ever since we were kids. Every relationship he's been in has ended there because he was thinking about me.

Coming back to me.

I wait for some silent explanation as to why Liam would bring *her* there, of all places, but he breaks eye contact with me to stare at the floor.

"And when Lee Lee took me to the playground, I thought for sure we were done," Corah continues. "I followed him out of the car, practically tripping over my feet because my eyes were blurry with tears. And you know what he said to me?"

"What?" Please tell me, because I can't fathom why he would taint what's ours with this trash.

Corah looks up at Liam, doe-eyed, and smiles. "He said it was on the playground that he first fell in love."

Her voice fades into the background. My pulse thunders through my body with loud, almost deafening thrums. It takes every ounce of willpower I have not to run and jump into his arms but I can't do that because no one knows about Liam and me. We chose to keep our unorthodox relationship a secret so high school doesn't ruin it. Things between us aren't ideal and, to keep appearances, Liam has to date. I could see other people too, but it's easier if I don't.

I chew on the inside of my cheek and silently plead to the universe for Liam to look at me. He needs to understand that I love him too. I don't care if it took three years of secretly pining after him and another five years of him sneaking through my window late at night for us to get here, but his gaze is glued to the ground.

"That's why Liam took me there, because that silly playground was where he found his first love, and he thinks I might be his last." Corah clasps her hands over her heart, feigning happy tears.

Dark spots cloud my vision but, at the moment, they are better than tears because my internal compass is spinning in circles and I'm a ball of emotions. I want to scream. I want to yank Corah by the hair out of Liam's arms and then, of course, I want to cry.

Somehow I manage to force it all down—the humiliation, the self-pity, the tears, and most of all, the anger— and make myself smile again.

"I know what you're thinking." Corah beams.

No. I highly doubt she does. If she did, she wouldn't be hanging on the arm of the man I love. Gloating. She would be running, because the things I want to do to her, to both of them, aren't legal in fifty states.

"It wasn't a big, fancy promposal, but I didn't need anything glamorous. The way Lee Lee asked, it came from the heart and that's what matters most." Corah snuggles into Liam's side and looks up at him like the sun rises and sets because he exists.

I know it does in my world. I shiver, feeling a chill as the actual sun dips behind a cloud. Ironic considering we're inside and its rays barely shine through a nearby window. Still, I feel the darkness nonetheless.

"You must have been thrilled." I force the words out, dying a little with each syllable.

Liam finally lifts his emerald gaze to meet mine. There's no remorse in his expression. No regret for breaking my heart into unmendable pieces. What I find is worse.

Pity.

The bell rings and, for once, I couldn't be more grateful there are only two and a half minutes between classes. If I have to stand here any longer pretending to be happy for these two, I might crack.

"We should go," Liam says, leading both him and Corah towards A-hall. The same hallway I should be going to, but I can't seem to make my feet move. I can't bring myself to walk behind them and watch their happiness. Their circle of friends follow like peasants, eager for the attention of the king and his new queen. A few steps down the hallway, Liam looks over his shoulder at me. "See you tonight."

"Are you okay?" Maggie asks once Liam has turned down the hallway. Her hand reaches out and I watch her fingers touch my arm. I feel nothing. My mind is too busy keeping my head above the swell of tears and holding onto a smile to process anything else.

"Yeah." I don't sound like myself. My voice is strained, cracking with emotion while coming out an octave higher than normal. "I just need a minute."

Maggie's perfectly plucked eyebrows knit together. Everything she wants to say is written on her face.

Don't let that jerk get to you. He never deserved your heart. You'll get through this. Everything will be okay.

But she keeps it all to herself. "Alright. I have my extra credit thing with Mr. Alverson today, but I'll try to be done in time for lunch." She pauses, studying me a little longer. "Are you sure you're okay?"

I nod, my lips stretched tight across my face. The smile couldn't be faker, but Maggie doesn't press the issue.

After what feels like an eternity, she sighs and says, "Okay, sweetie. I'll see you later, but text me if you need me."

"Will do."

The moment she rounds the corner of B-hall, the dam of tears I was holding together with scotch tape and band-aids cracks. The world around me blurs into starbursts of light as liquid pain trails down my cheeks.

I run into the nearest bathroom and press my back against the wall. I squeeze my eyes shut, forcing myself to take slow, steady breaths—a tactic my therapist taught me back in middle school when my social phobia controlled my life. *Deep breath in. And let it out. One. Two. Three. Four. Five.* It takes a few cycles for the pressure in my chest to decrease and the waterworks to dry up, but eventually I start to feel better.

A toilet flushes in a nearby stall and the nervous needles under my skin spring back to life. I can't bring myself to look at who is here and see either a smug smile or a look of pity from someone who thinks they know what has happened. I keep my eyes closed, using eight-year-old logic of, *if I can't see you, you can't see me.* I know that's not how the world works, but it makes me feel better.

The lock on the stall door slides open, metal scraping inside itself. Heavy footfalls take one step, and then two, and then stop. Silence eats away at my resolve to stay strong and keep my eyes closed. After the slowest five seconds of my life, I hear, "You look like shit."

You've got to be kidding me!

My eyes snap open at the deep rumble that is uniquely Asher Anderson's. He's got this smoked-a pack-a-day rasp, paired with a knee-knocking baritone pitch. If Snow White and the Prince ever had a son, it would be him. With hair as dark as a starless sky and moon kissed skin, the contrast is striking. But then you add in his eyes, a unique shade of amethyst that looks too perfect to be real. The girls around here all but melt at the sight of him. Liam may be the shining king of the school, but Asher is the prince wearing a crown of thorns.

Asher crosses the bathroom to wash his hands in the sink, shaking loose water droplets into the porcelain bowl when he's done, never breaking eye contact. Not even when he reaches for a paper towel from the dispenser.

"Get out!" I scream, unable to take his patronizing stare any longer. This is the girl's bathroom, for Christ's sake. Is this man so heartless as to beat me here just to inflict more pain on my already bleeding heart?

Wouldn't put it past him.

I've known Asher all my life. Our parents—mine, Liam's, and Asher's mom—used to be friends. I still remember the stories my mother would tell about how excited she was for all of them to be pregnant around the same time. We were a heartbeat away from being a B-rated version of the sitcom *Friends* if they'd all had kids.

Until one day when everything imploded.

As for Asher and I, we drifted apart in the sixth grade after he ridiculed me for getting my first period. As if I wasn't embarrassed enough to find a puddle of red when I stood to jump into the pool, Asher let everyone at that birthday party know what happened. He even went as far as calling me shark bait the rest of the year. Liam thought it was hilarious. I wanted to die.

"Perhaps I should say the same to you." Asher chuckles and leans his ass against the sink, crossing his long, muscular arms.

My jaw drops. This is my bathroom. He... My train of thought is lost as I take in my surroundings. The girl's bathroom has more than two stalls and it doesn't have urinals.

No. No. No! I cover my face with my hands, mortified. *Could today get any worse?*

"It's cool." Asher guffaws. "No one will walk in on us, if that's what you're worried about. Besides, it looks like you need a moment."

I let my hands fall to my sides, shoulders rolling forward. I know Asher's sympathy will come with a price, but I do need a minute's peace. I don't know how I'm going to make it through lunch and my next three classes. Everyone is talking about prom and now all I'll be able to think about is Liam and his stupid promposal. "It's girl shit. I'm fine."

"You don't look fine." Asher steps closer, crossing the tiny bathroom in only three strides.

I turn my head and stare at a phone number someone scribed onto one of the stalls. I hate looking at Asher. He makes my stomach jump and my heart flutter at the same time. One a feeling of irritation. The other... not going there.

Asher tucks his knuckle under my chin and lifts, forcing my gaze back to him. "You look like Liam stomped all over your heart. Again."

I jerk my chin free of his grasp and lean back against the wall. I'd rather touch the cream-colored tiles with all its grimy germs than him. I hate him. I don't hate him. I don't know how I feel about Asher. Things between us are... complicated. Always have been.

"You don't know what you're talking about."

"Don't I though?" Asher chuckles again. The dude laughs a lot, only it never sounds happy. There's always a hidden layer of darkness or sorrow or something straight up evil in it.

Asher steps back and grabs the door's handle. He tugs it open and steps out, leaving me alone in the boy's bathroom. I take a second to gather my thoughts, grateful to finally be alone.

I shake my head, irritated that he thinks he knows me. Knows what I'm feeling. Asher doesn't know jack shit about having a broken heart. He's the heartbreaker, just like Liam, leaving a trail of tears wherever he goes.

I click the side arrow on my Roku TV remote, aimlessly searching through Netflix's movie options for the millionth time tonight, but nothing grabs my attention. I glance at the clock sitting on my desk. Tonight is dragging, only three minutes have passed since the last time I looked at it. When Liam said we would talk, I assumed it would be earlier than this. That me and our conversation was a priority.

Apparently not.

I groan and throw myself back on the bed. Nervous energy buzzing through my veins keeps me from sleeping even though my eyelids are heavy. It doesn't help that my brain won't stop micro-analyzing Liam's stoic expression during Corah's story either. How his glistening green eyes were trained on the floor. The way his lips turned down into a subtle frown. Nothing about what happened in the hallway felt right.

I sit up with a start, a jolt of adrenaline pumping through my brain. I think I figured it out.

Corah's tale was just a story.

In all probability, Liam didn't correct her because he didn't want to embarrass her. I let out a small relieved breath and laugh at myself for being worried. Liam is my best friend. He would never ruin Riverside for me, let alone settle down with someone like Corah.

I laugh at my own stupidity and lie back down, my mind finally at ease. Unable to find something of interest on TV, I scroll through Tik-Tok until my window slides open at quarter to one. I set my phone on the small table beside me and sit up, crossing my legs. *This is it.*

Liam twists his broad shoulders to fit through my window frame, then hoists himself inside. I expect him to greet me with a hug. To sit beside me in my bed, possibly even lay back, pull me into his arms, and talk until we fall asleep. He's done that so many times over the years, I've lost count. Not tonight. Instead, he chooses to sit in my desk chair, spinning it to face me.

The tiny hairs on my arms stand on edge. A feeling of unease I can't shake weighs me down. It's heavy on my chest, heart, and mind. I think I would prefer a night with my thoughts, drowning in wonder, than have whatever conversation Liam wants to have.

"Did you have a good night?"

Liam lets out a long sigh and slouches until his head rests against the edge of the backrest. He stares up at my ceiling, at what's left of the glow in the dark stars I never bothered to take down from when we were kids. A small smile tugs at his lips but leaves as quickly as it came. "I don't want to do this anymore, Lainey."

All of my senses hone in on the pang of fear rippling through me. I can't breathe, can't think, let alone speak. My mind races a million miles a minute, unable to focus on one thought for more than a second. Liam is not breaking up with me. He can't. He wouldn't throw years of, whatever you'd call us, away for a *girl*. A stupid girl he just started dating. This has to be some sort of misunderstanding.

"Do what anymore?"

"Us." Liam pushes up out of the chair. He runs a hand through his blonde hair, shaved on the sides, long on top.

I hated the cut when he first got it. I thought it made him look like a tool, but it grew on me. Now it's at the stage where it needs to be styled again. Even so, in his flustered state and through my emotional turmoil, I can't help that my heart beats for him.

"It's not fair to Corah."

To Corah?

My lips turn down into a frown. What about me? What about us? We never explicitly talked about it, but we were going to go to college together. Get married. Be that one percent that stays with their childhood sweetheart. My mind reels. Images of the future I've dreamed about since middle school flicker, then shatter into tiny pieces, along with my heart.

When I don't say anything, Liam adds, "I like her too much to hurt her. I think I might even love her."

I stop breathing, stop thinking, and force myself to meet Liam's gaze. His eyes are red and glassy. His lips turned down. He looks upset. Then again, he could be high.

"You can't love her," I whisper. Finding the courage to speak is like looking for a needle in a haystack; hard but not impossible. I clear my throat and force myself to talk louder. "It's only been a few weeks."

"It's been seven." He huffs.

I twist the edge of my comforter between my fingers, anxious to distract myself from the despair threatening to eat me alive. My diversion is not working. I still feel the pang of jealousy, the hurt of betrayal, and the desperation to make Liam realize that we belong together. "That's not love, Liam. It's lust and hormones."

Liam's dark brows pull together. Perfect plump lips press into a tight line. He's angry with me. He's never been angry with me, not even after I spilt red Kool-Aid all over his favorite baseball card when we were kids. Or when I slammed the window shut, breaking two of his fingers a week before playoffs last year.

"You don't know what love is, Lainey. You've never even dated."

"I love you."

I've said those words a million times in my head, but never out loud. My heart races, pumping my blood so fast I'm dizzy. I think I might die if he doesn't say it back. He has to say it back. When he does, he'll know; it'll hit him how perfect we are together and all of this nonsense with Corah will be over.

Liam lets out a strained breath. He steps forward and takes my hands in his, only there's no tingle with his touch tonight. No zing of excitement. "I love you too, Lainey, but not like I love her."

The tiny cloud of hope I was floating on dissipates. I pull my hands from his and hook my thumbs behind my back, under the elastic of my pajama shorts. I can't touch Liam, not if I intend to keep my composure. "I don't get it. What makes her different?"

Liam shrugs and walks over to my desk, then picks up a framed picture of us from last summer. We'd borrowed his dad's boat and spent the day drinking with his friends at the sandbar. When the sun began to set, we found a tiny island to explore before exploring each other for the hundredth time. It was perfect. We were perfect. *What happened to us?*

"I don't know. Corah just is, and I can't do this with you anymore." He looks up at me and sighs. "You don't cheat on someone you love."

Liam's words knock me back a step. Every whisper, every rumor I'd told myself wasn't true floods my brain.

He pities her. She's his fallback girl. She's pathetic; who lets her boyfriend kiss another girl? He'll never date her.

Anger fights its way through the pain, morphing into a hungry beast. I taught Liam how to kiss. I gave him his first blow job. I helped him figure out that when you finger a girl, you don't twirl it around like you're mixing tea. I should be the person he's worried about hurting because I came first! "But it's okay to cheat on me?"

Liam puts the picture back on my desk. He turns to me, confusion etched across his face and the fact that he's so ignorant pisses me off even more. "We were never dating, Lane. It's not cheating if you're not together."

All the air leaves my lungs. My jaw drops as I struggle to take another breath. Never dating? We've been hooking up in one way or another for the better part of five years! How can he say we weren't together?

"That's not fair."

"Isn't it?" Liam crosses his arms. He's not being facetious. In his mind, I honestly believe he thinks everything between us is kosher. That this conversation would have been as easy as breathing if I wasn't fighting for us the way I am.

Unlike him, my every breath is strained as I wrestle with the onslaught of emotions at war within myself. For the first time in my life, I'm seeing a side of Liam I don't like. I think I put him on a pedestal, dismissing the stories about him and the flavor of the week. I knew he was playing the bases with these girls, but I assumed the only person he was sleeping with was me. I should have listened to the rumors, heeded the bright red flags that told me I was being used.

Oh god.

We never used a condom. I'm on the pill, but that doesn't stop diseases. How many girls has he been with? How much has he exposed me to? My stomach twists and this time I think I might actually puke. "Get out."

"Lane." Liam's arms fall to his sides. He steps forward and reaches for me.

The thought of his hands on my body sends a bubble of bile into my throat but I swallow it down. I lean back and out of his reach. "Don't touch me, Gilliam."

Liam's jaw squares. He hates his full name almost as much as I hate mine. "Don't be such a bitch, Elaine. We were having fun. That's it."

My fists ball at my sides. I'm trying hard to keep myself together because if I yell, I'll wake my parents, and then we'll both be in trouble. My dad likes Liam, but I doubt that affection would last if he caught him in my room in the middle of the night.

If I cry, Liam will know how much he's hurt me and I don't want that, either. I force a smile and stand from my place on my bed. With a restrained touch, I take Liam by the arm and lead him to my window, resisting the urge to shove him out of it. "Liam, I'm tired. Go home."

He shakes his head but begrudgingly climbs out of my window. The pressure in my chest decreases with every inch that increases between us. Like this, I don't have to look up to meet his gaze. We're eye to eye. Equal, but apparently worlds apart.

"Want a ride to school in the morning?"

I nod, not trusting my words. I fear my voice will squeak and expose me for the mess that I am. I'm hanging onto my composure by a tattered thread. I need Liam to leave so I can hide under my blanket and cry.

Cry for all the years I've wasted and the lies I told myself.

I opt for a seat in the back of Ms. Honey's homeroom class instead of my usual middle row table. The chances of anyone knowing about my conversation with Liam last night are slim, but this is high school. All it would take is for him to tell Corah we had the talk and rumors would spread like wildfire. People are pathetic, finding joy in other's suffering, and I can't stand the thought of anyone looking at me today, laughing at me.

I hug myself, pulling the oversized 5 Seconds of Summer hoodie I found in the back of my closet around me. It's Liam's, which both infuriates and depresses me at the same time. I'm pissed at him for how things ended. How he so carelessly threw us away. But the reality of it is, I'm more hurt than mad.

I thought what we had was unbreakable. I assumed the years we'd spent together, both as friends and more, were as important to Liam as they are to me. I guess it's true what they say about assuming, because I was nothing to him. Just a warm body to hold when someone better wasn't available.

Maggie strides into the room a few minutes before the bell rings. Her gaze skirts over the tables when she realizes I'm not at our usual spot. She finds me in the furthest corner of the room a half-second later and frowns.

"So, it's true. Liam asked Corah to prom and dropped the L-bomb," she says.

The realization of how serious Liam is about Corah knocks the wind from my lungs. I didn't think he'd said those three words yet. Although, if he was willing to throw us away, it makes sense. I guess I just hoped he'd take some time to wallow at the end of our chapter. Maybe even think about everything he's given up before jumping feet-first into a serious relationship. What he ended between us deserves at least a day of mourning.

I need to stop thinking this way. Clearly, there was no us. No secret romance. And certainly, no midnight serenades. It was all in my head. "Yup. I'm sooo happy for them."

"Sweetie." Maggie sits in the open chair beside me and wraps her arms around my shoulders. "I'm so sorry. Are you okay?"

I fight back a horde of tears and force a smile.

I.

Am.

Fine.

I'm fine. Me, yeah, this girl here, she's fine. Completely unfazed that the guy I've been in love with since middle school doesn't feel the same way.

I.

Am.

Great.

How many times do I need to tell myself that for it to be true? "Do I look that bad?"

"Yes." Maggie grimaces.

I exhale a laugh that sounds more like a whimper, then fold my arms over the desk, and drop my head. My eyelids are heavy, but I keep them open, fearful of what I might see when I finally give in. I don't think I slept more than an hour last night. I couldn't. My mind kept pelting me with the names and faces of girls. Some I knew Liam to be with. Others rumored.

"Enough of this." Maggie tugs at the hood on my sweater until I stand and she grabs my backpack. "You're not going through the day looking like you got into a fight with a raccoon. Let's go, missy."

Normally I'd argue with Maggie. Most days, I don't wear much more than mascara and keep my hair in a high ponytail. I don't see the point in spending hours making myself look like someone I'm not. For one, I absolutely suck at makeup, and my hair never does what I want it to. But the main reason I don't bother with that stuff is because Liam says I'm prettier without it. Today, though, I'm too tired to fight her on it.

Maggie walks with the confidence of a model on the catwalk as we cross the room. She's beautiful, but not in a shove it in your face kind of way. She's smart and witty too, which is what attracted Russell, her long term boyfriend, in the first place. But it was her bravery that drew me to Maggie freshman year. She defended a girl she didn't know and put an end to her bullying. Maggie is my hero.

"We need to go to the bathroom," she says the moment the bell stops ringing. "It's an emergency."

Ms. Honey closes the door and turns to face us. She takes one look at me. A real look, not the quick glance over she gave me when I walked in, and frowns.

Do I look that bad?

"Is everything okay, girls?" Ms. Honey asks.

"No," Maggie declares, "but it will be. Please, Ms. Honey. You know Lainey. She's a good girl. I wouldn't be asking for a pass if it wasn't important. I mean... look at her."

I wasn't worried about how I looked until now. I glance down at my hoodie and notice how people avoid eye contact with me when I raise my gaze again. The familiar sting of tears pooling makes me bite my bottom lip. I can't cry. Not here, in front of eighteen people who are probably chomping at the bit to pull their phones out and record my breakdown.

After what feels like an eternity, Ms. Honey agrees to excuse Maggie and me and writes us a pass.

"Thanks, Ms. Honey," Maggie says, pulling me by the hand out of the room. "You're the best."

Maggie takes me to the locker rooms down C-hallway, beside the gym. She twists the spindle on her lock and pulls out a big, black, duffel bag. When she unzips it, I almost laugh. It's a freaking bedroom in a bag. There's a curling iron. A straightener. Six magnetic mirrors to make a haphazard full length one. A complete set of makeup. Extra clothes, shoes, and even undergarments.

"Sit," she orders, pushing me down onto one of the locker room benches. "We have some work to do."

Maggie spends all of homeroom straightening my hair to tame my flyaways, then twisting my thin strands into a loose side braid. She covers the dark circles under my eyes with concealer, then spends a solid fifteen minutes on my eyeshadow. She swaps my loose button-up with a fitted white polo and trades my baggy school pants with a thigh-length skirt. She even takes my sweatshirt—*Liam's sweatshirt*—because, quote, "it makes me look like a hobo."

When she's done, I look better than I did at homecoming, which is insane because I paid my makeup artist a small fortune to make me beautiful that night. Money wasted, because Liam was too busy with the girl of the moment to notice me.

A high pitched shrill bounces off the walls around us when the bell rings. Maggie grabs my shoulders and looks me dead in the eye. "You have three classes until lunch. Everyone will be watching you. Micro-analyzing every detail for the rumor mill."

Great.

"Don't give them anything to talk about. Smile. Laugh. Pretend the sun is shining out of your ass. If these people want something to talk about, let them wonder why you're not the same mess you were forty-five minutes ago."

Maggie pulls me into a hug and I bite my lip to keep it from quivering. I can't do this. I can't face the wolves alone. I need her by my side, to keep me strong, but this is the only class we have together. I feel stupid and used by that jerk I thought was my best friend.

"No more of that." Maggie pulls back and wipes my tears away before they run down my cheeks. "Liam doesn't deserve your tears. Besides, it'll ruin your makeup."

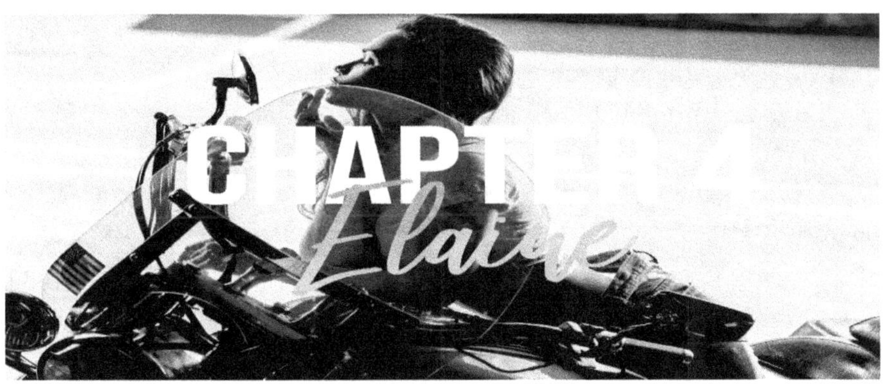

I raise my gaze from my phone at the sound of a plastic tray settling on the table. I've managed not to cry in front of anyone this morning. A miracle if you ask me. I held it together when I saw Liam and Corah making out against his locker and even when I overheard the whispers of people asking if I'd cracked yet.

Apparently, the whole school knew I was Liam's secret lover. If someone didn't, they do now, because damn near every time I turn a corner, the conversation stops. Rumors about me are spreading faster than I can wrap my head around and, from what I can tell, Liam is doing nothing to stop them.

I hate today.

"You look hot." Asher tucks his long, denim-clad, legs under the table. There's a full meal on his tray, including a bag of chips and a Coke, which is odd because he rarely eats at school. He pulls the tab of his soda then lifts the can to his lips. "I mean, you always look nice, but today... wow."

"Jeez, Asher, what the hell are you doing over here?" I don't have the energy to deal with him. I'm barely keeping it together as it is, and Asher will likely be the straw that breaks the camel's back.

Like Liam, he draws the attention of those around us merely by existing. It's part of the reason I chose to sit by myself today. At the furthest open table from our usual one that I could find.

"See, this is why I don't give you compliments." Asher smirks and sets the soda on his tray.

I have no food in front of me and can't stomach the thought of eating.

He notices and tosses his bag of potato crisps across the table. It lands an inch away from the edge and bumps into my elbow.

"I don't have the patience to deal with your crap today, Asher. What do you want?"

"I want to know why you're sitting all alone like a lost puppy in a cardboard box and not at our table." He points to where a few of the cheerleaders have perched in the center of the cafeteria. They laugh at each other's jokes while waiting for either Liam or Asher to join them. "Just because Liam pushed you to the back burner again doesn't mean you've been exiled."

I grab the bag of chips, having every intention of shoving it back at him, until my stomach rumbles. The pain from not having eaten anything since breakfast yesterday sets in and almost makes me double over. I begrudgingly open the bag of sour cream and cheddar and crunch on the first crisp I grab. It's like heaven in my mouth, making my stomach rumble again, begging for more.

"I've never belonged with you guys. I'm not pretty like those girls, or popular," I finally say.

"Don't do that," Asher demands, his tone serious and cold.

It startles me because, in Asher's mind, I either don't exist or have been put on the earth for his amusement. He takes pleasure in exploiting my quirks as entertainment for him and whoever else may be around. This new, somber side is unnerving.

"Do what?"

"Put yourself down. You're prettier than every girl in this room. Never forget that."

I'm taken back by the compliment. I can't tell if Asher is sincere or trying to make me feel better because of how shitty today has been. Either way, I don't need him or his faux sympathy. I roll my eyes then crumble the newly empty chip bag and toss it back onto his tray. "Yeah, okay."

Asher shakes his head, the brooding expression he's known for back in place. That's better. Too much more of this mood swing and I might be fooled into thinking he cares. "Why do you hate me?"

I look around the cafeteria, scanning the lunch line for Maggie's fire engine red hair. She should have been here five minutes ago. I exhale a sigh, realizing she probably got caught up with Mr. Alverson and that Asher is going to keep his I-am-your-friend charade going. "You ripped the head off my favorite doll."

Asher leans his elbows on the table. His dark brows pull together, amethyst eyes staring into my soul. I shudder from the intensity but don't look away because, in this light, they almost have a blue hue. It's not often that I'm this close to Asher, actually paying attention to him. They're fascinating.

"First of all, I never ripped her head off," he states so matter of factly, I would have believed him had I not seen him clutching baby Ariel's hair in his hands all those years ago. "And we were seven. Don't you think it's time to let that go?"

In truth, I have let it go, but in my head, this excuse doesn't sound as pathetic as admitting he hurt my feelings. That I haven't gotten over being called shark bait. "Liam told me I shouldn't be alone with you. He says you're not the guy you pretend to be."

Asher picks up his burger with both hands, then takes a bite. Something so natural as eating should not be so fascinating, but the man moves with fluidity and grace. I never noticed it before and can't stop watching. Grease drips onto the paper plate and down his arm. He sets the burger down, wipes his arm with a napkin, and then his mouth.

"Tell me, how is blindly following Liam working out for you again?"

He smirks and something inside me flutters. My lips turn down into a frown. I must be emotionally traumatized if I'm finding Asher appealing. I refuse to fall into the mosh pit of girls that lose their minds because they think he is attractive. Nope. Just nope.

I look around the cafeteria, desperate to find Maggie. She would set me straight and shoo him away. Unfortunately, it doesn't seem like she is going to make it in time for lunch today.

My ears perk at the sound of a boisterous laugh that's cut short. I look up and over to the door, already knowing what I'll find. Liam stares at me, teeth clenched, fists balled at his sides. While he and Asher may be friends, there's a lot of tension between them. Sometimes I wonder if they have the keep-your-friends-close-enemies-closer thing going on.

Liam shakes free from Corah's love hold and storms across the cafeteria. People move out of the way because they aren't used to seeing this side of him off the football field. They don't know about his temper. Liam works hard to hold the persona he's created.

"What the fuck are you doing over here?"

I can't tell if Liam is talking to me or Asher. It doesn't matter, he looks murderous. His broad chest heaves up and down with each strained breath. He ignores Corah as she snakes her arms around his waist again, focusing on me for an extra second. For a moment, I can't help but wonder, *Is he jealous*?

"Ellie and I wanted some alone time. Didn't we, El?" Asher winks at me and my cheeks flush against my will. Being alone with Asher is the last thing I want. He's arrogant and selfish and has a crude sense of humor. *What's he playing at?*

"You're joking." Liam all but laughs. He's pissed and it puts me on edge. Twice now he's gotten mad at me, and I don't know how to feel. Especially since I haven't done anything wrong. "Him? Of all the people you could be fucking, you chose him? What the hell, Lainey?"

"I... um..." A balloon inflates in my lungs pushing on the magic button that starts my waterworks. I hate that Liam is upset with me, but I'm crushed he'd assume I'm screwing someone else. Does he think I'm that easy?

"I knew it," Liam mumbles when I can't formulate a sentence that doesn't betray how hurt I am. He runs a hand through his hair, then shakes his head. His eyes narrow and fixate on Asher and I fully understand the phrase *if looks could kill*. "You're just like your mom. You can't stay away from what isn't yours."

I don't have time to figure out what Liam means before Asher stands, fists balled at his side, and says, "Really? You're going there?" He runs his tongue over his teeth and then makes a clicking sound. "Fine. You're no better than your dad. Can't keep your dick in your pants."

"Fucking prick!" Liam smacks Asher's soda off of his tray and the carbonated drink sprays everywhere. Once the can stops spinning, what's left of the brown liquid spreads across the table, sliding off the edge and into my lap. My lip quivers as I look down at the mess that was Maggie's clothes. Her skirt is soaked and her blouse is ruined, the front now more brown than white.

"Shit," Asher mumbles under his breath. He stands and pulls his shirt over his head, lifting his undershirt in the process and exposing the hard lines of his stomach. For a moment, I'm stunned. The man truly is gorgeous. His fair skin pops against the contrast of his black skinny jeans. Hard lines exasperate the six-pack he's worked hard to build the past few years. Every inch of him pulls me in, and those are just the parts of his body I can see.

Asher has always been attractive, drawing the eyes of anyone who dared to look. I'm looking. Really looking and wondering, *When did he go from boyish cute to 'make my heart race handsome'?*

"Put this on," he insists, tossing the white button-down at me.

I catch the fabric and hold it in my hands. I look to Liam for guidance because I'm more confused than a chameleon in a bag of Skittles. That was a mistake. Liam's neck flushes red as he removes Corah's arm again. She's trying to comfort him, to soothe him back into the calm, collected king the school knows. It's not working. He's too far into the red zone to see clearly.

"Lainey is fine!" Liam yells.

I am not fine.

I'm embarrassed, and wet, and sticky, and on the edge of losing the composure I've fought all morning to hold. Even though Liam is looking at me in a way he never has before, he made it clear last night that we are *just friends.* I shouldn't have to worry about him getting pissed at me for having lunch with Asher. He eats at our table all the time. Why is today any different? And why does he care if I put on Asher's shirt? Besides, if Liam hadn't thrown the soda, I wouldn't need something to cover up with!

I slip my arms through the holes and pull the button down over my head. Asher isn't a big guy but his shirt swallows me, falling halfway down my thighs, covering my skirt. His lingering scent swirls through me, a mixture of laundry detergent and beach musk. I like it. I don't want to, but I do.

The corner of Asher's mouth lifts into a delicious smile that makes my heart flutter. I bite my bottom lip and look from one boy to the other. I don't know what I'm feeling right now, let alone why. All I know is Liam has gone from looking like he wants to kill Asher to looking at me with disgust and a little bit of desire.

"Come on, babe. Let's get out of here." Asher rounds the table and puts his arm over my shoulders.

Liam grabs me by my elbow before we can take more than a step and spins me to face him. He is the only person to ever hold me the way Asher is and it has never been in public. Our moments were stolen in the dark, away from prying eyes.

"Lainey, what the hell is wrong with you? You hate Asher."

I don't hate Asher, but that doesn't mean there is anything going on between the two of us either. I know I should say something to let Liam know that Asher and I are just friends, and that is a stretch, but I don't want to feel like this anymore. Like my every breath hangs on Liam's approval or that my heart beats for his sideways glances. Maggie was right all along; I deserve to be more than someone's dirty little secret.

"Why does it matter? You and I are only friends. Remember?"

"I know that." Liam huffs. "I don't think Asher is good enough for you."

"Lee Lee," Corah coos. She steps in front of him, silently demanding his attention, but Liam looks past her. To us. "Don't be silly. You should be thrilled your two best friends are together. We can double date now!"

"Yeah." Asher wraps his arms around my waist and pulls me out of Liam's reach. "That sounds like fun. What are you two doing next Friday night?"

Liam's eyes widen and then narrow on me. His reaction to double dating makes me feel like I've been gutted under the weight of his gaze. I hate it. I want the strength I had moments ago, when I shoved it in his face that he lost all say in what I do when he made us friends. I want to be the girl who lives freely without worrying about what a guy who never gave two shits about her, until now, thinks. Most importantly, I want Liam to realize that he's an idiot for giving up on us and I think the way to do that is to make him jealous. That's the only logical explanation for why he's acting this way. He's jealous.

Maybe that's why I reach my hand up and cup the back of Asher's neck.

Maybe I'm intrigued by the tiny flutter in my stomach from when Asher's head dips.

And maybe, just maybe, I like the rush of adrenaline that shoots through me when Asher's mouth presses against mine.

The kiss lasts a fraction of a second, but it's long enough to set me on fire. Even without tongue, Asher's lips make me weak at the knees. I don't understand why he has this effect on me. I gave up on my pathetic excuse of a crush when he called me shark bait, but something inside me stirs to life. Something I'm not ready to acknowledge.

Asher pulls back and rests his chin on my shoulder. His heart beats wildly in his chest, and mine mimics the rhythm. Hard thumps. Fast thrums.

"Liam." He smirks. "It's been fun, but there are only five minutes left of lunch and I plan to use every minute of it. If you know what I mean."

Asher takes my hand in his. He pulls me out of the cafeteria and we run down the hallway then duck into the empty art room. He closes the door behind us and that bubble in my chest pops. An invisible noose wraps around my neck, tightening with every strained breath. Breaths that, no matter how big, never fill my lungs. So I take another and another. Each one faster than the last, but there's never enough air.

I kissed Asher.

I let Liam and everyone else in the cafeteria think I moved on with his best friend.

I. Ruined. Everything.

"Breathe, Ellie." Asher rubs his hands down my arms. I look into his eyes, tears streaming down my cheeks.

This can't be happening.

He seems so calm. Like everything that just happened is normal, but nothing about today has been normal. Normal was on another planet and we've moved two galaxies away.

Asher takes a large, exaggerated breath that spans the time of four of mine. He does that again and says, "Like this."

I copy him, forcing my breathing to match his slow and steady pace. After a few seconds, I feel my lungs fill and a weight lift from my chest. Today has been a whirlwind. I don't know which part was worse— coming to school looking and feeling like I'd been run over by a truck, pissing Liam off; or needing Asher, of all people, to talk me through a panic attack.

Asher pulls a couple of stools out from one of the tables and sits across from me. "You good?"

"Yeah." As good as I can be from emotional whiplash. I've gone from Liam's closet girlfriend to Asher's newest conquest in a matter of hours. At least only half of the rumors are true. I sit onto the other stool and brush my cheeks with the back of my hand. Black water stains my skin and I realize the makeup Maggie worked so hard on this morning is ruined. I run my fingers under my eyes then wipe them on my skirt. "Thank you."

"For what?"

"Going along with all that craziness." I flick my wrist, indicating I'm talking about what went down in the cafeteria. I don't know what to call it besides crazy.

Asher's lips lift in the corner. I like his smile, which is terrifying because, before today, it's been years since I've noticed it. "It's cool. It was kind of fun."

"Why'd you do it? Say we're together?"

Asher rubs his jaw. He stares at the wall behind me, searching his thoughts. After too many moments of quiet, he meets my gaze again. "I didn't like what people were saying about you today."

Panic slithers down my spine. I've known all day that my name has been in people's mouths, but no one has had the balls to say any of it to my face. Everything I know about today's gossip is speculation based on snippets I've caught. "What are they saying?"

Asher shakes his head and looks down at his hands. "Nothing. It doesn't matter, because everyone thinks you're mine now."

"We aren't together, Asher. Don't you think people will be suspicious when they see you hooking up with someone else?" They might not. I mean, I was Liam's backup girl. Their words, not mine. Would it be so hard to imagine that I could be the same for Asher? I shudder. I don't want people to think I'm an easy lay with no morals.

"We've only got a few weeks left, Ellie. I can keep my hands to myself."

"But why would you want to?"

I'm trembling, only I'm not cold. My nerves are shot and the thought of being Asher's girlfriend is too much to handle. Even if it is fake. We aren't enemies but we haven't exactly been friends either. Outside of lunch, I don't hang out with him. We have nothing in common. Asher spends all of his free time at parties or down some hussy's pants. Whereas I am either with Liam, Maggie, or at home.

I shake my head, finding more flaws with Asher's plan the longer I think about it. "Liam will never forgive us if we do this. Are you willing to throw years of friendship away over a fake girlfriend? Because I can promise you nothing is gonna happen between us, Asher."

"Liam's dad slept with my mom. He's not my friend, Ellie. He's my half-brother."

"What?" I stare at Asher in disbelief and wait for him to elaborate because there is no way in hell I heard him right.

Asher shrugs like this bit of information is no big deal. It's a HUGE fucking deal. A mind-blowing, world tipping big deal. Everything makes sense now. The fights with our parents. Them forbidding us to see Asher and yet, except for the third grade, we've always been in the same school. Even though he's never lived in the right school zone. "How long have you known?"

"Since the sixth grade. The only reason I was able to come to Ridgewater freshman year is because Derek pulled some strings. The old principal was adamant that, because I was out of zone, I couldn't come here." Asher pauses to flash a wicked grin. "I obviously got my way."

That smile falls and Asher rubs his palms across his thighs, then rests his hands on his knees. "Anyway, Liam likes to throw it in my face that I'm a home-wrecking bastard. I didn't intend to drag you into our drama, Ellie. I just wanted to know why you were sitting by yourself today, but then Liam started with his usual malarkey and I snapped. He acts like he owns you."

"He's just protective." I look down at my hands, embarrassed. Liam can be possessive at times, but it's only because he loves me. At least, that's what I've always told myself. Now, I'm not so sure.

"No, Liam wants to have his cake and eat it too, which is bullshit." Asher stands and pushes his stool back under the table. "What do you say?" He holds out his hand. "Be my fake girlfriend for the last few weeks of school."

I take it and let him help me to my feet. On a normal day, I'd be thrown by Asher's show of chivalry. Today, however, I think I've gone numb. He pushes my stool back under the table, beside his, but doesn't let me go. A tingle of... something... trickles through my veins. Like the kiss, I don't want to think about the feeling, let alone figure out what it means. "I don't know."

"Come on, Ellie. By now, the rumors will be running rampant. Everyone probably thinks we're together anyway." He pauses, waiting for my response but I'm still unsure. "Did you see the way Liam looked at us?"

"Yeah." I sigh, thinking about the way Liam's eyes narrowed on me. "He was pissed."

"No, he was jealous. Guys want what they can't have, and I publicly took you off the market."

I tuck both of my lips between my teeth and fight a smirk. I hoped as much, but hearing my suspicions confirmed is nice. I swallow hard, not sure what's crazier: Asher's suggestion or that I'm actually considering it. If Asher is right, and Liam was jealous of us, there is a chance I can get him to see me as more than... whatever I am to him. "You think he was jealous?"

Asher laughs and puts his arm over my shoulder. He opens the door with his free hand and we step out into the hallway. Those lips, the ones I just had on mine only minutes ago, hover close to my ear. He's putting on a show for anyone who's looking, and people are looking.

"I know he was."

I stare at the four text messages I've sent Liam, waiting for his reply bubbles to pop onto my screen. I've been standing at the front entrance of the school for thirty minutes with fleeting hope that we are okay. He ignores me, which I should have expected after what happened in the cafeteria, except now I'm stuck at school without a ride home.

I squeeze my phone between my fingers and glance over my shoulder at the football field. Maggie still has another hour of band practice. It wouldn't be the end of the world to wait for her, but then I'd have to explain how Liam stood me up and she'll sing the *get under someone to get over him* tune. Kissing Asher today was one thing, but sleeping with him, or anyone else for that matter, is a horse of a different color.

My ears perk at the sound of an engine. It's too loud to be Liam's Range Rover and no one at this school has enough money for a classic muscle car. Which means it could only be one thing: a motorcycle. And there is only one person in our school who rides one.

I take that back. Plenty of girls have ridden it. Too many, if the rumors are right. My stomach twists at the thought. Yet again, I refuse to acknowledge that the sensation is from anything other than disgust. I squashed what stupid feelings I had for Asher years ago. There is no way in hell I'm letting them come back. Especially now.

I stand up straighter as a flat black motorcycle roars into the front of the school parking lot, stopping less than a meter away from me. It's a nice bike. Sleek, with enough room for someone to ride on the back. Fire burns through me again as a faceless girl wraps her arms around Asher's waist. I bite the insides of my cheeks, using the physical pain as a distraction. I must be mentally exhausted to be jealous of an imaginary girl.

Asher's grey combat boots kiss the pavement as he balances the bike between his legs before killing the engine. I haven't seen him since we left the art room. Not surprising, since we don't have any classes together. He lifts the face shield on his helmet, revealing those amethyst eyes that capture my gaze. In this light, bright yet shadowed, they look like ice. Pale. Clear. With a hint of blue. "Need a ride?"

"Not on that death mobile."

"Come on, Ellie. It's not that bad. Here." Asher takes his helmet off and holds it out to me, white with blue flames. It matches his jacket, but not the bike, which makes me wonder, *Why?*

It's no secret that Asher lives on the sketchy side of the tracks. While most of the families at my school aren't rich, they're comfortable. Once you cross the tracks, however, things are bleak. It's common knowledge the families over there are barely getting by, which makes Asher having a motorcycle unusual.

I would think that *if* he saved all of his money to buy the bike, and *if* he was able to scrounge up the extra cash for a matching helmet and jacket, that it would go with the bike. I'm being stupid. Asher's attire shouldn't bother me, but it does. *Maybe Mr. Heiter bought it.*

"You wear this and I promise to go five miles under the speed limit," he adds.

I shift on my feet again, narrowing my eyes. I don't trust Asher. He's the kind of guy who has an ulterior motive behind everything he does. I don't believe for one second that our fake dating is to make Liam jealous. Until I figure out what it is he wants, I'm not agreeing to anything. Not even a ride home. "You're being oddly nice today. What do you want from me?"

The corner of Asher's lips lift and he chuckles. The sound is light and carefree, devoid of the usual malice dancing behind it. He holds his hand out, waiting for me to take the helmet. My fingers tingle. I want to take his hand in mine and hug him. I want to thank him for having my back today in his own preposterous way, but I don't.

Asher sighs and drops his arm. His chin tilts down but I can't read his expression. "I know I'm a dick to you more often than not, and for that I'm sorry, but I'm trying to do the right thing. Liam is a jerk and it kills me to see you so upset. So, please, let me take you home."

I look back at the football field where Maggie is. I should wait for her, but Asher has never apologized to me. Seeing him like this, so open and almost vulnerable, melts the wall of ice keeping him out. I'm probably going to regret it, but I say, "Okay."

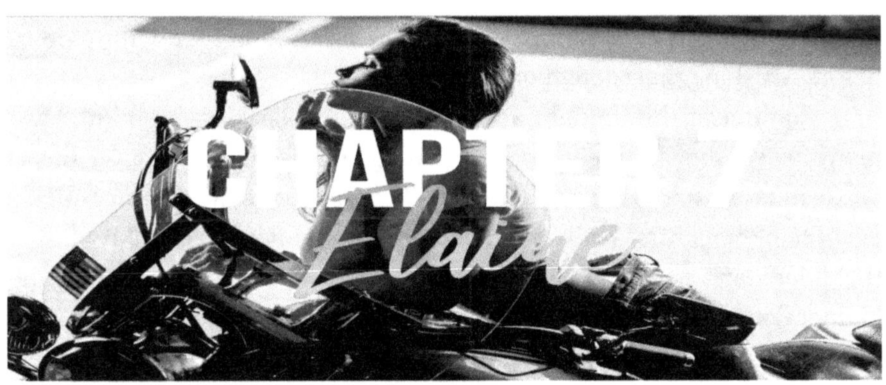

"**A**sher Blaine Anderson!" Mom squeals the moment his motorcycle comes to a stop. She hurries down the front porch steps, then bounces on her toes, waiting for him to steady his bike. She holds out her arms once both of his feet are on the ground and tugs him into a hug. She squeezes him tight, then pulls back and gives him another glance over, her grin stretching with each passing millisecond. "My, how you've grown."

"Hello, Mrs. Walker." Asher pulls the key from his ignition, silencing the roaring metal beast between his legs.

Riding a motorcycle wasn't as scary as I thought it would be. Asher kept his promise and stayed five miles under the speed limit at all times. I told myself that I wasn't going to be like those other girls and hang onto him for dear life. I did well to keep my word, but once we started going faster than fifteen miles per hour I didn't have a choice. It was either hold onto his waist or fall off. I'll never tell him, because riding on his motorcycle will never happen again, but it was kind of fun.

"You haven't aged a day." He grins. "What's your secret?"

I pull Asher's helmet off and catch Mom blushing. She shakes her head and runs her hands down her apron, which is stained with years of cooking mishaps. Most of which were mine. I can bake a mean batch of brownies, but I'm useless when it comes to real food.

"A smooth talker, just like your   " Mom presses her lips into a tight line, cutting herself off. "Would you like to come inside? We're having lasagna tonight, and I have enough to feed an army."

Asher smiles politely, eating up the attention and handling it like a pro. I wonder, *How many times has he done this?* Schmoozed with parents before whisking their daughters away.

I shudder at the thought and push it to the back of my mind. How many girls Asher has been with doesn't matter because, whatever this is between us, it isn't real. It's practice for *if* I agree to the fake dating thing.

"Thank you, Mrs. Walker, but I should probably get going. My shift at the diner starts soon and I can't be late." Asher holds his hand out for the helmet I'm hugging.

I give it to him, feeling stupid for holding it like that, and take a few steps towards the garage.

"Are you sure?" Mom pleads. She looks desperate, scared that she may never see Asher again.

I get it. I see Asher every day, but for her it's been ten years, and he's a far cry from the boy she used to babysit.

When he nods, Mom adds, "At least let me send some home with you. Your mother used to love my lasagna. That is, if you think she'll take it."

Asher smiles sympathetically. Mary Anne, Asher's mom, is a sore subject. Before their falling out, Mom was closer to Mary Anne than she was Rayna, Liam's mom. I never figured out why she chose Liam's mom over Asher's. It's a shame because over the last year, Rayna began to avoid us. Sometimes to the point of crossing the grocery store to get away. Now, we never see her.

"Mom is working the graveyard shift tonight and our fridge is on the fritz. Even if I did bring some home for her, it would probably go bad. Thank you anyway." Asher reaches out and touches Mom's arm. If he has any hard feelings towards her about the way things went down, he hides it well.

"Thanks for the ride." I quickly step towards Asher and hold my arms out for a hug.

I'm doing him a solid, saving him from any more awkwardness from my mother. Asher smiles, his eyes twinkling like stars in the sky as he leans in. I expected our embrace to be one of those awkward side hugs, but Asher goes all out. He squeezes me tight, with both arms around my waist, while pressing his lips to a tender spot under my ear. When he pulls back, I find myself wrestling with a strange, unwanted case of longing. I like the way it feels, being in his arms.

Asher puts his helmet on and pushes the faceplate up, exposing his amethyst eyes. "See you tomorrow, Ellie. Bye, Mrs. Walker."

Asher slides the face shield down again and brings his bike to life. Mom and I watch as he drives away and eventually disappears out of sight. I'm glad he's gone. I need some space to figure out how I'm going to make Liam come back to me without needing Asher's ridiculous plan. For some reason, I can't think straight when he's around.

Mom shakes her head, still thinking about Asher and mumbles, "He looks so much like his father did at that age, it's scary."

It's hard to picture Derek Heiter as a teenager. The man is so uptight, if you tried to shove a stick up his ass, it would break. I bite back a laugh but then remember, I'm not supposed to know the secret of Asher's father. "You know who Asher's dad is?"

"What?" Mom jumps and looks at me wide-eyed. "No. Of course not. Mary Anne never told any of us who he was. Why?"

I shake my head. I can't imagine Asher would lie about Derek. It would be too weird, but it's still hard to believe that Derek and Mary Anne had a secret affair. I didn't expect Mom to tell me the truth about Asher's dad, but it would have been nice if she could shed some light on the situation. "No reason, but you looked at Asher like you'd seen a ghost."

Mom chuckles and throws her arm around me, pulling me in for a hug. "It felt like it. The last time I saw you two together, you were waist high with pigtails. I vote you stop growing. I don't think I can take much more of it."

"Mom." I roll my eyes and pull out of her embrace. "You say that every year."

"And every year I mean it more."

We walk up the front steps and into the kitchen. I settle onto a stool while she goes behind the counter and pulls dinner out of the oven. Dad is working late again, as usual, so it's just me and her until about eight.

Mom sets a plate of lasagna in front of me, then leans against the kitchen counter with her own in hand. "Why didn't Liam give you a ride home? He picked you up this morning. Didn't he?"

I shrug, shoveling a forkful of noodles into my mouth. How do I explain to her what happened without spilling the beans that Liam and I have been hooking up the past five years in secret? I can't. I have no option but to lie. "I think he and his girlfriend were going dress shopping for prom."

Mom chokes on the food in her mouth. She sets the plate on the counter and opens the cabinet behind her. After grabbing a cup and filling it with water to wash it down, she gets her bearings again. "He can't be serious with that Corah girl, is he?"

I shrug and stab at my plate. Corah is the last person I want to talk about. She's going to prom. *Stab.* She got Liam to break up with me. *Stab. Stab.* She ruined everything! *Stab. Stab. Stab.*

"Are you going to the dance?" Mom asks, in a tone that implies she's up to something.

"No," I say, flatly. "I need a date to go to a dance." I'm not making the same mistake I made at homecoming. Being the third wheel with Maggie while watching Liam dance with another girl from my loser table for one is not my idea of fun.

Mom smiles again and picks up her plate. Like Mr. and Mrs. Heiter, she's always known Asher goes to school with us. Everyone just likes to pretend he doesn't exist and avoids asking any and all questions when it comes to him. Until now. "Asher is cute. You could go with him."

"Not if I plan on staying friends with Liam," I say, more to myself than to her. I slide off my stool and walk around the counter to put my plate in the sink.

Mom reaches out, taking my hand in hers. "Liam is a great guy, Lainey, and a good friend, but that's probably all he'll ever be. Don't let a man who doesn't see how great you are hold you back from finding happiness."

"Mom—"

"No, Laine." She shakes her head. "Don't 'Mom' me. I know you have a crush on Liam. I'm old, not blind. You're eighteen and have never had a boyfriend, and I think that's because of him."

She's right, but I don't want to admit it out loud. Liam and I may have only started sleeping together sophomore year, but I've been giving him all my other firsts since I was thirteen. Knowing he never cared for me the way I care for him is embarrassing. "Guys don't see me like that, that's all."

"Bullshit. You're a beautiful young lady and I saw firsthand how Asher looked at you."

Mom didn't see anything. Nothing is going on between Asher and me. We're friends. Barley. And yet, my stomach flutters to life. "How did he look at me?"

"Like you have the power to crush him."

Beep! Beep!

"Bye, Mom!" I yell, running out the door.

The music from Maggie's red VW Beetle hums through the closed windows. I open the door and my ears are assaulted by her latest obsession, Machine Gun Kelly. Don't get me wrong, I like a lot of the songs he's made, but Maggie has a problem. She can listen to the same song over and over for hours, trying to find new aspects to it. Hidden messages. Musical genius. I don't know what she's looking for. All I know is after the fifth time of listening to 'Bloody Valentine' in a row the other day, I was over it. She twists the knob on the stereo, turning the music low enough that we can talk when I get in.

"For the record, I'm mad at you."

Maggie being mad at me is as shocking as waking up to find the sky blue. She has had an opinion about my relationship with Liam since we were fourteen, landing me in her hot seat almost daily. Considering everyone thinks Liam and I are on the outs, I'm curious about what I've done now. "Oh, yeah? Why's that?"

Maggie huffs impatiently, like I should already know. "You didn't tell me that you and Asher are hooking up! I had to hear it from Marley, who heard it from Alandra, who heard it from Karen, who saw him give you a ride somewhere yesterday."

I groan and drop my head against the headrest. I haven't made up my mind about Asher's offer yet. In the unlikely event I don't go through with it, this newest rumor isn't going to help my reputation. "Do people have nothing better to do than gossip about me?"

Maggie shrugs, a shit-eating grin stretched across her face. "I think you two getting together is brilliant."

"We are not together," I insist because, despite what the whole school must think, we aren't. We're just... seeing if we can stand to be around each other for more than five minutes. Yeah, that's it.

"Too bad. You dating Liam's best friend would have been dope. It's the ultimate fuck you, in my opinion." Maggie flicks her blinker and turns right.

She's right, the situation would be the perfect f-you if Liam and Asher were actually friends, but they're not. They're brothers, and I haven't decided if that makes everything better or worse. "Asher asked me to be his girlfriend yesterday." Sort of. "But...I don't know."

Maggie slams on the breaks at the stop sign, launching me forward and into the dashboard, only to be yanked back by the seat belt. "Ow! What?"

I rub the sore spot on my collarbone then stretch the seat belt loose again. "Calm your tits, lady. It's no big deal."

"Lainey!" She gasps. "Asher has never had a girlfriend. It's a huge deal if he wants you to be his first."

I roll my eyes and try not to think about the heaviness of being Asher's first girlfriend. Fake or not, the implication makes my stomach flip. Just another reason why fake dating is a bad idea. "He's been with plenty of girls. I wouldn't be his first anything."

"Yeah, hookups, but none of those bitches got the coveted title of girl-friend." She groans and rolls her eyes. "What happened when Asher gave you a ride home? I know your mamma; she wouldn't let you just show up on the back of a motorcycle, no questions asked. Did she freak?"

The car behind us honks, forcing Maggie to focus on the road instead of me. She sticks her hand out the window, flipping off the person behind us, then shifts into gear again.

"No. Mom was fine with it. She seemed more excited to have Asher at the house than me."

"Weird."

"I know. Right? So, what's Russell up to lately?" I ask, trying to change the subject. Talking about Asher is almost as uncomfortable as talking about Liam. I love Maggie to death, but it's no secret she and I don't see eye to eye when it comes to boys.

Maggie groans as she turns into the school parking lot. "Russell who?" She finds an open parking space then reaches into the backseat for her backpack. I don't budge, instead opting to stare at her, expectedly, until she spills the beans. "We broke up."

"What?" I shriek, my mind spinning. Maggie and Russell have been in love with each other since Mr. Tabor sat them next to each other in Biology class freshman year. They are that perfect, nauseating couple you can't help but love to hate. "Why?"

Maggie shrugs and looks down at her hands. She puts up a good front, but I know she loves Russell. They were each other's first everything. That kind of love never dies. Everyone after is a band-aid, covering the wound of a broken heart, but never filling the hole. "What am I supposed to do, Lainey? He's going to Berkeley in a few weeks and I'm not."

I shake my head, not believing what I'm hearing. They can't break up. They're meant to be together, like Freddie Prinze Jr. and Sarah Michelle Gellar. "That's stupid, Maggie. People do long distance all the time."

"And it never works. Someone ends up ignored or cheated on." She reaches over and takes my hand, comforting me through her break up. "It's okay. Besides, what am I supposed to do? Follow him to New York?"

"Yes!" Finally, she's seeing reason! "Mags, there are tons of colleges in New York. You only need to get into one and you'll have your happily ever after!"

Maggie's lips stretch into a tight smile. She gazes out across the courtyard, probably spotting Russell as easily as I do. He stands with his friends, hands in his pockets, head hung low. One of the guys nudges Russell's shoulder and he looks up. He smiles, but there's no joy in it. Even from here, he lacks the charismatic presence that makes him so endearing. I feel bad for him. For her.

"Asher's bike isn't here," Maggie says, nodding towards his usual parking spot.

"Well, that's a relief."

It's not. Bees buzz inside me, creating an almost painful unease. I thought I was worried about how Asher would act around me today. Worried that he may try to kiss me again because I opened that door. I thought I was nervous to see how Liam would react to me after everything that happened yesterday. Turns out, those nerves are competing with the disappointment of Asher not being at school today.

"Miss me?"

I look up from the beef stroganoff I've yet to touch, unable to fight the smile that lifts my lips. I don't want to be excited to see Asher. We aren't friends, more like forced acquaintances, but the bees transcending into butterflies inside me don't seem to know this.

"I didn't think you were coming today. Your bike wasn't out front."

Asher tucks his long legs under the bench and sits across from me. He twists the cap off his water, swallows, then pops a stick of gum in his mouth. "Had some shit to deal with at home, but I'm here now. Isn't that what counts?"

"Just so we're on the same page, there will not be a repeat of yesterday," I warn. "If that's what you're looking for, then you might as well leave."

I've thought about the way Liam reacted to seeing Asher and me together all morning. As mad as Liam was, I think I can fix things between us if I cut all ties with Asher. Easy enough, considering we don't have that many ties to begin with, but I don't want to go back to what Liam and I were. I want to transcend into what we should have been all along—a real couple—and I don't think that's possible unless I make Liam change the way he sees me.

Asher's brows knit together. "Ellie, what are you talking about?"

"The kiss," I whisper.

He laughs, really laughs, and my heart soars. I haven't heard Asher this carefree since we were kids. There's nothing behind the sound except pure amusement. No hints of judgment, or ulterior motives, or wicked scheming. He leans his elbows on the table and glances at the apple on my tray. "You gonna eat that?"

I shake my head. Asher stretches out his long arm and takes the fruit. His breath wafts across the table, and I catch the distinct smell of beer lingering under mint. My smile falls, my mood souring with concern. "Are you drunk?"

Asher takes a bite and wipes away the juice that drips down his chin. "No, beautiful, not drunk."

My brows furrow as I take in his disheveled appearance. Messy hair. Wrinkled shirt. Asher wears the rugged bad boy look well. Today, however, he's teetering on hobo. "But you have been drinking."

Asher groans and tosses the half-eaten apple back onto my tray. "Let it go, El."

"Asher!" I whisper-yell. "It's eleven-thirty! What the hell is wrong with you?"

"Aw." He covers his heart with his hands and juts his bottom lip out like a lovesick cartoon character. "You care."

I roll my eyes. He's so frustrating. I can't believe I thought for a fraction of a second yesterday that he was cute. I'm pleading temporary insanity. Asher is not cute. He's annoying. "Rumors are spreading that I'm your girlfriend. I never agreed to that."

Asher flashes a cocky grin that says he's convinced I'm going to give in. I may. Might. In all likelihood, I'll probably agree to the fake girlfriend thing, but I'm not going to make things easy.

"Pretty sure you agreed when you kissed me yesterday. Or have you forgotten?" he asks.

Of course I haven't forgotten. I've only kissed two people in my entire life! I roll my eyes and pretend he doesn't get under my skin. I'm not even sure I should count yesterday as a kiss. Without tongue, it was more like our mouths hugged for two-point-five seconds. "Was I supposed to dream about it all night? It was a kiss, not some mind-blowing orgasm."

"I can give you one of those if you'd like." Asher wiggles his eyebrows and licks his lips.

My cheeks heat. Liam and I have been fooling around for years, but I can't say with certainty I've ever reached the big O. However, that doesn't mean I'm ready to jump feet first into bed with Asher. Even if he could make that happen.

"Hard pass." I glance around the cafeteria for Liam. I am sitting at our usual table today, hoping to mend the bridge I demolished yesterday. "You need to leave and put a stop to these rumors before it's too late."

"Why do you have to be so difficult?" Asher groans. "Why can't you be like 'thanks for having my back'?" He pauses, expecting me to thank him. When I don't, he grunts and adds, "Liam has never done anything for you. Hell, he's the reason half of the school thinks you're a slut. Me," Asher taps his chest with one finger, "I beat the shit out of the kids who were placing bets on how quickly you'd spread your legs for them. I saved you from a hell you didn't even know was coming by making you mine."

"Wait, what?" People are taking bets on me? Does Liam know? Is he doing anything to stop it? My stomach churns. Based on how things went down yesterday, both with the cafeteria and with the whispers, I'd say no.

"Just fucking forget it. I should have known you'd pick him," Asher mumbles. He shakes his head and pushes up from the table.

"Trouble in paradise?" Liam gloats as he approaches. His smug smile is aggravating. I get that he may not like seeing Asher and me together, but as my friend, he should want to see me happy, even if the happiness is fake. Not find my discord amusing.

"No," Asher growls at the same time I say, "Yes."

Liam's temperament changes. That smile I was just complaining about, it falls faster than a tower of cards on a windy day. He puffs his chest and shoves Asher back a step. "Did you hurt her?"

"Of course not. I'm not like you, dickhead." Asher guffaws.

"What the fuck did you say?"

"Guys, stop!" I can see where this is headed, and it's not good. Mixing Liam's short temper with Asher's lack of sobriety means we're one smart-ass comment short of a fight. These two have been pretty good about keeping their cool in public, considering they're half brothers and all. I don't know what things are like behind closed doors, when no one is around. Judging by the tension that's always looming, I'd say these two aren't as close as I thought they were.

There's chaos brewing in his eyes and it terrifies me. He's got a wild streak he keeps hidden, but we all know it's there. You can't grow up on that side of the tracks and not get your hands dirty one way or another.

"I said," Asher taunts, "I'm not like you. I don't make a sport out of fucking with girls' emotions."

Liam crosses his arms and chuckles darkly. "Right, you just get them knocked up and then pressure them into abortions."

Without warning, Asher swings, catching Liam off guard with a jab to the nose. Liam staggers back a step. Asher barely gives him time to find his footing before tackling him football style. Asher's shoulder rams Liam in the stomach and they slam into a trash can.

People stand and gather in a circle, chanting "Fight! Fight! Fight!"

I run to the nearest cafeteria monitor, a paraprofessional in her first year of teaching, who looks absolutely terrified. "Aren't you going to do something?"

The woman stands there, mouth slack, watching it all go down. It's no secret we are short-staffed, which is probably why there are only two teachers on lunch duty. I don't know where the other one is, but this lady is useless. I snap my fingers in her face. She blinks twice, noticing for the first time that I'm in front of her, then reaches for her radio.

"Uh, Ms. Grant to the office."

"Go ahead," someone replies through the speaker.

"We have a fight in the cafeteria," she says.

"I'm on my way," a different, deeper, voice replies. I recognize it as our assistant principal and nervous tingles take over. If Liam gets caught fighting, he won't be allowed to go to prom, which should make me happy. Except, I know he wants to go and, no matter how mad or hurt I am, I still want to see Liam happy.

I push my way through the crowd of people to the center of the circle of onlookers. Asher has Liam pinned. He's sitting on his lap, throwing blow after blow into Liam's face. Liam has his arms up, attempting to offset the impact, but it's not doing much good. His lip is busted and his left eye is already swelling shut.

"Stop!" I scream, but my words are lost among the sound of the crowd. I take a breath, trying to settle the nervous energy searing through me, and step closer. "Asher, stop."

He still doesn't hear me. I take another step and reach for his arm, thinking I can pull him off of Liam. Asher's arm rears back and his elbow smacks me in the nose. Pain clouds my vision with purple spots. I cover my nose with my hands, adding pressure in an attempt to alleviate the sensation rippling through my face. It doesn't take long before my hands are covered in blood. I must have made a noise because Asher stops hitting Liam and looks over his shoulder at me.

"Shit, Ellie, I'm so sorry!" Asher climbs off of Liam and cradles my cheeks in his hands. His thumb brushes over the side of my nose and I flinch. He grimaces. I want to be mad, but can't. Asher's eyes are a pool of pain that runs deeper than him accidentally hitting me. He looks miserable.

"You three," Mr. Roper, our assistant principal, declares, "come with me."

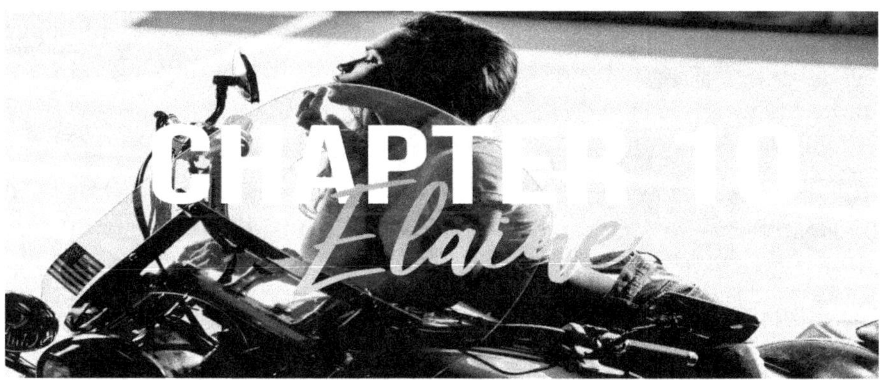

Nurse Bell cups my cheeks in her hands, lifting my head towards the light to look at my nose. She presses her thumbs along the ridge, turns my face again to inspect what I'm assuming is bruising, then releases me to scribble something on a notepad. When she's done, she grabs a handful of paper towels then holds them out to me. "It looks like most of the bleeding has stopped, but pinch your nose with these just in case."

I don't need a mirror to know I look like an extra from a horror movie. I've always been a bleeder, from scrapes to dental work: this is no different. However, just because I'm not freaking out about the amount of blood covering my shirt doesn't mean I like it. "Is it broken?"

Nurse Bell shakes her head then meanders over to her rolling chair. She swipes her badge along the screen, probably to open my file and document that I was here. "It doesn't seem that way, but with the amount of blood you lost, I can't be sure. I'm going to recommend that your parents take you to a doctor to be sure."

I groan and let the napkin fall from my face. It's saturated. Not surprising, considering the brown paper towels our school buys are crap. They don't even absorb water. They hold just enough to seem wet while spreading the rest of the liquid around like a toddler with his vegetables. "Do you have to call my mom? I could go to the doctor myself and bring you back the note. Will that work?"

Nurse Bells leans back into her chair, a playful smirk tugging at her tickle-me-pink lips. "Tell you what, I'll wait to call until after Principal Baxa has made contact. That way you can play the sympathy card."

I groan again and fall back against the hard clinic bed. The paper barrier separating me from the shittiest cushions in this universe crinkles under my weight. *I'm so dead.*

It takes thirty minutes of constant pressure to get my capillaries to stop leaking. We were doing good, until I sneezed and reopened the floodgates. By the time I make it to the chairs outside of Principal Baxa's office, Liam and Asher are gone, probably suspended for the rest of the week. Before my ass can sit in the folding plastic chair, my name is called. With heavy footsteps, I walk into the room.

Principal Baxa is a tired-looking woman. Closer to thirty than she is forty, running a school with nine-hundred and twenty-two kids has taken its toll. Her foundation cracks where wrinkles have forced their way through. Her lips are always turned down into a frown, and then there are her eyes. What were probably once sparkling pools of blue are now empty holes of grey.

"Sit, Miss Walker."

I follow her directions, taking the black rolling chair across from her. I look around the room, noticing the lack of personal decorations. For a woman who's been in this position for four years, she's made no attempt at making her office feel welcoming. If not for her degree on the wall nearest the door, there would be nothing hanging in the room. Even her desk is absent of photos or trinkets. I've never been in here before, but I get the feeling that this wasn't supposed to be a permanent position.

"In light of everything that happened in the cafeteria, and your unruly appearance, you are excused from the rest of your classes today."

My throat goes dry as nervous needles tickle my spine. Sending me home means it will go in my file that I was suspended. I've never been in trouble before. I have no idea how this will affect my future.

What if the University of Florida pulls my scholarship? Or worse, what if they rescind my acceptance? Heat claims my neck, making me break out into a cold sweat. Going to UF has been my dream since the third grade. I don't know what I'll do if they kick me out because of this.

"Please, Mrs. Baxa, you can't suspend me. I didn't do anything wrong. Asher and I were just sitting there, having a conversation, when Liam came up. I'm sure he didn't mean to cause a fight, but Liam and Asher are like oil and water. They don't mix sometimes. I tried to get help. I tried to break it up. I don't deserve to be suspended."

Mrs. Baxa exhales an impatient breath. "I know all of this, Miss Walker. Both boys insisted you had nothing but good intentions this afternoon."

"Then why are you sending me home?" Tears of frustration pool behind my eyes. My future can't be ruined because of a cockfight. I won't let it.

"Because you were physically assaulted and are covered in blood." Principal Baxa huffs. She glances at her watch and her lips turn down into a frown, probably from reading a message. I don't think she's intentionally being rude. If I had to guess, I'd say the woman is at the end of her rope. At our school, something is always happening. Be it a fight or a spontaneous electrical fire in the woodshop, shit here is never ending.

"Oh," I say, relaxing a little. "So I'm not in trouble?"

"No."

"And you don't have to call my parents?" It's a long shot, but a girl can hope.

"The nurse needs to call them to explain the incident, but no. I don't have to." She pauses and stares at me skeptically. "Unless that's what you want."

"No!" I shout, jumping to the edge of my seat.

Mrs. Baxa's lips lift into an amused smirk. She's pretty when she smiles. Too bad the sight is as rare as an A on my report card. "May I offer some advice?"

I nod, not sure what words of wisdom she could offer.

"The sooner you end your lover's quarrel with those boys, the better. I'm very much aware of the tension between Mr. Heiter and Mr. Anderson. Their situation warrants as much, but you don't need to add to it."

"What situation?" Does she know about their dad? Is Derek Heiter a three-timing scum, sleeping with Ms. Baxa too? I bet he is. I bet that's why she transitioned from assistant principal to principal our freshman year, and I'd bet she is why Asher was able to come to school with us. I press my palm to my forehead. This is too much to process.

Mrs. Baxa pales and my suspicions are confirmed. "Never mind. Collect your things, Miss Walker, and have a good day."

Twenty minutes later, I'm outside the school's entrance. I look around at the overflowing student lot and weigh my options. It's a five-mile hike to my house. Five long miles in the blistering Florida heat, but I'd rather walk than tell my mom I was sent home. First, she'll freak out about my nose, and then she'll scold me for trying to break up a fight. Her disappointment is worse than any punishment she or Mrs. Baxa could hand out.

Convinced I've made the best decision, I shoulder my backpack but barely make it to the front gates before the distinct rumble of a motorcycle stops beside me. I keep my gaze forward, not wanting to see the damage Liam inflicted, or vice versa. Today's fight was uncalled for. I understand that these two have issues that stretch beyond me, but they need to deal with it when I'm not around.

"Where the hell have you been?" Asher asks, silencing the motorcycle. "I've been waiting outside for you for almost an hour. I was starting to think you took a ride with Liam."

"I ran into Russell. We were talking."

Russell confirmed everything Asher said in the cafeteria. Right down to Asher beating the snot out of a group of guys in the boy's bathroom yesterday. It's all the more reason I need space from everyone. Liam was supposed to be my best friend. Why didn't he stick up for me? Why is he letting people make me out to be a cheap slut? I'm so angry, I could easily do something I'll probably regret, like agreeing to Asher's fake-dating proposal.

"I didn't know you were waiting for me."

"Of course I was waiting for you!" Asher takes his helmet off and holds it against his stomach.

He barely has a mark on him, and I'm surprised at the relief that comes over me. That feeling is short lived when I see the bruises on his knuckles. He may not look like anything happened in the cafeteria today, but I don't think the same can be said for Liam.

"Ellie." He reaches out and touches my arm. "I'm so sorry. Are you okay?"

"I'm fine."

Asher frowns and holds his helmet out to me. "Can I take you home? I feel like shit. I never meant for you to get hurt."

"No." My feet carry me forward. I grit my teeth and turn my head. I might be angry with Liam, but I'm not exactly happy with Asher, either. He started a fight. He freaking elbowed me in the nose. And, apparently, he got some girl pregnant. It couldn't have been someone from our school, that kind of juiciness doesn't stay secret for long, but the fact that I didn't know makes me inexplicably frustrated. I spin on my heels and stare him down. "Tell me about the girl, Asher. The one you got pregnant."

Asher grits his teeth and runs a hand through his dark hair. "Let it go, Ellie. That's not anything you need to worry about."

I don't need to worry about it? For someone who wants to be my fake-boyfriend, he sure has a lot of secrets. I have no secrets. My life is an open book that, apparently, everyone has read the Cliffnotes on. I'm so mad I could scream, and the only person around to take my frustrations out on is Asher. "My name is Lainey. Why can't you get that through your head, Asher? L. A. I. N. E. Y. Lainey."

Asher's hand, still holding the helmet, falls to his side. "You weren't Lainey until *he* decided El wasn't a good enough nickname. Until *he* changed you and turned you into his perfect groupie. Even as a kid, your head was so far up Liam's ass you couldn't see through all his shit. I will never call you Lainey because you are so much more than what he's made you to be."

"Stop it!" I scream, my emotions getting the best of me. My internal compass is spinning from mad to sad and right back to mad again, over and over. "I won't let you ruin the memories I have. Liam was my best friend. He looked out for me. Kept me safe from jerks like you."

"I'm the jerk?" Asher stares at me, shocked. He shakes his head, equal parts frustration and anger passing over his face. "El, everyone knows you two were fucking. Liam bragged to anyone who would listen about how easy it was to get you into bed. How all he had to do was make empty promises you both knew would never come true."

"You're lying," I yell through a pool of tears. I don't want to believe

Liam would do that, even if I know it's true. I want to hold onto the illusion that he was my best friend who loved me.

"You already know I'm not lying, Ellie." Asher's face falls.

The way he's looking at me, it's like he can feel my pain and it makes this conversation hurt more. No one should have their heart ripped apart the way mine is.

"I've never lied to you, not once, in all the years we've known each other."

I wipe my nose with the back of my hand and sniffle. "You're right. You just kept things from me, like who your dad is, and became a royal asshole in the process."

Asher reaches for my arm but I pull it away. His brows furrow and then he sighs. "I know, and I'm sorry. If I could go back in time and change how I've treated you, I would. But I'm trying to be a better person, Ellie. And I'm trying to make sure no one fucks with you. Guys are assholes. They're only after one thing."

"What about you? Doesn't that mean you're only here for one thing too?"

I arch my brows at him and cross my arms again. A feeling burns its way through the darkness eating me up from the inside out. The feeling of desire makes my skin squirm with delight. It's a feeling I have no business experiencing. I bite my lip and calculate the date in my head. Maybe my period is coming. Maybe that's why I'm such a mess.

"If I thought I had a shot with you, then maybe." He smirks and my treacherous heart speeds up. How I can go from angry, to crying, to nervous is beyond me. Thankfully, Asher doesn't notice because he adds, "But I know better."

I force the heady butterflies fluttering inside me back into the dark cave they flew out of. I wipe the tears from my cheeks and say, "You humiliated me in the sixth grade, called me shark bait, and made fun of me more times than I can count. Don't get me started on the daggers you shoot from across the hall. How do you expect me to forget all of that and be your friend, let alone your fake girlfriend, Asher?"

"First of all, I was fifteen for ninety percent of your accusations. I was pissed off at the world and jealous as a mother fucker."

"Jealous?" Maybe I could accept that excuse if his animosity had been directed towards Liam, or Russell, or any of the guys he hangs out with that have a functioning family with two parents. But me? On the outside, it would appear that I fall into that category, but Asher knows better. He saw firsthand when we were kids how much my dad works. It got so bad last year, Mom thought he was having an affair. My life isn't anything to be jealous of. "Of what?"

"It doesn't matter." Asher shakes his head and climbs off his motorcycle. "What matters is that I'm sorry. For all of it."

"You hurt my feelings. I know that sounds lame, but I had serious self-esteem issues because of you." My self-esteem issues are still a problem, but they're better, so there's no point in going there.

Asher reaches for my hand and threads his fingers with mine. He steps close, until we're toe to toe and tilts his head down to look me in the eye. "I'm a dick, but I'm trying, Ellie."

I glance over to the senior parking lot and scan it for Liam's car. From the looks of things, he's already gone for the day. If Liam were thinking about anybody but himself, he would have offered me a ride home but, as usual, I am forgotten. I look back at Asher, feeling more confused than ever. He was always supposed to be the jerk in our unorthodox trio. So why is he the one waiting for me and not Liam?

"I forgive you, I guess."

"As for the daggers." Asher chortles. "Those were always meant for Liam. Never you, Ellie. So..." He reaches up and tucks a strand of hair behind my ears. Tiny bolts of electricity zing from his fingers into my chest. My heart skips a beat and I realize there was never any question as to what I was going to do. "Will you reconsider that ride home?"

I take the helmet and climb onto the back of his bike, wrapping my arms around Asher's waist. He smells good, like freshly sprayed cologne. I close my eyes and breathe him in. I'm treading on dangerous waters, making a deal like this, but I'll pay the price. Asher hasn't admitted what he wants from me, but this man always has an angle. Our arrangement benefits him in some way and I will figure out how.

"I should probably get used to this thing."

"Oh?" he asks. "And why is that?"

"Because no one is going to believe I'm your girlfriend if I'm scared to ride with you." My stomach drops. Asher's girlfriend, not Liam's. *Lord, I hope I'm not making a mistake.*

Asher looks over his shoulder and smiles. "Girlfriend. Huh?"

"Fake girlfriend, but yeah."

Asher reaches back and grips my thigh. That zing of electricity, the same one that traveled from my cheek to my chest, shoots to my center. "Things are gonna get fun."

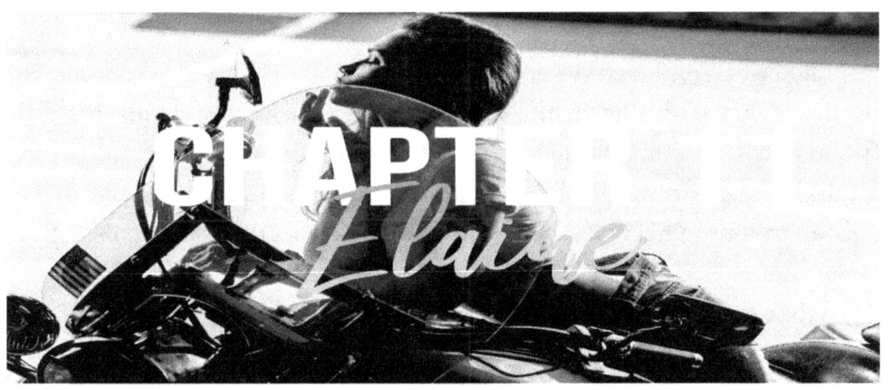

The doorbell rings and I yell, "It's open," without bothering to get up. The only people who come to my house are Maggie—and she's at work—or Liam and his dad. Either way, they've been around long enough to know the routine: come on in and make yourself at home.

"You look adorable." Asher chuckles.

I turn my head to the sound of his voice, horrified. Never in a million years did I think Asher Anderson would be at my house on a Friday night. For one, there's the issue with our parents that he seems to have forgotten. But also, I imagine curling up at seven PM with a rom-com and a half-empty bowl of popcorn isn't his thing.

I reach for one of the three throw blankets Mom keeps on the couch to cover up with. I'm not indecent, but the flannel Rudolf the Red Nosed Reindeer pajama pants I'm wearing aren't exactly flattering and, most importantly, I'm not wearing a bra. I'm sure Asher has seen his fair share of boobs, but the thought of him seeing my nipples through my red tank top is unnerving.

"What are you doing here?"

Asher glides across my living room and lifts my stretched out legs to sit on the far end of the couch. I pull my knees in to give him more space, but he grabs my ankles and sets my feet in his lap. At first, I'm too stunned to pull them back, but then he speaks and my stomach drops. "It's been a week. We have a double date with Liam and Corah. Remember?"

"Oh, no, we do not!"

The last thing I want to do is hang around with those two tonight. I'm used to Liam cuddling in the hallway and occasionally giving his girlfriend of the moment a quick kiss. With Corah, though, every time I turn around, they're in a full-blown make out session. Her hands are always on him, roaming his body. Hair. Shoulders. Stomach. Between his legs. It makes me physically sick to watch.

Asher smiles and reaches for my green fuzzy-sock-clad foot. He digs his thumb into the sole of my heel and rubs out knots I didn't know existed. My head falls back against the armrest of the couch, a quiet moan escaping my lips.

I close my eyes and let myself forget that, a little over a week ago, this wouldn't have been possible because I severely disliked Asher. I wouldn't say hate, because there were times he surprised me, but it was close.

I will say that Asher has blown me away the past two weeks. If he ever decided to have a girlfriend, for real, he'd be a pretty great boyfriend. He's abandoned our old lunch table, with Liam and the cheerleaders, to sit with me and my friends at the far end of the cafeteria. Whenever he gets the chance, which is more often than I expected, he finds me in the hallway to escort me to class, all while trying to hold my hand. And, much to my surprise, every time he touches my skin, something deep inside me stirs to life. Feelings I'd squandered years ago rear their ugly heads, and I don't like it.

"El?" Asher queries, his voice soft and soothing.

"Hmm?" I don't want to open my eyes. When I do I'll have to acknowledge the feelings inside me by pretending they don't exist. I thought fake dating Asher would be easy—I haven't liked him since fifth grade, haven't even considered us friends since sixth—but separating what's real and what's not is turning out to be harder than I thought.

Asher switches to my other foot and I melt deeper into the couch.

"Will you please come to Kyler's party with me tonight? Now that I have a fake girlfriend, I'll look like a total dick if I go without you."

I exhale a heavy breath and open my eyes. I've been to a total of two parties during my high school life and both were disasters. I expect tonight to be no different. I rarely drink and don't have the patience for blubbering idiots. Also, when Liam brought me, I would end up ditched and have to find a way home. Asher looks at me, patiently waiting for my response with my foot in his hand.

"I'm not the party type." I'm sure he already knows this. Just like he knows why I don't like going out.

"Me either."

That can't be true. All Asher does on the weekends is party and find girls to swap spit with. *Along with other juices.*

"Between football and work, I haven't gone to a party since January. I've worked every spare minute I could during the season. Now that it's over, I'm supposed to cover the weekend shift, but I convinced my manager at Lindy's Diner to give me Friday nights off until the end of the semester. People need to see us together, outside of school, to believe we are a real couple." Asher sets my foot down but still holds onto my legs.

"Do you think that's necessary? Things have been fine the past few weeks. Maybe we should keep them how they are." I'm having a hard time grappling with the fact that if Asher is telling the truth, he doesn't fit into the mold I've crafted for him. It's jarring. First Asher is sweet and considerate and now he doesn't party. What's next? Is his revolving door of girls a lie too?

"Are you ashamed to be seen with me, Ellie?"

"Not ashamed, just getting used to it," I confess. "You've got to admit, this is weird."

Asher shakes his head and flashes a playful smile.

I tuck my lips between my teeth, fighting a grin of my own. When he looks at me like this, I don't see the jerk who thought picking on me was funny. I see the kid I used to watch movies with after school. The kid who braided my hair and ate all the chocolate chip cookies then blamed me so he wouldn't get in trouble. I miss that Asher.

"Not weird, Ellie. This is fate. We were always supposed to be in each other's lives. We just got a little off track."

"If we're going to do this, go to parties and be together outside of school, there needs to be rules." Because if I don't set some kind of guidelines, this could go horribly wrong. The last thing I need is to be caught in a whirlwind of hormones and let Asher down my pants. I'm human. I have needs.

But not with him.

"Rules are meant to be broken."

"Asher," I warn. He may be a rule-breaker, but I'm not. I've never smoked a cigarette, let alone tried drugs. I've never stolen anything, not even on accident; I've never even skipped school. Asher can break all the rules he wants, but not when it comes to me.

"Fine. Fine." He exhales a sigh of impatience but, judging by the smile on his face, it's all for show. "Lay them on me."

"I just have one." Or ten, but I figure we should start with the big one and add more as needed. So far, Asher has been sweet, caring, and most importantly, respectful, but we've been at school. There's only so much you can do with hallway monitors around every corner. In the outside world, there's no telling what could happen, which is why I'm starting with the big one.

"Really?" One dark eyebrow arches. "I find that hard to believe."

"Well, we've already kissed. So, people are going to expect more of that, and you're not exactly known for keeping your hands to yourself." I pause to gauge his reaction. True or not, Asher is rumored to be as much of a player as Liam. People may not be questioning the validity of our relationship yet, but if we go to a party and he's not touching me somewhere scandalous, they will be. "So, your only rule is: above the clothes."

"Really?" Asher pushes my legs open and scoots between them, close enough to make my heart race but still leaving a few inches between us. His eyes take me in, scanning their way from my belly button to my face. He's got a look, one that matches how I'm feeling: confused, anxious, and a little turned on.

"What?" I laugh, nervously.

Asher stays there for a breath, likely gauging my reaction. I bet he expects me to push him away. I won't, because I need to get used to him being this close if we're going to pull this off, but that doesn't mean I'm going to throw myself at the man and invite his tongue down my throat.

"Can't handle being this close to me?"

Asher's playful grin turns sinister. He runs his hand over the inside of my thigh, stopping dangerously close to my center and the air gets caught in my lungs. Warmth radiates from his hand to my core. It's been weeks since Liam and I had sex. I've handled things myself in his absence, but feeling Asher's fingers makes me shudder in delight. "So, I can do this?"

I swallow hard but hold my poker face. Asher squeezes my thigh and rubs his thumb across the soft flannel over my panties. I may be coming unglued with need, but that's my secret. If Asher ever found out he can turn me on, this whole fake dating thing would be ruined. You can't have feelings for your fake boyfriend. It's in the rule book. Okay, so there isn't a rule book, or if there is I haven't found it. But I have seen *No Strings Attached* and *Friends with Benefits*. In both movies, someone caught feelings and, even though they were only hooking up and not fake dating, it ruined them. Good golly, I'm rambling. My thoughts aren't even making sense. "Yup, that's okay."

Asher smirks and slides his hand upward and over my hip. He pulls my blanket away and discards it on the floor beside me. I hold my breath as his hand glides up my side. He stares at me, watching for a reaction when he cups my chest, purposely capturing my nipple between his fingers. "And this?"

"Um..." I might as well not have a shirt on. The cotton spaghetti strap could be made of air at this point. My other nipple hardens, impatiently waiting for attention. I've never wanted Asher like this before.

Thought he was cute? Yes.

Had a childhood crush? Of course.

But this feeling is different. It's like poison in my veins, tangling and fighting with the existing desire I have for Liam. I know it's wrong. I know they're brothers. I know that this is all fake, but the way my hips instinctively buck to find Asher's, and the way his hard length strains beneath his jeans, adding pressure in all the right places, it all feels too real.

"That's fine too." My voice cracks and Asher smirks. The desire to kiss him and see how far he'll walk the line between what's allowed and what's not is strong. Too strong.

Asher grins, but his jaw is tight. A dark chuckle vibrates in his throat as he retreats to his side of the couch. I bite my lip to hold in a whimper. This cannot be happening. I cannot be falling in like with Asher.

"If I didn't know any better, I'd say you liked that."

I roll my eyes and push myself off the couch. I'm in trouble. Deep, deep trouble if Asher can unravel me like that with a simple touch. I need some space before I do something I'll regret. "Don't be ridiculous. I'm going to get ready. Give me about twenty minutes and we can leave."

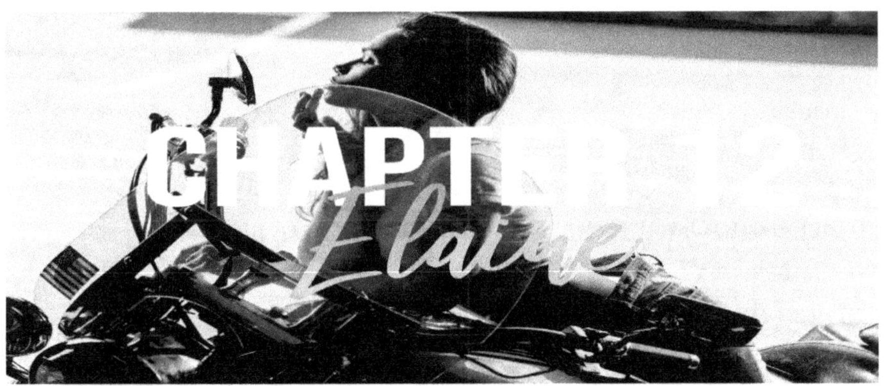

"**O**h, my gosh!" I yell over the music when we walk into the party. I don't know who's house we're at, but it's big and filled with people. Dozens of cars are haphazardly parked in the front yard and a quarter of the way down the mile-long driveway, lining both sides. This house, it's too ostentatious to belong to anybody we know. I mean, it has pillars on the front porch. Colonial style pillars! In Florida! Whoever lives here, they've got that fuck-you-money.

My fingers tangle with Asher's as he leads me deeper into the house. He's obviously been here before because he has no trouble navigating his way through the maze of a first floor to the back yard. I glance up at him, slightly jealous of the confidence Asher radiates. I want to hide inside myself right now. I've never been good with crowds, or strange people, but he seems at home here.

Asher must sense the anxiety beginning to bubble inside me, because he unlaces our fingers and wraps his arm around my waist. My cheeks heat, but the building pressure in my chest dissipates. I thought it would take longer to transition Asher from jerk to friend in my mind. To my surprise, the switch was seamless. It's like everything that happened between us the last few years is a fading nightmare and I've woken to the man Asher was always meant to be.

But then my stomach drops when I spot Liam a few feet in front of us and I remember everything about what Asher and I are doing is fake. I swallow my anxiety and get my game face ready. Tonight, I am Asher's girlfriend. I took the title everyone wanted but never got.

I.

Will.

Make.

Liam.

Jealous.

"There they are," I whisper more to myself than him.

Liam tosses a ping pong ball into a red cup on a plastic table at the center of the patio. He shoots his fists into the air then grabs Corah's face and pulls it to his. My stomach twists watching them together. I've never seen how Liam acts with a girl because the few times we went to a party together, he ditched me. The more I watch, the stupider I feel as I realize he's been using me all of these years.

"Who's next?" Liam asks when the guy across the table finishes drinking a can of beer.

"We are." Asher takes my hand and pulls me to the plastic party table with him. I drag my feet, not ready to face Liam, but then Asher turns to me, his eyes shining with challenge, and asks, "What do you say, Ellie? Do you wanna be my beer pong partner?"

"She doesn't play beer pong." Liam turns his gaze to me, a smile tugging at his lips. "Do you? *Lainey*?" He emphasizes my name and stares me down.

I force my lips upward into a smile to fight the scowl brewing.

I shrug my shoulders and hope I look more confident than I feel. I've drank before, a glass of champagne every New Year and a White Claw every once in a while when boating, but this is different. Intimidating. "There's a first time for everything."

"That's my girl." Asher drapes his arm over my shoulders, pulls me close, and presses his lips to my temple. I smile up at him, ignoring the fluttering inside me while watching Liam glare at us through my peripheral vision.

"Whatever." Liam tosses his first ball and sinks it into a water filled cup on our side of the table.

Asher drops his arm and reaches across the table for the cup. Someone hands Asher a can of beer from a cooler under the table. He finishes it before the next ball sinks into its home. Asher reaches for that cup too but, of course, Liam has something to say. "She wants to play, she can drink."

Asher scowls at Liam. I lift the top of the cooler and dip my hand into the ice. "It's fine."

My fingers wrap around a skinny can. I pop the tab and sniff the opening. Beer has a unique, pungent smell that is anything but appealing. I tip the can back, squeezing my eyes shut, and almost gag as I choke it down. It takes like hell, but at least it's cold. I think it would taste worse warm. Thankfully, the beers are mini cans, so I finish it in four quick swallows.

I wipe my mouth with the back of my hand and open my eyes. Liam looks murderous, but that seems to be his expression whenever I'm around these days. I set my empty can beside Asher's and raise my gaze to him.

He's smiling, almost proudly, and says, "That was hot."

I ignore the comment and grab one of the ping pong balls that have found their way into a cup of water on our side of the table. "Is it our turn?"

"Yup." Asher takes a step back and holds his hand out at the table. "Ladies first."

I toss my ball and miss. It bounces on the table twice then rolls across the floor. Corah goes chasing after it like a cat to a laser light. I bite my lip and look up at Asher. Hopefully he isn't upset. We could lose because of me.

Asher chuckles and shakes his head. "You're going to be the death of me tonight." He throws his ball and it sinks into the cup in the center of the cup-triangle on Liam's side of the table.

Liam grabs the cup and pulls the ping-pong ball out. He guzzles his beer in a matter of seconds and tosses the ball back without dipping it in the water cup. It lands on our side and Asher is forced to drink again.

"My turn!" Corah bounces on her toes then tosses the ball. She misses by a mile, hitting Asher in the chest, and giggles. "Oops."

"What the hell was that?" Liam roars. The music is loud. Most people probably can't hear how angry Liam is, but I can. I see it in his pinched brows, hear it in the dip of his tone. The muscles of my shoulders tighten and I hold my breath,

"Relax, Lee Lee. It's just a game." Corah rolls her eyes and ignores Liam's accusatory tone.

He hates to lose and Corah's nonchalant attitude towards this game isn't helping matters. But Liam isn't my problem tonight. I'm here with my *boyfriend*, not the asshole who didn't bat an eye when he broke my heart.

"Our turn," Asher says with a smirk. He sinks his ball into the first cup.

Corah bends down for a beer and Liam smacks her hand. He steals the beer, glaring at her, then chugs it.

My turn. I refuse to be dead weight on our team. If I could land one stupid ball into just one stupid cup, I won't be a lost cause. I close one eye and focus on the cup nearest Liam's crotch. I practice throwing twice, not letting go of the ball until I'm sure it will go in. It does. I'm so excited I reach for Asher's cheeks. My lips press against his in a moment of pure excitement. It happens so fast, he barely has time to register what I've done before I pull away.

Liam's face is fire-engine red when I look back at him. If there were any doubts in my mind that he's jealous, they're gone. Asher was right. Guys want what they can't have, and I'd bet it's killing Liam to watch me with someone else. If we do this right, he might break up with Corah before prom and take me instead.

"Get a fucking room," Liam growls.

"With pleasure." Asher grabs my hand and takes a step like we're going to leave the table.

"Hey!" Liam yells through gritted teeth. "Finish the game first."

Asher chuckles and hovers his mouth to my ear. "I love watching him squirm." He kisses my temple then turns back to the table and faces Liam. "Didn't realize you wanted to lose so badly."

I'm stunned, my feet cemented to the floor. Was Asher going to take me into a bedroom? What would happen then? Would we kiss? Would he test his boundaries, even with no one around? Better question, do I want him to?

Liam smirks and rotates both ping pong balls in his palm. "I'm just getting warmed up."

"Easy there, killer." Asher's hands settle on my waist. They're like fire against my skin, sending a heatwave throughout my body.

I, apparently, am what he calls a lightweight, because after two mini beers my head felt lighter. After the third, I couldn't stop smiling. I may be the worst beer pong player in the history of the game but, by that point, I didn't care. Before long, Asher and I had two cups left on Liam's side of the table. All courtesy of Asher's killer skills. I landed my ball into the target once tonight. *Go me!*

Liam, of course, made his ball into the last cup on our side of the table, which meant he won. I took that cup about three minutes ago, beer number four, and now the world moves a half-second slower than my brain.

I turn my head to the left and giggle as I watch the room catch up to me. I'm the fucking Flash, faster than everyone else in the house. I speed from the patio to the kitchen in less than a second, then watch as everyone tries to catch up.

"Up you go."

The floor separates from my feet and I'm suspended in the air. I'm not flying, although if drinking could make that happen I'd be fucking drunk all day every day.

Asher's fingers grip my sides as he sets me on the counter. He rests his hands on my knees and pulls my legs apart to stand between them. "Are you good?"

"I'm fucking fabulous."

Asher's brows knit together. He's cute like this, all pouty and protective. I tap him on the cheek and notice how baby smooth his skin feels under my fingers. I bet it would be even smoother if I licked him.

I refrain, laughing at my ridiculous thoughts, and say, "You're adorable. You know that?"

His lips lift into a delicate smile. *Such a nice smile!* "You need water."

"Nooo." I pout, reaching for Asher's hand and holding it in both of mine. "Don't leave me. I'll be lonely when you go."

"I'm just walking to the fridge." He shakes free of my grasp and rounds the counter. I watch as he opens the fridge and procures a water bottle. My jaw falls open in amazement. How did Asher know there would be water in there? He crosses the kitchen again and returns to his place between my legs. He twists the cap off, then hands the bottle to me. "See. I'm still here."

"You know..." I tip the bottle but miss my mouth. Cold water spills down my shirt. Normally, I'd be freaking out. I hate being dirty or wet, always have. Don't get me started on sand. The tiny grains sticking to my skin...ugh. It's the main reason I don't like the beach, but beer does funny things. I find that I don't care if my shirt is wet and laugh.

"You're drunk."

"Am not." I giggle. I don't know what's wrong with me, but that's something else I don't care about right now.

"What are we, eight again?" Asher is trying to sound mad but I think he finds me amusing. His lips twitch, like he's fighting a smile and his hands are on my knees.

My skin tingles. The sensation climbs up my thighs and into my stomach. If I thought there was an inkling of attraction between us at the house before, it's been magnified tenfold. I blame the beer, but just like everything else I don't care. Asher is hot. No, he's sexy. I should be able to appreciate all the sexiness my fake boyfriend has to offer.

I smile and shrug, taking a sip of water, this time finding my mouth. The cold liquid slithering down my throat feels better than I anticipated. I'm suddenly aware of how hot I am and pour some of the cold water down the back of my neck.

"You're a hot mess tonight." Asher sighs and shakes his head. "Give me your phone."

"Oh, are we taking a picture?" I shift onto one hip and pull it out of my back pocket. I like pictures, although I never seem to take any. *What's up with that?* Freshman year, my iPhone had so many pictures on it, Mom had to buy additional cloud storage. I can't remember the last picture I've taken this year.

Asher holds his hand out. Palm up. "Sure, after it unlocks."

I give Asher my iPhone and he lifts the camera to my face. I smile but I realize this wasn't a photo op. He was using facial recognition to unlock it.

Asher twists the screen back towards him. His thumbs tap against the glass for a few moments, and then he turns around. His back presses against my chest and for a moment, I don't know what to do. There's a churning at the bottom of my stomach that is not harmless butterflies. It's pure desire, something I have no business feeling for Asher, but it's there whether or not I want it to be.

"Smile for the camera."

I push my doubts away, drape my arms over Asher's shoulders, and grin. Liam hated taking pictures with me. He's always making some excuse to get out of it or he'll pull someone else into the shot. The photo sitting on my desk is the only one I have of the two of us that's even remotely recent.

"Wait!" I insist. "I want one more."

Asher sighs again but doesn't close out of the app. I turn my head and press my lips to his cheek. I can't see his reaction, because my eyes are closed, but can hear the smile on his face when he says, "Alright now, drunky-drunk."

My phone dings before he can darken the screen. I look at him puzzled because I haven't texted anyone in hours. Liam is here, clearly not in the mood to text me, and Maggie is probably in bed asleep by now. "Who's that?"

"Maggie." Asher thumbs hover over the glass. Tap. Tap. Tapping.

"Why is she texting you? Me?" No. Not me, him. Maggie is texting Asher and I want to fight her and throw up at the same time. This has to be a side effect of the beer because I love Maggie. I shouldn't be jealous of her right now, but I am. "You. Why is she texting you?"

Asher presses the side button, darkening my screen, then sets my phone facedown on the counter. The fact that I can't see their conversation makes me irrationally mad. He has a phone. If he wants to fake-cheat on me, then he can do it from his own device. I cross my arms.

Asher slides his hands from my knees, up my thighs, and all that anger is lost in a haze of lust again. "I needed her to cover for us."

I bite my lip, wanting Asher to say he's taking me home for more than a sleepover. Nervous needles prick my skin and desire floods my brain again, sending waves of longing between my legs. I look into his eyes, those same eyes I've seen day in and day out for years, and wonder if he can tell how much I want him. I wonder if he feels the same pull that I do, right now, and I wonder if he's drunk enough to break my over the clothes rule tonight. "Why?"

"Because you, love, are drunk and if your mom is anything like she used to be, she'll kill both of us. So, I told her Maggie needed an emergency girl's night and asked Maggie to cover for you."

I huff out my nose and roll my eyes. "My mom is never going to buy that."

"She would, and she did, because I told your mom that Maggie and Russell broke up." He reaches up and pushes a lock of hair that fell into my eyes behind my ear. "I may have also implied that Maggie is a mess, crying into a carton of strawberry ice cream. Your mom said to send Maggie her love."

"How do you know these things?" I ask, thoroughly impressed. Asher stays out of people's business. He's popular in part because he's hot as hell, but also because he has this mysterious thing going for him. The ice cream though, that's Maggie's favorite, and a detail Mom would have caught. Had he said something like vanilla or cookies and cream, she would have known I was lying.

"It's pretty obvious." Asher points to the living room where Russell sits in an oversized armchair. His face is crestfallen. "See that? He's moping."

I drag my gaze across the room to Russell again. He holds a red plastic cup in one hand and stares at his feet while Tabitha, a girl that's in the marching band with Maggie, runs her mouth. She touches his arm and Russell meets her gaze. He shakes his head, then looks back at his feet.

"No, Russell isn't," I insist. "He's avoiding that skank, Tabitha, who should know better than to make a move on what's not hers."

"And?"

"And she needs an ass kicking because Russell is off limits!" I scoot towards the edge of the counter but don't get far.

Asher's hands settle on my hips. His fingers dip under the hem of my shirt, brushing against the skin of my stomach, and I forget what I'm supposed to be doing.

"And moping. Guys don't ignore hot pussy unless they're thinking about someone else." He hitches his thumb over his shoulder. "Russell is thinking about Maggie."

My smile falls. Images of Tabitha straddling Asher flicker in my mind. She dips her head and claims his lips, only breaking the kiss for him to pull her shirt over her head. I shudder and close my eyes. I don't like it or the way they make me feel. When I open them again I ask, "You think Tabitha is hot?"

Asher laughs and the sound soothes my worries. There's no malicious intent behind it, or snarkiness, just pure amusement at me acting like a fool. I'd be embarrassed if the fluttering in my stomach wasn't overpowering every other emotion.

"All of that, and that's what you take away?"

I shrug and look down at my lap. I grip the counter because I have nothing to do with my hands, then realize I'm staring at Asher's zipper. Not on purpose, but he's between my legs and I've legit been looking at it for a solid three seconds now. I dart my gaze up, unexpectedly meeting his. I suck in a breath then look past him, to Tabitha, who is still trying to coerce Russell into bed. I watch her, seriously considering the consequences of breaking into her house and shaving her head. I might not have to break in anywhere. If she gets someone in bed tonight, they should fall asleep and no one would know it was me. Just some evil party prank. I smirk. No one would like her then.

"Jealousy looks good on you."

My gaze snaps back to Asher. Heat claims my neck and ears. "I'm not jealous."

"Sure you're not." He chuckles

"Bite me."

"Tell me when." He smirks but silence falls between us again, only this time there's a new type of tension. My lips tingle. I want him to kiss me and I want it to be real, with tongue and accidental hair pulling. I want to lose myself in his kiss because that's what every girl says happens when you meet Asher Anderson's lips.

"Ellie, I need… "

I twist on the counter when someone walks by with a tray of tiny cups. I know Asher was about to say something serious, but it can wait. Tonight isn't a night where we should be having heavy conversations. "What are those?"

"Jell-O shots, and you don't need any."

I ignore him and slide off of the counter. Mary, I think that's her name, hands me a pink one. I loosen the gelatinous goo with my finger then dump it into my mouth. It tastes amazing. I finish it and grab a second one before Asher grabs hold of my hips again. "You are going to hate life in the morning."

I stick my tongue out at him and he rolls his eyes. He pushes me onto the couch and says, "Don't move. I'm taking a piss and then we're leaving."

"You're no fun." I jut my bottom lip out, then close my eyes. My head falls back onto the cushion. The world around me is nothing but darkness, but everything spins. It's not a good feeling. Too much more of this and I think I might puke.

"Want a beer?" someone asks.

I open my eyes and a guy I've never seen before stands in front of me, a red solo cup in hand. I felt good until Asher took my Jell-O away. Maybe all I need is another drink to make the world stop turning. "Sure."

The guy hands me the cup and walks away. I hold the beer in my hand, distracted by a gray blob across the room that looks eerily familiar. After a few seconds, it becomes clearer and I recognize the blob as Corah. She's straddling Liam, practically humping him on the loveseat.

"Where did you get that?" Asher queries. I don't know when he came up beside me, but I'm glad he's here. I don't want to be a loser alone on the couch while Liam has the time of his life with his new girlfriend. Pretty girlfriend. *Is it wrong to hate her?*

"I don't know; does it matter?" I spit. My happy drunk feeling is teetering, slowly morphing into a pissed off cat. I want to claw Corah's eyes out and set her hair on fire.

"Yes." Asher takes my drink and sets it on the coffee table between the couch and the loveseat. "Guys are sketchy. You don't know what could be in it."

I fold my arms, mostly because I don't know what to do with them, and stare across the room.

Corah and Liam are still making out. His hand slinks up the back of her shirt while hers pull at his hair. The space between my legs tingle. I miss having Liam in my arms like that. I miss feeling the warmth of his body against mine. Most of all, I miss him.

"Are you pouting because I took your beer?" Asher teases. "Because even if there wasn't a drug in your cup, you don't need it."

"I'm not pouting," I declare, raking my gaze back to him.

"Oh, you totally are." He chuckles.

I sigh and let my guard down. Asher is supposed to be my boyfriend but what I need right now is a friend. I feel abandoned by Liam. Rejected. And it sucks. "It's just... look at them." I hold my hand out to where Liam and Corah are going at it. "It's not fair."

Asher wrinkles his nose. I guess he doesn't like watching those two get it on either. "What's not?"

"I'm drunk and horny and he's over there making a C-rated porn." I pause to glance up at Asher. I hate that I have tears in my eyes. I hate that Liam turned what was probably the most fun night of my life into a horrible experience. I might have considered coming to a party again if they were all like this, but now all I want to do is curl into a ball and cry. "Why can't Liam look at me like that?"

"Like a fucking steak?" Asher growls. He sounds angry, but I don't have it in me to care why. My emotions are tumbling faster than a deck of cards and there's nothing I can do to stop them.

"No, like something he wants." I bite my bottom lip to keep it from trembling.

"Well, then let's make him want you." Asher sits on the couch beside me. He cups my cheek with his hand, turning my face towards his, and presses his lips against mine. For a full heartbeat, we're both stiff. But then his tongue traces the seam of my lips and I melt into him. I tilt my head and open my mouth and his tongue slides against mine.

Asher wraps his arms around me and I slide onto his lap. My hands glide across his shoulders and to his neck. This feels too good. I've wanted to do this longer than I'll let my sober self admit. A crush on a guy in middle school isn't supposed to create deep-rooted feelings. I buried all thoughts of Asher in the trenches of hell when he went from sweet to jerk. Those feelings must have been lying dormant, because kissing Asher is better than anything I could have ever imagined.

Our mouths tangle, tongues dancing in unison. I vaguely remember we are in the living room of a strange house. An even further thought is Liam and what he might think. I don't care. I'm going to kiss the hell out of this man because we feel right together.

Gradually, Asher pulls away. We stare at each other for a long moment, foreheads touching. "You good?"

"Yeah," I reply breathlessly.

"Awesome. Let's get out of here." Asher takes my hand and hugs me close. We pause in front of Liam and I notice his eyes are open, he was watching us while making out with Corah.

Asher smirks as we pass them and says, "Get a room."

I force my eyes open when the overhead light in my car turns on. I don't know when I fell asleep, but at some point on the drive to Asher's house, I must have. I rub my eyes, clearing the fog from them as I'm cloaked in darkness again. I like the dark. It doesn't make my head hurt, but then the light comes on again and I wince at the brightness.

"Come on, beautiful. Let's get you inside." Asher leans across me and unclicks my seatbelt.

I smile at him like a doe-eyed pre-teen, too drunk to care if I look stupid. Asher has a nice face. I should tell him.

"Youuve gawt a naish faysssss."

Asher looks at me funny. Maybe right now isn't the best time to tell him. My words aren't cooperating as they should. My legs feel like Jell-o when Asher takes my hands and pulls me onto my feet. I'm not sure if I'm the one moving or if the world is doing it on its own, but the trees behind Asher are swaying.

Asher hooks his arm around my waist and I hang onto him. Pretty sure I'd be on my ass if he wasn't by my side. He was right, I should not have taken those shots.

"Watch your step," he instructs as we climb the four wooden steps to the door of his double-wide.

I've always known Asher lived on the sketchy side of town, but I've never been here. With our parents being on the outs, there was no reason for me to come over and Mom never brought me for a play date when we were little. I turn my head to look around the neighborhood while Asher fishes for his keys in his pocket. My vision is a little blurry, but from what I can tell we are on some sort of cul de sac. Three, no four, double wides sit around a giant concrete circle, with a singular yellow street light illuminating the shadows. It's not as scary as I expected, but it isn't home, either.

Asher's front door squeaks when he pushes it open. The sound isn't loud, but it hurts my ears nonetheless. "Mom is working and Clint should be gone until sometime tomorrow afternoon. It's just us tonight."

"Okay." I'm not sure if I said that right. My voice sounds funny to my ears, slow and garbled. I don't think I like drinking anymore. At first, everything felt great, but now the world moves too fast.

"Careful," Asher says, moving us a foot to the right. "Don't step there."

I let him lead us through the dark to what I'm assuming will be his room. I can't see anything but shadows, but he knows where he's going. I close my eyes and lean my head against Asher's shoulder, listening to him ramble and letting my feet carry me.

"That's a bad spot too." His voice is soothing. I could fall asleep to it, but I force my brain to focus on what he's saying because this feels important. Asher may bring girls here all the time, but he's sharing a piece of himself with me.

"When I was a kid," he says, almost nervously, "I used to try and avoid the soft spots by playing the game 'the floor is lava'. I hated that spongy feeling under my toes. Now, it's a miracle when I step on a firm section. Mom and I have been in this trailer for as long as I can remember. We need a new floor. And a roof. And air conditioning." Asher shakes his head, and his whole body moves. Or maybe I'm swaying. It's hard to tell at this point. "The list goes on, but the money to fix the problems doesn't exist."

We stop walking. I try to lift my head and open my eyes, but they are too heavy. Asher's keys jingle again. It almost sounds like he's unlocking another door, but that's silly. People don't put those kinds of locks on bedroom doors.

We're moving again, and then a bright light shines past my eyelids. Something in my brain clicks to life, because I'm able to lift them open again. It takes a second for the world to come into focus but when it does, I realize we are in Asher's room.

He leads me to the bed, where I sit down and he turns back to the door. He turns a deadbolt, slides a chain, and then for good measure twists the lock on the door handle.

"That's a lot of locks," I try to say. It sounds like *thafs awat ov lawks*, but at least it's close.

Asher chuckles and pulls the rolling chair from his desk in front of me. He takes a seat, then lifts my foot into his lap. I watch him untie the laces of my red Converse sneaker, then pull my sock off and tuck it inside my shoe. He sets my foot on the ground, then takes the other and does the same. "Do you want to sleep in that or borrow something of mine?"

"Yours." I grasp the end of my shirt and lift to pull it over my head. My arms don't work as they should because my shirt gets caught, both on my earrings and my ponytail. Asher chuckles again at my pathetic attempt to free myself. I wiggle and pull, but it becomes apparent that I'm not getting out of this by myself. "I think I'm stuck."

"Mmm-hhmm," is all he says.

I wait a few seconds, hoping he'll pick up on the not so subtle hint that I want him to get me out of the mess I've gotten myself into, but like most men, he needs me to spell it out for him. I try to wiggle and pull myself free again but it's no use. "Can you help me?"

"I don't know." The bed dips beside me, but Asher doesn't touch my shirt or my arms. My skin pricks with anticipation. I can't see anything, but I can feel the heat bouncing off his body. "I kind of like the view."

"Asher!" I scold, but it comes out breathy and weak. Something is happening inside me. Excited flutters spring to life. I'm exposed, in nothing but a lace bra, and I think he likes what he sees.

Asher chuckles again. This time I feel his fingers fumbling with my earrings. As soon as they are free, he maneuvers my arms and pulls my shirt off. I fall back onto the bed, thoroughly exhausted from my entanglement.

"You good?" Asher trails his finger from the band of my bra down my side.

I shudder as a jolt of need zings through my body. Each feather light touch feeds the desire growing within me. I blame the alcohol. Under normal circumstances, I'd never relish the way Asher's hand feels on my body or relive our kiss in my mind. That kiss was nothing like I've ever had before. I close my eyes and smile. "Yeah, I'm good."

Asher stands and the bed shifts. I open my eyes and push onto my elbows. I bite my lip to keep the turndown of a frown hidden. I want him to come back and keep touching me, but I can't say any of that. I can't explain what I'm feeling, but if this is one-sided, I'll be humiliated.

Asher crosses the room to his dresser and pulls out a shirt and a pair of gym shorts. He turns around, smirks then hands them to me. "Here."

I sit up and take the outstretched clothes. Asher turns around and faces the wall. He still has his jeans and shirt on from earlier in the night. My gaze falls to his ass, and how the denim hugs it just perfectly. Feeling brave, I ask, "You don't want to watch?"

Asher peeks over his shoulder, a flash of purple meets my gaze before darting to my chest. "Do you want me to?"

I reach back, unclasping my bra, and let it fall to my feet. I'm not sure how much of me Asher can see, but I hope he likes this view better than the last. I shimmy out of my jeans and stand there in my matching lace panties. I crave the feel of Asher's hands. I want him to hold me and let that fire that comes from his hands spread throughout my body. "I don't know. Aren't you supposed to want to see your girlfriend naked?"

He's quiet for a long minute, then finally says, "Fake girlfriend."

"Oh." I'm gutted. It dawns on me that what I'm feeling is one-sided and everything that happened between Asher and me tonight was for show. I guess I can say we've officially crossed the line into friendship, but aren't going any further. *Friend Zoned.* "Right."

I pull Asher's shirt over my head and slip my arms through the holes. It smells like what I assume he smells like first thing in the morning, before sweat and deodorant changes his scent, not that that's a bad fragrance. This shirt smells like fresh laundry detergent and a hint of spicy cologne. I take a second to sniff it again, then pull his gym shorts over my hips. They hang loose, so I roll the waistband a few times to keep them from falling off. "Done."

Asher turns around. He stares at me, eyes trailing over my body, down to my toes, then up to my face again. I've slipped into Liam's shirt a few times after sex. He'd always get the same goofy expression Asher has, one that says he likes what he sees. I smirk, then step backward until I feel the edge of his bed behind my knees.

"I'll... uh," Asher stammers as a flush of pink colors his cheeks. I bite my bottom lip to keep from grinning. I've never seen Asher like this before. He seems nervous, which is crazy, because I know he's been with other women. Besides, it's not like we're about to have sex. He wouldn't even look at me when I gave him the chance. "I'll take the floor. You can have the bed."

I scoot across the mattress, closer to the wall, then cross my legs in a sitting position. "It's a big bed. You don't have to sleep down there."

Asher sighs and rubs the back of his neck. He looks pained and I can't for the life of me figure out why. "I told you I'd keep my hands to myself tonight. I don't know if I'll be able to keep that promise sleeping next to you."

"Is that such a bad thing?" Ellie queries.

I run my hand across my jaw and groan. I've never brought a girl home. I'm not embarrassed about where I live. A house, even if it is falling apart, is still a house. If some bitch is going to dump me because I live on the shit side of the tracks in a crappy trailer, then she can go fuck herself. No, the reason I've never brought anyone around is because of that *Thing* of a stepfather I have. He's a piece of shit and I don't trust him. Ellie will be safe though because he's a long-distance truck driver and out on a job until late tomorrow.

Ellie tugs the edge of the blanket back and pats the mattress. I want to curl up beside her, drape my arm over her waist, and back her up until her ass is pressed against my thighs. I've wanted this girl since we were kids. Back then, I thought teasing a girl was how you showed them you were interested. Where I got that fucked up idea, I don't know, but I inadvertently made Ellie's life miserable throughout middle school. In my mind, how often I poked at her equated to how much I liked her. Turns out, girls don't like to be made fun of. All I did was drive a wedge between us I've never been able to budge. Until now.

I don't know how I did it, but I convinced Ellie to be my fake girlfriend. Not exactly what I want, but I hope that if I do a good job, she'll realize that Liam was never the guy for her. It's always been me. My piece of shit half-brother has never cared about Ellie. He used her, let people talk shit about her, and never once thought about how his other relationships were breaking her heart.

Every time he laid claim to a new girl at school, I watched Ellie fall apart.

When Liam and that chick would break up, because he has never wanted to keep a girl longer than a few weeks lest they get attached, he'd run back to Ellie and she would glow. I may hate seeing those two together, but for those few days, Ellie being filled with such joy was worth the knot in my stomach.

"Are you scared, Asher?" she taunts.

Yes, I want to say—I'm fucking terrified. I've hooked up with girls but never slept beside them. That's a level of intimacy I only want with Ellie. Now, we're here with her stupid over the clothes rule and I'm scared I'm going to fuck it up in my sleep and lose the girl of my dreams before I've really got her.

I take a tentative step forward, my jeans feeling too tight, and stop at the edge of my bed. I force a chuckle to let Ellie know the idea of being scared is ridiculous, then stare her down. "You should be the one who's scared."

"You ain't shit, Anderson." She huffs. "I'm more scared of a butterfly than I am of you."

Ellie loves butterflies. Monarchs to be precise. In the second grade, we had a life cycle unit where we grew the damn things from a worm. Ellie was fascinated.

Back then, I used to go over to her house after school. She would grab her tablet and we'd look at pictures for hours, talking about the different wing colors and patterns. She said once I must have been a butterfly in a past life because my eyes are so unique. I laughed and shoved her shoulder because that's what kids do.

Eight years later, on my sixteenth birthday, I got a butterfly tattooed on my arm. It's interwoven within the half sleeve I'm working to turn into a full, so if you weren't looking you'd miss it, but it's there.

I reach for the button on my jeans and Ellie's eyes widen. I fight back a laugh as I unbutton and step out of them. I watch her, taking in every micro reaction, committing it to memory, because If I fuck things up tonight, at least I'll have the image of her in my bed, wearing my shirt, for the rest of my life. I pull my shirt over my head and toss it by my feet.

"I usually sleep nude." That's a lie. I like to sleep in the shorts she's wearing, just in case I have to run out of my room in the middle of the night, but I love seeing Ellie's cheeks flush pink. "But I'll keep my boxers on tonight."

"Well, aren't you a gentleman." She rolls her eyes but chews her bottom lip as I crawl under the covers.

I turn my back to her and face the other side of the room. I hear Ellie shift to do the same. My bed isn't big. It's a full, which means there's enough room for two, but only just. Her butt presses against my backside. I hold my breath for as long as I can stand it and think about everything but her. Cars. My new work schedule. The money I owe Bane McCarron for running my neighbor's piece of shit stepbrother out of town. Statistics.

I try everything not to notice Ellie's shallow breathing. Or how she smells sweet like candy but also a little like beer. I do my best not to let myself get hard because that would make tonight awkward as fuck.

"Asher?" The mattress squeaks as she shifts. Her warm body molds against mine and we fit together like a fucking puzzle piece. I always knew we would. Even in this reverse spoon position, we were made for each other.

"El?" I look over my shoulder then decide to turn. I face her and drape my arm over her waist.

She wiggles closer until her stomach presses against mine. That bottom lip of hers slips between her teeth as she looks up at me. I can't read her face but wish I could, because I know she can feel my hardness pressed against her. I can't help it. I'm a guy.

"How difficult would it be for you to pretend I'm one of those girls?" she whispers. That lip of hers slips between her teeth again. She's nervous. I am too, but I have a feeling it's for a different reason.

"What girls?"

Ellie closes her eyes and sucks in a breath. I wait, feeling my heart ravage my rib cage, and wonder if she can feel it too. If she can tell how excited I am to finally have her in my arms. When she opens her eyes again, that bottom lip is quivering. "The girls you bring home. Could you pretend I'm one of them and…" She lets out a shaky breath. "And touch me?"

I clench my teeth and exhale through my nose. This girl, she's trying to kill me. My restraint can only last so long, but instead of being as tormented as I anticipated, my stomach twists. Liam must have fucked with Ellie's head hard if she thinks I would choose another girl over her. She's beautiful. I just wish she knew that.

I push her honey-colored locks back from her face. I want to see her eyes. I want her to look into mine, and find the truth of my words. "I don't have to pretend, Ellie."

She looks at me through hooded eyes and grins. "Really?"

"Ellie," I cup her cheek with my hand. Tomorrow is going to suck. Tomorrow I have to live knowing what those lips taste like. I didn't think twice about claiming them at the party. People were around, so I could easily chalk up our embrace as a performance. Here, though, it's just me and her. There is no excuse I could make up to justify how much I want to taste her mouth again. "You're gorgeous. I would choose you over any other girl in the world every day of the week."

Ellie gasps. Her beautiful brown eyes search mine, probably for a sign that I'm lying or doing what guys do. You know, saying what they think girls want to hear to get them into bed.

I refuse to blink. I want her to know I mean every word. My eyes burn with the need to close them but I don't.

Ellie smiles again and presses her mouth to mine. I let my eyes drift closed and fall into her lips. I could kiss this girl for hours and never come up for air. I move my hand from her cheek to the base of her neck and thread my fingers through her hair. She moans and shifts on top of me.

I rest my hands on her hips. Ellie sits up and flips her hair. Her back arches, hips rocking over mine, and I grunt. *Jesus, this girl feels good.*

Ellie leans down to kiss me again. She shifts her hips and rubs herself along my hard length. My fingers dig into her skin, guiding her, knowing at some point I need to put a stop to this. I'm not breaking her rule. We are over the clothes, but I don't want Ellie to do anything she'll regret in the morning.

Even with the thin cotton barriers between us, the friction is intense. Pressure builds in my balls. If I don't end this now, I'm going to come in my pants like a fucking twelve-year-old.

Ellie's body shakes with pleasure and she groans into my mouth. "Holy shit."

I swallow hard as she pulls back and gaze into her hooded eyes. This is the defining moment. She has this look, like a feral cat in heat ready to pounce. I'm going to have the worst case of blue balls, but I can't sleep with her. Not yet. Not like this.

Ellie scoots down my thigh and reaches for the band of my boxers. I take her wrist between my fingers. She looks down at me, head slightly cocked to the side. "Not tonight."

"But..." She pouts, not bothering to finish her sentence. Her bottom lip quivers as tears pool behind her eyes. She thinks I don't want her, but she couldn't be more wrong.

I sit up and wrap my arms around her waist. I look into her eyes and hope to God she's not so drunk she can't understand why I'm saying this. "Ask me tomorrow, when you're sober. That way I know this is what you want."

"But I want you." Ellie cups her hands behind my head. My skin vibrates with need. I want her more than I've wanted anything in my life, but it would be wrong to take her like this.

"Good. Then we're going to have a great day tomorrow." I tilt my head to taste Ellie's lips again. This kiss is short and to the point. A goodnight kiss.

I roll her onto the mattress and hold her body against mine. She curls into me, molding to fit. I close my eyes, knowing I'll dream of her face. Every night my mind torments me with what could have been if I wasn't an idiot all those years ago, and every day I wake knowing it was just a dream.

Tonight is different.

Tonight, the girl I've loved since before I understood what this feeling was is in my arms, and it's better than anything I could have imagined.

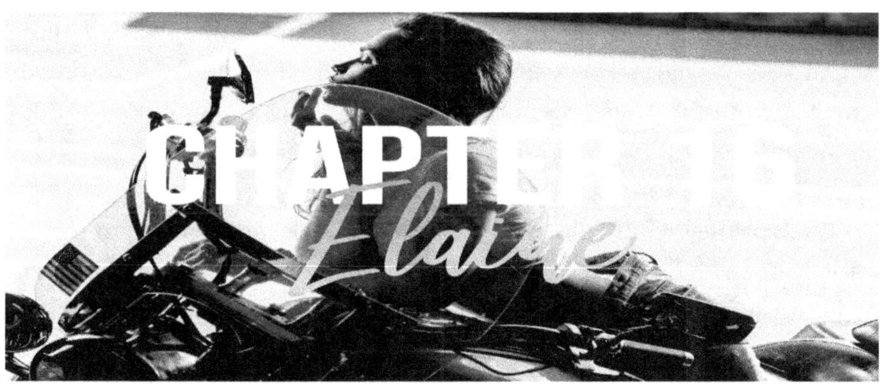

I groan and pull the covers over my face. There's a pounding at the door. Or maybe it's in my head. Either way, it sucks.

Asher's arm is across my waist. It's warm and heavy and, as soon as I realize it's there, nervous flutters consume me. He pulls me tight against his body and grunts. I think he's still asleep so I don't move to wake him. This used to be my favorite part about mornings, waking up in Liam's arms. Being here with Asher is like a twisted *deja vu*. It's almost comforting, even with his morning wood pressing against my thigh.

Someone bangs against the door again. This time, there's no denying the sound isn't in my head. "Get your fucking slut out of my house, Asher."

Asher's fists curl around the fabric of my shirt. *His shirt.* He releases me and pushes out of bed.

"Stay here," he warns without so much as looking at me. Asher's fingers unlock his door with precision. The slide of the chain and flick of the lock on the doorknob takes less than a second. I was too drunk last night to question all the locks, but I think I understand. That man outside the door, the one banging against it like he's trying to break it down, must be Asher's stepdad. From the looks of things, I don't think they like each other much.

I slip out of Asher's shorts and pull on my jeans, listening to the conversation in the hallway. I don't bother changing my shirt. The only reason I'm fussing with my bottoms is so the gym shorts don't fall off when I stand up.

"Get your slut out of my house, boy," Asher's stepdad says. I think Asher said his name was Clint. Whatever it is, the man sounds drunk, which I shouldn't judge, because the way my head is spinning, I think I might still be too.

"Ellie is not a slut," Asher scolds. "And I'm not your boy."

I search the cream-colored carpet for my socks and find them tucked into my shoes by the foot of the bed. I grab them and hurry to put them on because things sound like they are heating up in the living room.

"Thank god for that. You're a piece of shit."

My breath catches in my chest. Did Clint really say that? His blatant dislike for Asher tears me up inside. Asher is a good man, with a kind heart. He doesn't deserve to be talked to like this, let alone woken up this way. I hope this isn't an everyday thing for him.

"Whatever." Asher huffs. "We'll be out of your hair in five minutes."

"You owe me this week's rent," Clint demands.

My ears prick, curiosity spiked. Why does Asher have to pay rent in his mother's home? Is he choosing to stay in this falling down trailer and abusive environment? Something about their conversation feels off. I hurry to finish tying the laces of my Converse.

"I don't have it yet."

Clint chuckles darkly. "I'm not opposed to other forms of payment. I'm sure we can work something out with that slut of yours."

There's a scuffling and then something made of glass shatters. I run out of Asher's room, almost twisting my ankle on a soft spot when the floor dips. Clint has Asher pinned to the ground in the kitchen with the edge of a broken beer bottle against his neck.

"Hey!" I yell, storming across the double-wide. The kitchen, dining room, and living room are all one area, separated by the change from carpet to linoleum tile. "Get the hell off him!"

Clint ignores me and presses the edge of the broken glass harder against Asher's neck. A trickle of blood leaks, staining his pristine skin red. Clint laughs at the sight while Asher is chillingly still. Fueled by rage, I kick the man in the side.

Clint grunts and turns his attention to me. "You're a stupid little bitch."

He stands and drops the beer bottle to the floor. His sweat-stained tank top barely covers his stomach. Blue jeans streaked black hang off his hips. His breath stinks from a mix of not brushing his teeth and alcohol. I absorb all of this in a fraction of a second, while he grabs me by the hair and pulls my face to his until we're nose to nose.

From my peripheral vision, I see Asher scurry to his feet, but I keep my eyes trained on Clint. I'm not scared. I know without a doubt that Asher won't let anything happen to me.

The distinct sound of metal sliding against metal as a bullet is chambered into a gun causes Clint to flinch. He lets my hair go, dropping me to the ground, and turns around.

Asher stands a foot away, one leg behind the other, pointing a small black gun at Clint. "Get your things, Ellie. We're leaving."

I scramble to my feet then run into Asher's room. I grab my shirt, keys, and phone, then reach for Asher's shoes. I dart out of his room and to the front door. The scene in the kitchen hasn't changed. Clint is staring at Asher like he wants to murder him, but he seems to have enough sense not to push Asher's buttons this morning.

"I'm ready." I pull the front door open and press the unlock button on my wireless key fob. The lights of my sedan blink, letting me know that everything is open.

Asher steps towards me, never taking his gaze off of Clint. His gun stays trained on the man who literally had me in his grasp minutes ago. When Asher reaches the front door he says, "Get in the car, Ellie. I'm not moving until you do."

I race down the front steps to my car and whip the door open. I start the engine and park as close to the porch steps as possible. Asher pulls the front door shut then takes the steps two at a time. He hops in and I peel out of his driveway before the passenger door is closed. Dust kicks up behind my tires. There's no point in looking in the rearview mirror. I can't see anything. But I feel Clint's eyes watching us as we speed away.

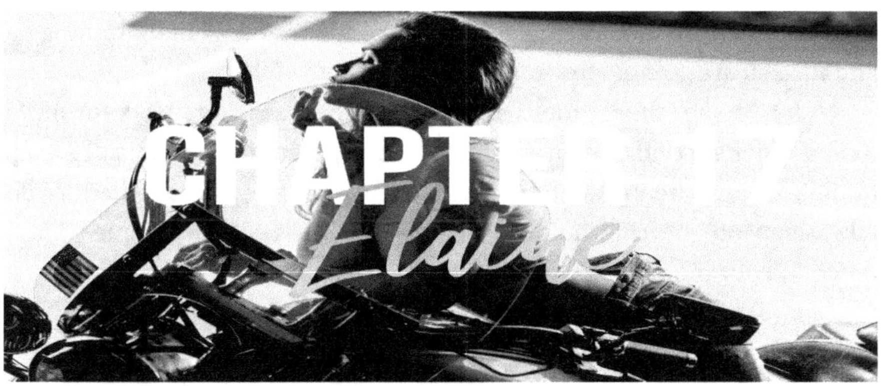

sher opens my glove box and shoves his pistol inside. I want to ask him how long he's had a gun, where it came from, and if he's ever used it before, but I'm scared of the answers. That side of the tracks is like a world of its own. Everyone knows the cops there are dirty. I wouldn't say we have a mob, because this isn't the nineteen-twenties, but there are some scary guys over there who control what happens.

Dad talks about it all the time. Being a prosecuting lawyer, it's his job to make sure the bad guys are put behind bars and stay there. He doesn't get into details at home, but two names always light dad up: McCarron and Michlovich. Whoever those guys are, they are big players in everything that happens over here.

"We're supposed to meet Maggie and Russell at the beach in ten minutes," Asher says, breaking the silence once I cross over the railroad tracks that separate the good side of town from the bad.

"Wait? What?" I pull up to a stoplight and peer over at Asher. He stares out the window, his hands clasped together in his lap. We need to talk about what happened this morning but I have a feeling now isn't the time. "I don't have a bathing suit."

"I'm sure Maggie has one you can borrow," Asher replies, his face expressionless. I can't tell if this was the first time he's pulled a gun on his stepdad or if things like this happen all the time. Whatever the case, Asher is deep in his thoughts and that frightens me.

He's shaking, likely from coming down from the adrenaline rush. I need to keep him talking, to get him out of his head. "Wait, both Maggie and Russell are going? How much did I miss last night?"

"A lot." Asher finally looks at me. Too bad I can't stare back for more than a quick second because the light turns green. I bring my gaze back to the road and he looks out the window again. "Maggie called after you fell asleep on the ride home. I answered because I was worried Liam ratted to your mom about how you got wasted."

"Oh, okay." I vaguely remember Asher texting Mom last night. If he hadn't, she would be blowing up my phone, wondering where I am. I need to look through my text messages later to see what he said and get my story straight.

"I guess Russell went over to Maggie's house after the party."

I sit straighter in my seat. Russell and Maggie are perfect together. Her breaking up with him was stupid. But if Russell went over there last night and she tried to call me, I hope that means they decided to work things out. "And?"

"And she's going to Berkley now with him, so they can be together."

What? *Oh, my gosh! Oh, my gosh! Oh, my gosh!* This is amazing! "Wait, Maggie didn't apply to Berkley. That's why they broke up to begin with."

Asher reclines the passenger seat back and closes his eyes. "You'll have to ask Maggie to give you all the details. I hung up the call when I realized the conversation wasn't about you and shut your phone off. That way you could tell your mom it died."

MAGGIE IS ALREADY at the beach, reclined under an umbrella, by the time we arrive. Asher looks ready to relax, without a shirt and in a pair of shorts he grabbed from the gas station. I never paid attention to the tourist section each one has, but apparently, they sell bathing suits, flip-flops, and shirts with bikini bottoms painted on. Unlike him, though, I look and feel one hundred percent out of place in my jeans and an over-sized shirt.

"You're functioning better than I did after my first time being drunk," Maggie teases.

I ignore her dig and wave at Russell, who tosses a football with a few guys I recognize but don't know. "It's been a morning."

"I see this." Maggie wiggles her eyebrows, probably referring to the fact that I am still wearing Asher's shirt. I shoot her a look that says *hell no* and she giggles.

"Come on." Maggie stands and grabs her oversized beach bag. "Let's get you changed. We have some catching up to do."

"Yeah we do!" I insist. "Berkley?"

"He applied for me and I got in. Can you believe it?" Maggie squeals with excitement as she gathers her bag that's filled to the brim with odds and ends. She lifts it onto her shoulder then places a hat on her head.

"We'll be back soon," I yell to Asher. He waves at me then jumps into a volleyball game like this morning never happened. *How often does he do that? Push his shitty mornings to the back burner and pretend like life is great in front of his peers?*

Maggie links her arm with mine once we're up the stairs and safely on the boardwalk. Everyone has her faults, and Maggie, she has two left feet. It's a wonder how that woman can play the trombone and march at the same time. "All right, sweetie, I need all of the dirty details. What happened last night?"

"I need breakfast. I'm starving," I deflect. Just because I can remember every painful, humiliating detail about last night's party doesn't mean I want to relive it. "Can we talk about this after we eat?"

"Nuh-uh. We can walk over to the Red Onion and grab some brunch after you get changed. I want to know everything, like yesterday."

I fill Maggie in on the party, and how I opened myself up to Asher by practically stripping only to be shot down, but I leave out what happened this morning. I don't think Asher would want anyone to know how much of a jerk his stepdad is. Besides, there's still the matter of the gun in my glove box.

"I don't have anything to say about last night; everything seems different when you're drunk," Maggie replies from the other side of the stall in the bathroom. "But going off of how he acted on your couch before the party, it sounds like Asher might like you, sweetie."

I switch my Converse sneakers with a pair of pink flip-flops Maggie brought, then slide the lock on my stall and step out. "I don't know. He was pretty adamant last night that I was just his fake girlfriend."

Maggie pulls a hair tie off her wrist and hands it to me. I usually have one on my wrist too, but there's no telling where it disappeared to. Her lips purse together as I twist my long strands into a braid. When I'm done she says, "Maybe he was trying to be nice. I mean, you were pretty wasted last night."

"How would you know?" I raise my eyebrows at her. Just because I've only ever had one beer before last night and a few sips of champagne doesn't mean I was a babbling idiot. I think I held my own pretty well, all things considered. Okay... that's a lie, but she doesn't need to know it. "You weren't there."

Maggie smirks and unzips a pocket on her beach bag. She pulls out her phone and shows me a video message I sent her last night, sometime between Asher's texts and the ride home. I cringe watching myself tell her how amazing Russell was for ignoring Tabitha's advances. I press the side button, darkening the screen, not needing to see more, and hand the phone back.

"See. Wasted." Maggie snickers then slips her phone back into its hiding spot. "Let's drop this off at your car. Then we can grab some brunch."

When we get back from the Red Onion, Asher and Russell are playing against Liam and this guy named Kevin in a volleyball game. My stomach knots at the sight of Liam. I feel guilty for throwing myself at Asher like I did last night. I have to remind myself that Liam and I aren't together anymore, and he was all over Corah. I didn't do anything wrong because, in Liam's eyes, Asher is my boyfriend. If he doesn't like what he saw, he should break up with Corah and do something about it.

"I didn't invite them." Maggie grimaces. Even if she does think Asher's and my relationship is real, I'm sure she understands how hard it is to be around Liam. "I swear."

"It's fine." I take a sip of my soda. I can do this. I can be loving and sweet on Asher if I have to. I just hope Liam and Corah don't put on as much of a show this morning as they did yesterday. "I should have expected to see them. It is, after all, Saturday."

"You're right. It will be fine, because you have hunky Asher to distract you from Liam's shenanigans." Maggie hooks her arm through mine and we trek across the sand together. My steps falter when I realize Corah has set up her umbrella next to ours, but Maggie pulls me forward.

"Lainey." Corah tilts her sunglasses down and greets me with a fake smile. She reaches across and sets her hand on my arm. "How are you feeling, love? You looked a little rough last night."

"I'm fine." I pull my arm free of Corah's grasp. Just her skin on mine makes me want to throw up, but I'm not a bitch. It's not Corah's fault I hate her, it's Liam's. So, I mask the movement by pretending to need something out of Maggie's beach bag. I grab a can of sunscreen and spray my legs. "How are you?"

"Oh, I'm great." Corah giggles. "You know I can't drink anymore."

Maggie and I exchange a look, not having any clue what Corah is talking about. I rack my brain to recall the details of last night. She's right. She didn't drink a drop during our game of beer pong. But why?

"Oh!" Corah says with a titter. "Liam didn't tell you?" She waits for Maggie and me to respond. When we don't she rests her hand on her stomach and says, "We're expecting."

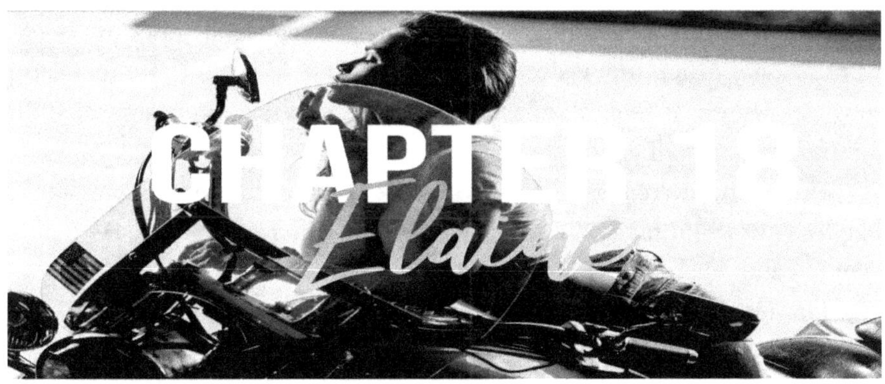

I can't breathe.

My pulse ravages every inch of my body while my ribs compress my lungs and the world spins into a blur of colors. I take a ragged breath that spans a lifetime as what Corah said sinks in.

Liam is having a baby.

A goddamn baby.

The weak foundation supporting my plan to win Liam back crumbles. My reason to spend time with Asher, to let him hold and cuddle up against me, is officially moot. As many faults as Liam has, he will do the right thing. He will stay with Corah, probably even marry her before the baby is born, and I will officially be nothing.

"Lainey?" Maggie's voice distorts in my ears. I turn my head to where she sits beside me, my vision tunneling. Her brows knit together, a wrinkle of concern appearing between them. "Sweetie, you don't look so good."

I don't feel good. Liam is having a baby!

"I..." I stand, my body on autopilot, and turn on my heels. I run across the sand, up the steps of the boardwalk, and keep going. I can't feel the burn of the hot Florida asphalt under my bare feet or the sting of tears as they stream down my cheeks. I don't look at the oncoming cars as I dart across the road or wave apologetically when they honk their horns at me.

I.

Just.

Run.

Until a hand forcefully grabs onto my forearm and jerks me backward. The tunnel my vision narrowed into widens as my feet stop moving. My chest feels like it's on fire, not able to get enough air and fighting what little I give it.

"Holy shit, you're fast!" Asher pants. He holds onto me with one hand, like he's afraid I'll take off again, and sets the other on his hip. He bends over to catch his breath and asks, "What the fuck happened?"

"Liam is having a baby," I say in one breath.

My heart breaks all over again for him. For me. Hell, for that baby that's going to grow up in the middle of a loveless marriage. As much as Liam thinks he loves Corah, he doesn't. He's infatuated and, if he's not careful, he'll follow in his father's footsteps. I run my hand through my hair and push my wayward strands back. This can't be happening. How could he be so reckless?

Oh. My. God.

We never used condoms and he clearly didn't use one with Corah, considering she's pregnant. The fear I had two weeks ago about Liam giving me a disease hits me twofold. Thank God I have an appointment on Tuesday to get tested. If Liam gave me anything because of his carelessness, I'll kill him.

"Good for him." Asher lets my arm go and sits on a nearby parking block. At some point during the volleyball game, he took off his shirt and left it behind when he came chasing after me.

Images of last night's dream flicker in my mind. It felt so real, straddling Asher's lap and kissing him until I made myself come. My heart sinks further into my stomach. Liam is starting a family and I'm having wet dreams about a guy who is using me for one thing or another.

I walk over and slump down on the stoop beside him and glance at the leaves of the oak towering above us. I don't want to have this conversation, but I can't deny the truth of my situation, it has to happen. "You don't understand. Liam will never come back to me now."

"Oh," Asher mumbles, realizing where this is going. He stretches his legs out, crossing them at the ankles. Sand dusts his bare feet and calves. I don't think I've seen Asher in shorts since that sixth-grade pool party. He has nice legs. Thick and muscular. "So, that's it then?"

"What? No!" The thought of being alone right now is crippling. Asher and I may have been fake dating for only two weeks, according to our classmates, but I can't imagine walking through the halls on Monday without him by my side. Everyone will accuse him of being with me to make Liam jealous, which is true, but having people say it out loud makes me sound that much more pathetic. Thank God no one knows this is fake. "Not unless you want it to be."

Asher presses his lips into a tight line. Fear that he thinks I want to keep our charade going because I have feelings for him sends a shiver through me. Last night unearthed a bunch of emotions I'm not ready to deal with yet. I haven't had the time to figure out if I like him or if the beer I drank last night does. *If,* and that's a big if, I'm starting to like my fake boyfriend, the last thing I want is for him to find out.

"I just... I enjoy spending time with you. Things between us are easy, kind of like they were when we were kids. And...um... I was hoping you'd want to keep fake dating me because being dumped as soon as Liam and Corah announce their love child will suck. Not because I'm jealous of them. I don't want to be in her shoes, but I think people will assume you don't want me anymore because Liam won't come back to me. Am I rambling? I'm rambling."

I cover my face with my hands, humiliated that I am losing all control, and take a deep breath. I can't lose Asher, not yet. Not when he's become the crutch I didn't know I needed. *Please don't leave me.* After a moment to collect myself, I look at him again "I'm sorry. I guess you make me nervous."

The corner of Asher's lip lifts. It's the first smile I've seen today that doesn't look forced. "I do?"

"Okay, not you." I roll my eyes because I'm laying too many cards on the table. "But this conversation. I feel pathetic begging you to keep up this fake boyfriend charade, yet am terrified you will say no."

"Ellie." Asher takes my hand and pulls me into a hug.

I wrap my arms around his waist and allow myself to melt into his embrace. I close my eyes, letting the world fall away, and just enjoy what might be our last hug. I doubt Asher will keep touching me like this once things go back to normal, and I'm surprised at how sad that makes me. I really like being Asher's friend. I don't want to lose this.

"I promise I won't fake break up with you until you're ready to call it quits." Asher presses his lips to my temple then pulls back and forces me to look up at him. "And so you don't start thinking this thing we have is one-sided, I like spending time with you too. At this point, you're the only person I'd call my friend."

"You have friends, Asher. Quit playing."

"No." He shakes his head. "I have acquaintances, people I'm forced to be around, and Liam. None of them I'd consider a friend. You, Ellie, are the only person I've ever brought to my house. The only girl to ever sleep beside me at night, in any bed. And my only friend."

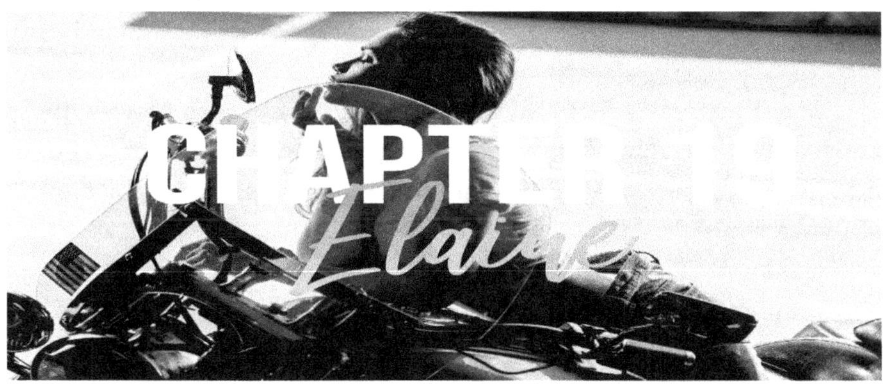

Asher leans against an oak tree at the front entrance of Ridgewater High, arms crossed across his chest. Khaki, school-issued slacks hang low on his hips, even with a belt, and the navy blue button-down falls near his waist, untucked. He's got his usual 'just had sex' air to him, and I can't look away.

I sit in my car for a few extra seconds to watch him scan the faces of our classmates as they enter the building. I realized this weekend that there's more to Asher than I originally thought.

Sure, he's handsome. I particularly like the strong curves of his jawline and how the tip of his nose has a small droop, but I understand, now, why he looks on edge all the time, ready to fight. He has to live with a monster of a step-father while watching his half-brother live a life that should be his. A life of warm meals, lavish birthdays, and carefree existence. I would be pissed off and keep everyone at arm's length too.

But there's another side to Asher people don't ever see. A sweetness that I thought was lost as he transitioned from boy to man. Deep beneath that hard exterior is the kid I used to have staring contests with. I loved falling into Asher's eyes, looking for new colors in his bottomless irises. The same kid turned man, who drops what he's doing to chase after me when I'm upset. A man who would pull a gun on someone to keep me safe. A gun that is still in my glovebox.

I glance at the latch on my dash wondering, *When is Asher going to get rid of it?* He needs that with him, at home, more than I need it in my car. Also, Dad would kill me if I was unintentionally harboring a murder weapon. Knowing Asher, that's probably not the case, but it would be my luck.

Asher. I turn my gaze back to the courtyard and watch him a minute more. When we started this fake dating craziness, I said there would never be anything between us. I think I'm a liar and I can't blame the alcohol anymore.

I think I've caught feelings for my fake boyfriend, and it sucks.

I jump at the sound of my phone pinging beside me. I lift it from my backpack in the passenger seat and smile. I haven't seen Asher since we left the beach on Saturday afternoon. He had to work at the diner the rest of the weekend, probably to pay his shitty stepdad's rent. Unable to sleep Saturday night and with nothing to do on Sunday, I found myself comparing Asher to Liam more times than I should have. It's unnerving how I find myself attracted to both of them, even though they are so different.

Asher: I'm outside. Where are you?

Me: Just parked. Be there in a sec.

Asher turns his gaze to the student lot and scans the cars until he finds mine. He smiles when he notices my silver sedan and tucks his phone in his back pocket.

I grab my backpack and check the front pocket for my student ID, lunch money, and tampons. Thinking about Corah being pregnant reminded me that my period is due soon and the last thing I want is to be called shark bait again. By the time I'm situated and ready to go, Asher is at my door.

I press the unlock button and he opens it for me. He reaches across me, pressing a kiss to my cheek, and grabs my backpack. "I'll carry that."

"Who are you, and what have you done with Asher Anderson?" I tease.

"Well." He links his fingers with mine and closes the door behind me. I press the lock button on my key fob and zip them into a different pouch. Heaven forbid one of my girly products falls out in front of him. He waits until I'm ready then says, "I don't have the best track record of keeping girls around."

"Ugh. I don't need a reminder of why I thought you were gross." I know Asher has been with a lot of girls. I also know that he wasn't often caught around the same girl for more than one weekend. I groan and wrinkle my nose. Thinking about how many people he's probably been with makes me sick.

"Nice to know you thought so highly of me." He chuckles then bumps his hip with mine. "I'm just saying, in case anyone had any doubts that we are still together after our public display of affection on Friday, I thought I could walk you inside."

"A true gentleman," I tease, batting my lashes at him. "Where have you been all my life?"

"Sitting on the sidelines, waiting for you to notice me." Asher's smile falls and he looks me dead in the eyes.

My heart pounds in my chest. He's joking. He has to be joking. If Asher liked me, I would know. But he didn't. He poked fun at me and stopped rumors, and came to my rescue and... *oh, my God.*

Just as my internal freak out hits supernova level, Asher winks and says, "Just kidding."

I punch him in the shoulder and he laughs.

The morning goes by without a hitch. A few people whisper, but for the most part, everyone seems to have accepted that Asher and I are the real deal. It's strange because people that used to turn their noses at me for being *Liam's number one groupie* have looked me in the eye and smiled.

Asher is already in the cafeteria when the lunch bell rings, sitting at the table that has become ours when I arrive. Maggie and Russell are next to him, adopting this table too so we can be together, as have a few other random people. I stand in the food line, watching everyone mingle, and smile.

"We need to talk." Liam grabs my arm, like I'm some kid in trouble, and tilts his head towards the hallway.

"Can it wait? I'm hungry." It's almost my turn in line and my stomach rumbles. All I want is a salad and the cafeteria workers are almost out. If we go now, there's no telling how long we'll talk. They may be sold out by the time we get back, or worse, I might miss the whole lunch period.

"Asher already bought you lunch."

I look over at my table again and notice that Liam is right. Asher has a coke and an untouched salad beside him. I smile and wonder how he knew, but I'm not surprised. Asher just knows things, like my favorite chips and Maggie's choice of ice cream. I turn my attention back to Liam and his hand on me. He's never been like this, physically possessive. I don't like it. "Fine, but let me go."

Liam releases my arm and walks towards the cafeteria doors. I look over my shoulder again at Asher and our eyes lock. His face lights up when he sees me then falls upon noticing Liam. He must realize I'm not coming to the table. I don't think he likes it, but Liam won't leave me alone until we talk. I'd rather get this conversation over with now than have him crawl through my window tonight.

Liam pushes the door open but doesn't hold it for me. Something I probably wouldn't have noticed, until Asher. He turns on his heels once we're in the hallway and crosses his arms. "You've made your point. Are you done?"

"What are you talking about?"

"Asher," he says, impatiently. "You officially win. I didn't think it would bother me to see you with someone else, but it does. There. Are you happy?"

"Kind of." I smirk. I'm glad Liam is getting a taste of his own medicine. Watching him cuddle up with other girls in the hallway over the years has sucked and seeing him and Corah at the party was even worse. He deserves a little bit of suffering. "Hate to break it to you, Lee, but me being with Asher has nothing to do with you."

"Of course it does!" He snorts. He's right, sort of, but I'm not ready to admit it. "Why else would you choose him?"

"What's wrong with Asher?" I demand, crossing my arms. From what I've seen in the last few weeks, Liam and Asher aren't nearly as close as I thought they were. Now that football season is over and I sit at a different table, they aren't ever together.

"Everything, Lainey!" Liam shouts. He throws his hands in the air and storms down the hallway to the next set of lockers.

I follow him, needing to hear his explanation because I don't see it. Asher is kind and considerate. Now that he's done being a jerk, he puts my feelings first and, even though we don't talk much outside of school, he's really good at communicating with me. Something Liam never wanted to in public unless I initiated the conversation.

"What does that even mean?"

"Asher is not a good guy. Have you seen where he lives?" Liam runs a hand through his hair, freshly cut, and lets the long strands fall back into place. He looks good, but not as good as Asher. "He is nothing but trash."

I don't know what comes over me, but I shove Liam in the chest. He can't begin to relate to what Asher's life is like. Hell, I only got to see fifteen minutes of it, and what I witnessed blew my mind. "Asher is a good man, Liam." I push him again and force him back a step. "People can't help the circumstances they are born into." I shove him harder, growing more pissed off with each step we take. "You can't imagine the shit he's been through because you get to live the perfect life." *Shove.* "You have two parents who love you." *Shove.* "A best friend who deserves better." *Shove.* "And opportunities you squandered by knocking up that bitch of yours."

Liam backs into a locker. His eyes widen at the realization that I know his secret. The secret he should have told me because we were supposed to be best friends. I swear, the longer I look at him, the more infuriated I get.

"You can't tell anyone about Corah, Lainey. Promise me."

"You should know better," I jeer.

"Ellie?" Asher queries. I look over my shoulder, and my stomach twists. From the outside looking in, it would seem that I've got Liam pinned up against the lockers. I look like I'm making a move on someone's baby daddy.

I take a step back from Liam, guilt that I've done something wrong twisting my insides. I open my mouth to defend myself but stop short when Asher holds his hand out to me. He pulls me close and wraps me in a protective hug. I fold into his arms and try not to notice the way he smells or how our bodies fit together. Asher has shown me more affection in two weeks than Liam has in the last four years. I was naive to think Liam loved me.

Love doesn't hide someone away in the shadows. It doesn't make you question your every move, wondering if you're going to piss the other person off. Most importantly, love doesn't make you feel insecure.

I do not love Asher. I like him because he makes me happy. I don't have to worry about what I say or wear around him. He's proven that I can make a complete idiot of myself. I don't have to worry about him leaving me for someone else, because he blatantly ignores other girls when I'm around, excluding Maggie. I like Asher because he makes me feel like I'm special.

Liam never did that. Even if nothing comes out of our fake romance, I've at least learned what a real relationship shouldn't feel like.

"Are you good?" Asher asks me.

I look up into his eyes. That the turmoil I felt walking out of the cafeteria with Liam fades to dust when I'm in his arms. "Better now."

"Good." Asher dips his head and presses a kiss to my temple. His gaze follows movement behind us and I'm painfully aware Liam is still watching. Asher mustn't care because a moment later, he's looking at me again. "I bought lunch. We'd better hurry if we want to eat before the bell rings."

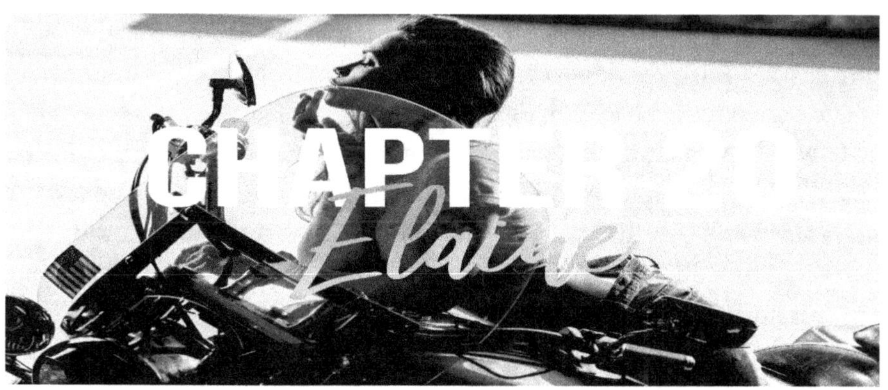

sher works every Tuesday, Wednesday, Thursday, and Saturday evening, and all day Sunday, which doesn't leave much time to hang out after school. We get out of class at two fifteen and he has to be at the diner by three for the start of his shift until eleven. All of which was fine, until the nagging need to see him crept in. I don't know what it is, but the more time I spend with him, the more it seems like it's never enough.

Asher meets me at my car every morning. Walks me to as many classes as he can. Sits with Maggie, Russell, and me at lunch. Hangs out with me after school on his days off while I do my homework. Takes me to the beach on Saturday mornings. Watches movies at my house on Friday nights.

I should be happy.

For a girl who wouldn't even consider her fake boyfriend an actual friend three weeks ago, I should be overjoyed to spend any time with him.

I'm not.

Every minute we're apart is a lifetime in itself. I fight the urge to text him because I don't want to come across as needy, and we don't text or talk when we aren't together. I have his number, but he hasn't opened that door, and I don't want to go first because I'm scared that if I seem clingy, he'll catch on to how I'm feeling and call this quits.

Despite all of my fears and insecurities, I'm parked in front of Lindy's Diner at seven-thirty on a Tuesday night, debating whether or not to go inside. Lindy's sits in a not so great part of town, but still on the good side of the tracks. It's the kind of place that draws in locals, but tourists or islanders wouldn't be caught dead here.

I watch Asher through the large paned window. It's him, a waitress, and an elderly couple inside. My stomach churns with nervous energy. I place my hand over my belly in a vain attempt to settle it. I shouldn't be nervous. After all, I spent most of my free time with Asher these days, but I'm crossing into his space. Uninvited.

My phone pings beside me, a new text message begging to be read.

Maggie: Get out of your car.

Me: I don't know what you're talking about.

Maggie: You told me thirty minutes ago you were going to Lindy's. Which means you got there ten minutes ago and since you're texting me back, you haven't gone in yet.

Maggie: Stop being a chicken and GO!

I roll my eyes and laugh.

Me: You know me too well.

Maggie: Duh. I'm your best friend.

Maggie: Seriously tho, Asher will be excited to see you.

Maggie: We both know no girl has ever surprised him like this before.

That's what I'm worried about. I take a deep breath and force myself out of the car. Maggie is right. I wanted to see Asher. I need to stop being a coward.

An over-the-door bell jingles as I step inside. I freeze on the welcome mat, my nerves finally getting the best of me.

"Welcome to..." Asher's words fall off when he sees me, and I begin to panic. I shouldn't have come. Showing up, unexpected like this, probably crosses some weird real-world-fake-dating line. "Ellie? What are you doing here?"

"I... uh..." My gaze darts around the room. My heart beats faster. Another panic attack is looming around the corner, and there are only two ways through it. Calm myself down and wait it out, or run. Right now, I really, really want to run.

Asher's lips lift into a heartbreakingly beautiful grin. He steps around the counter and pulls me into a hug and the tension in my chest fades away. "Are you hungry?"

"Sure," I answer as he ushers me onto a swivel stool at the counter. Lindy's Diner has a retro feel with its black and white tiles and baby blue vinyl booths. It's cute. Not something I'd want to see every day, but nice in a nostalgic kind of way. "What's good?"

"Everything." Asher slides a plastic menu over to me. He leans one arm on the counter and runs a hand through his hair. "The cook here is the best in town."

"Cool." I close the menu and lay it on the counter beside me. "Tell him to surprise me then."

"You got it, babe." Asher winks then walks through the swinging double doors. I wait a minute, expecting him to come back, but he stays hidden back there.

After five minutes with nothing to do, because I purposefully left my phone in the car, I start to feel anxious. My mind runs rampant with questions like, *Why hasn't he come back out? Is he hiding from me?* And the thought, *I shouldn't have come*, runs on a broken record.

The waitress I saw through the window taps the only other patron left, an old man, on the hand and walks over to me. "Hey there, sugar." She leans against the back counter, the one that has a nineties model fountain drink display on it, and tucks her hands into the pockets of her white apron. "Did Asher take your order already?"

"Yes, ma'am." I wish I had my phone to play with or a magazine to read, or something. Being left alone with my thoughts is never a good thing. They used to fixate on Liam, thinking about the future we'll never have or over analyzing our conversations. Now it seems my thoughts want to berate me for coming here. Despite Asher's smile, I can't help but feel like I've crossed some invisible line with us.

"That boy," the woman says with a smirk, shaking her head in amusement. "I've never seen him jump so fast to get behind the grill. You must be somethin' special."

"Wait, Asher is the cook?" The pressure in my chest decreases to where I can breathe without feeling my pulse race. I smile, feeling stupid having thought he was avoiding me. Asher isn't Liam. I should have known better.

"Yup," the woman says, stepping forward, "and he's the best one I've had in three years." She extends her hand across the counter. "The name's June Bell, but most people call me June-B."

"Ellie." I surprise myself, choosing the name Asher's given me over Lainey. I shake June-B's hand and her grin stretches wider.

"The infamous girlfriend." She reaches under the counter and pulls out a tall glass. "Strawberry or vanilla?"

"Uh..." I have no clue what she's asking for, but if I have to choose then, "Strawberry."

"A girl after my own heart." June-B winks then shuffles over to the ice cream bin and slides the glass top open. "I thought Asher was pulling my leg when he said he'd finally settled down, but here you are."

"Settled down?" I ask, my mind whirling. Asher told someone about me. About us. Does that mean he's having fun fake dating? Might he, maybe, want to take the fake part out of our arrangement? I squirm with excitement then take a breath. I have to calm down or I'm going to blow my cover.

"Oh, heavens." June-B stands upright and dumps the strawberry ice cream into the blender. She reaches for some milk, pours that in with a dash of sugar, and then tops her whittling machine. "You're not her, are you?"

June-B frowns, then flips a switch, bringing the blender to life. Once it's all mixed, she pours the shake into a glass, adds a touch of whipped cream, then tops it off with a cherry. She sets the milkshake in front of me and says, "on the house."

"Who did you think I was?" I pull the paper off my straw, then take a sip. It's perfect, not too sweet but still heavenly.

Asher pushes through the swinging double doors with a plate in his head. He beams at me as he sets it on the paper placemat in front of me. "One cold, black train. A cheese-stuffed patty topped with lettuce, tomato, a hearty onion ring, ketchup, and spicy mayo. No mustard because you hate the stuff."

My cheeks blush, amused that once again he knows something about my food preferences I haven't told him. And then I see the burger and my eyes 'bout bulge out of my head. "That burger is freaking huge!"

"Don't be intimidated, El. We both know it's not the biggest thing you've had in your mouth this week." He winks and I throw an onion ring at him. I hated giving Liam blow jobs. It was a chore that took a lifetime and he'd have a fit if I didn't swallow. But the idea of taking Asher in my mouth isn't as unappealing as I originally thought it would be. *Maybe one day.* I smirk and look down at my plate again.

"This looks amazing." I pick the burger up with both hands and sink my teeth in it. Warm and juicy, with a hint of spice but not so hot that it's unenjoyable.

Asher's grin stretches as he watches grease drip down my chin. "So, what kind of trouble were you stirring up, June-B?"

"Oh, you know." She flicks her wrist in my direction, then grabs a stack of napkins to refill the containers. "I was just about to ask this pretty thing if she was your girlfriend, or could at least tell me if the little lady exists."

Asher's cheeks flush. I've never seen him look so boyish and vulnerable. He tucks his lips between his teeth and I have the sudden urge to kiss them. We haven't kissed since the party. That was twelve long days ago. Sure, he's dropped sweet nothings against my cheek or shoulder at school, but those kisses are nothing compared to what we shared that night.

"And?" Asher asks expectantly. "What's it gonna be? Are you my girl, Ellie?"

The bite of burger in my mouth sticks in my throat. I chase it with a swallow of milkshake, then wipe my chin with a napkin. "Didn't we have this conversation a few weeks ago?"

Asher rests his elbows on the counter. He leans in close. So close that I can smell the mint gum in his mouth. "I'm making sure you haven't changed your mind."

I smile back at him feeling my heart flutter. "Never."

"You're late," Clint hollers from the couch as I stride through the doors of our twenty-year-old double wide. Mom and I, we've lived here my whole life, and each year something else in our home decides to break. It's not worth the cost to fix it, but it's also not our responsibility. We have a landlord, but all he's good for is collecting rent.

Clint, my mom's pathetic excuse for a boyfriend the last ten years, contributes by paying for the beer in his cooler. That's it. Mom, she busts her ass at the same diner I work at, day in and day out, just to keep us on our feet. She handles the rent and electricity. I help with the water and cable as well as pay for my cellphone and gas. Food is an afterthought, if there's any money left.

"I said," Clint huffs, a cloud of smoke seeping from the couch to the kitchen, "you're late."

Our trailer has two bedrooms, two bathrooms, and the rest is open space. The kitchen, dining room, and living room are all one area, separated by the change from carpet to fake tile. A long time ago, they matched, white to white. Now the vinyl has faded to tan and the carpet is brown from the dirt dragged in.

I like to think that at one time this was a nice home. If we had the money, it could be again, but priorities take place and as long as the leaks in the roof don't spread to the TV or over our beds, repairs stay at the bottom of the list. Besides, I'd have to hustle to get the money, and I try to stay out of the neighborhood's business.

"Work." I shut the fridge, wishing I had taken June-B up on her offer for a free meal. Every night she reminds me to eat before shift change and nine out of ten times, I refuse. I'd rather go to bed hungry than take a handout because I've learned nothing in life is free.

"That's no excuse, boy. Your curfew is eleven-thirty and it's after midnight. You were with that whore again. Weren't you?" Clint pushes himself out of his recliner.

When Mom and him first started dating, he seemed to have it all. A steady job working in construction, a new truck, strong hands, and motivation. He was everything my mother wanted: a partner, a role model, but most importantly, financial stability. It wasn't long before his true colors began to show.

I grit my teeth. Ellie is not a whore, but I'm too tired to fight. She left the dinner around nine, just in time, because Bane McCarron and his crew showed up fifteen minutes later. They claim they're not a gang, instead calling themselves vigilantes, but when you come into a restaurant, eat for two hours, and don't have to pay, you're no Robin Hood.

"I'm not your boy," I remind Clint, like I do every time he says it. "Thank God for that."

Last month, after getting fired from the only construction company within fifty miles willing to give him a chance, Clint found a job as a long distance truck driver. Best fucking job ever, and I'm counting down the days until he leaves again.

I take a step forward to walk around Clint's large frame and go to my room. He extends his arm, pushing me back that step and then some. "Where's this week's rent money?"

I grit my teeth and dig into my back pocket for my wallet. Mom doesn't know I pay seventy-five dollars a week to live in this shithole. I could take the three-hundred a month and find myself an efficiency in one of the apartment complexes a few blocks over, but that would leave her alone with this monster. A day or two is fine, but if I'm gone too much more, he gets lazy and doesn't care where he hits her. The last time they kicked me out, it took four days before Mom had a black eye. She, of course, refused to press charges so there wasn't much I could do.

I pull the tips I've been saving the past three days out and hand the cash over. Clint smirks and turns his back to me without so much as a thank you. I wait until he's planted himself into his chair, so worn that it molds to his body, before moving. After a solid minute, I shut myself in my room.

I turn the handle lock, my deadbolt, and then slide the chain into its holder on the door. One day I'm going to get out of this shithole town and take Mom with me.

GLASS SHATTERS IN THE KITCHEN, jolting me awake before my alarms go off. I sit upright, waiting, wondering if I'd dreamed it. A moment later something else breaks and Mom screams. I throw my blanket off and run across the room. My fingers brush across the locks, opening each one in less than a second.

Adrenaline pumps through my veins when I see Clint bent over my mother in the kitchen. I fist the back of his shirt as he draws back to hit Mom again and he elbows me in the face. I ignore the pain radiating from my eye, down my cheek, and throw Clint into the living room. He crashes against the recliner, knocking it on its side.

I turn to face him, squaring my shoulders, ready to fight. I've waited years to kick Clint's ass. He's the scum of the earth. The gum stuck on the bottom of my shoe, and I can't for the life of me figure out why my mother is still with the guy.

Mom rushes past me to be at his side. She places her hands on him, like he's a hurt child, assessing him for bumps and bruises. Clint presses his palm against Mom's chest and shoves her aside. "Get off me, woman."

"I swear to god, Clint, if you touch my mamma like that again, I'll fucking kill you." I ball my fists, ready for an attack. All I need is for him to purposely strike first. Then, when *he* calls the cops, I can claim everything was self-defense. He hurt Mom and attacked me. I'll press charges and he'll get locked up for domestic abuse for a few weeks. That'll be enough time to convince Mom to move and that we don't need Clint sucking the life out of us.

Clint stares me down. "What did you say, boy?"

Mom steps between us, her arms out wide. "Enough!"

"Get out of the way, Mom."

"No." She looks at me, one eye swollen shut and turning purple. I hate seeing her like this. Broken and beaten down. My mother is a shell of the woman she used to be because of this man. "You have school. Go before you're late."

"Mom!" I glare at her in disbelief. She can't be serious. I can't leave her alone with this monster. What if he hurts her again? What would happen if I'm not here to stop him? "You can't be serious."

Mom turns and cradles my cheeks in her hands. This close, I can see every tired line on her face. The purple hue spreading further down her cheek. Most importantly, I see her love, and it kills me. "You'll never get out of here if you don't go to school. I don't want this life for you."

I close my eyes, my shoulders hunching forward in defeat. I've heard the story my whole life, how if she had gone to college, things would have been different. How I'm her second chance. I would happily go to jail if it meant Clint would be out of our lives forever, but I know Mom. She would find a way to blame herself and fall back into depression. This last round nearly killed her. As much as I don't want to leave, I don't want her slipping down that slope again.

I open my eyes and stare into her tired browns. I don't look anything like her. All of my features, except for my nose, belong to Derek. I know it kills her to look at me, to live with a reminder of every mistake she's ever made, but she tries hard to hide the pain. "Okay, Mom. I'll go, but if he touches you, you call me."

She smiles, wordlessly telling me that she'll be alright. A lie neither of us believe, but we pretend to, for each other.

CHAPTER 22

The beach is my second home. The dugout underneath the boardwalk, my hidden bed. I learned a long time ago that my mother was always going to choose her boyfriend over me. I was twelve the first time she told me to find somewhere else to stay. On our side of the tracks, I knew better than to ask someone if I could sleep on their couch. Favors asked mean favors given, and I don't want to owe anybody anything over there. I already took a debt out with Bane McCarron once to help my neighbor, but he warned me. My next favor won't be as cheap, and getting rid of Clint isn't as easy as calling him, or I would have done it already.

I'm deep under the wooden planks, hidden behind a mound of sand I built to shield me from prying eyes. There aren't a lot of homeless people on this side of town. Someone sleeping out in the open would attract attention, but it's the safest place I've found. Unfortunately, even with all of my precautions in place, someone saw me crawl into my hideaway tonight and reported me. I raise my hand to shield my eyes from the bright light assaulting them.

"You can't be here," an authoritative voice says. Six years of sleeping in my hole, and now I get caught, when I'm eighteen and can be brought in. Figures.

I yawn, trying to catch a glimpse at my watch, and hold up my hands. I'm not a threat, just a tired kid with nowhere to go, and I want this guy to know as much. "I'm leaving."

I crawl out of my hole and slide down the sandy slope. The only thing I have with me is my helmet. My jacket is tucked into the compartment under the seat of my bike and it is parked in the Horizon Hotel's parking lot. I don't have to worry about someone stealing it there because they have security.

The officer tilts his light out of my face and down to my waist. "How old are you?"

I stare at the sand, waiting for my eyes to adjust to the darkness. When I can see again, I look up at him and say, "Eighteen."

"Fuck," the cop mumbles. He runs a hand through his hair then sets it on his hip. The man is quiet for a few minutes, probably deciding whether to fine me, bring me in, or let me go. I hope it's the latter. I can't afford the fine or bail, but a decent bed and breakfast would be nice.

A giggling couple walks past. I watch, in awe, as they cuddle against each other then ascend the wooden stairs. I've never had that. The few girls I've taken to bed I know by name, and there aren't as many as Ellie thinks. My reputation came about because of bruised egos and my lack of give-a-fucks. Just because a girl claims to have slept with me doesn't make it true. As for the seven ladies I have been with, they're in the same situation as me. Stuck. No wanting to drag anyone down with them and using a warm body to forget their problems for a night. These past few weeks with Ellie is the closest I've ever been to a normal relationship, and all we've done is lie to the world.

"What are you doing out here?" the cop asks, his tone a little lighter.

I recognize the sympathy in his voice. While I should be grateful, I'm no one's charity. I've fended for myself for years. Found ways to feed myself. Learned how to wash my clothes at the age of six because I didn't want anyone to know my mamma didn't have time for me. She loved me but worked too damn much. Now, as an adult trying to graduate, I'm sometimes homeless, but I'm used to that too. Two more months and everything will be different. In August I'll be at UF on a football scholarship, and no one will know I was once the kid who used to sleep in a hole in the sand. "Stepdad kicked me out. Needed a place to crash while Mom and him sorted shit out. I won't do it again, Officer."

"Is he the one to give you that shiner?" the cop asks. I bite my tongue but hold his gaze. I'm no rat. A cop crossing the tracks to sort a domestic disturbance will only attract attention I don't need. When I don't reply, he says, "Come with me."

"But I…"

"Relax, kid. You're not in trouble." He leads me past the boardwalk stairs and closer to the Horizon hotel's beach entrance. "Everything past those stairs is considered a private beach. While I can still harass you for being on the property, unless you're a danger to yourself or others, most cops will just ask you to leave."

"Why are you telling me this?" My eyes have fully adjusted now that the cop has turned his light off. We walk for a few minutes, past four sets of stairs, and are still going.

"Because I spent my fair share of nights in the sand when I was your age. Although, I was usually passed out drunk." He smirks as if remembering a better time. I'm jealous. Nothing about my overnights here is worth remembering. Especially the rainy Florida nights and soul-sucking mosquitos. "I'm going to go out on a limb and say you're a good kid because you don't look strung out or anything like that."

I'm far from strung out. Just tired and need life to cut me some slack. "Uh…thanks?"

"Let me put you up for a few nights. My wife would kill me if I brought you home, but I can get you a room here." He stops at the steps of the Horizon Hotel.

I look up at the string-lights that surround the patio. It's empty, the pool probably closed, but soft piano music hums from a set of speakers near the sand. I've only been in the Horizon Hotel's parking lot, thanks to a friend who does valet, and even that is classy. There's no self-parking. Every car is taken to a private, enclosed parking garage, with one way in and one way out that only employees, *and me*, have the keys to. I can't imagine what the hotel itself is like. "I can't let you do that, sir. I'm not your responsibility."

"No, you're not, but I've been in your shoes, kid. The difference was I had people in my corner to make sure I didn't nose dive into hell. Now, come on." He claps his hand on my shoulder and gives me a look that says this isn't up for discussion.

We walk up the steps to the pool deck. When we reach the door to the hotel's lobby, the cop digs into his back pocket and pulls out his wallet. Inside is a card, or a key of sorts, that he slides through the reader. A little light shines green and he pulls the door open. "After you."

My skin pricks as a chill slithers through me. The air inside is icy compared to the Florida heat. It feels nice, but takes a second to get adjusted to. The cop struts to the front counter where a pretty brunette smiles and greets him. "Logan! What are you doing here tonight?"

The concierge woman looks around like she's expecting someone to walk through the doors behind him. The cop—er, Logan—chuckles. "It's just me tonight, Misty. I need a room for the next week."

"Sir, I can't..." I start. This place is nice. As in, fresh flowers on the tables and chandeliers nice. It must be expensive. Cops make steady money, but they aren't rolling in it unless they're dirty. This guy seems too nice to be crooked.

Logan holds up his hand to silence me. "Family discount, kid. My sister's husband bought the place last year. I don't pay shit."

Misty, never once looking at me, smiles and hands Logan the room key. "Third floor, room three-oh-one. You're usual, Mr. Harris."

"Thanks, darlin'." Logan turns on his heels and leads us to the elevator. I follow, looking at decor. Ellie would love this place. One day, when what we have is real, I'm going to save up and bring her here.

"So your brother-in-law owns this place?" I ask as he pushes the button on the wall. The elevator is taking a ridiculously long time to get to our floor. Or maybe I'm nervous. It would be my luck this cop is some creepy child molester and I'm his new victim. This guy's got another thing coming if that's his angle.

"Trust me, no one was as shocked as I was. My sister was nearly murdered over there." He gestures to a spot in the lobby that has a set of black couches. "But when my brother-in-law, Rex, heard the owner was selling, they scooped it up."

"Must be nice, having a retreat like this."

Logan shrugs. "This place has just as many bad memories as it does good. My wife and I hardly ever come here, so we've racked up a shit ton of free nights." The elevator dings, silver-painted doors sliding open.

Logan hands me the key but doesn't step inside. "Stay as long as you need, just don't cause any trouble."

"Thanks again, Officer..." I glance at his chest for a name badge, but it looks like it was ripped off. There's a literal hole in his shirt where a name badge should be.

"It's Harris." His radio makes a static sound before a voice carries over. "I've got to go. See you around, kid."

My doorbell rings at an ungodly hour. I hear Dad grumbling something to Mom, then a shuffle across the living room. I finish pulling my hair into a ponytail, convinced that whoever is at our door at six fifteen in the morning either has a death wish or has some important news regarding Dad's latest case.

"It's a bit early, son," I hear my dad say from the living room. I strain my ears to hear the response of whoever is outside, but I can't discern the voice. The person is speaking in low, hushed tones. It must be work-related. Dad has a lot of informants, people that need to meet on the down-low. I cap the eyeliner pen, not giving our visitor anymore thought as Dad says, "Come on in."

"Asher!" my mom coos. "What a lovely surprise."

That catches my attention. I put down my tube of mascara and creep into the hallway. Asher takes an open stool at the counter as Mom sets a plateful of scrambled eggs, toast, and grits in front of him. The way she's smiling and going on about last night's dinner, telling him he should have been here, makes it seem like this is a normal morning for them.

For the record, it's not.

My insecurities send needles shooting down my spine. I never finished my makeup. Even though Asher has seen me with crazy hair and day-old eyeliner, that doesn't mean I'm ready for him to see me bare-faced. I may not wear much makeup—a little eye shadow, mascara, liner, and some lip stain—but that's become my go-to look now. I take a tentative step backward, hoping to slip into my room before anyone notices me.

Of course, Mom takes this moment to look away from the beautiful boy sitting in front of her and notices me. "Morning, Laine. Look who stopped by."

Asher swivels in his chair and meets my gaze with a grin. My heart falls to my feet. His left eye is bruised and swollen shut. *What happened after I left the diner last night?*

I no longer care about what I look like. I rush across the tile floors to be at his side. I already know who did this to him, but I want Asher to say it out loud, in front of my parents. I want them to put a stop to this. Dad has connections everywhere. He has to do something! "What happened to your face?"

Asher chuckles but he sounds sad. His smile doesn't reach his eyes. He reaches for my hand to comfort me but I take a step towards my dad. "I got into a fight with a squirrel."

"Asher! That's not funny." I look to my dad with pleading eyes. "Dad, can't we do something?"

"About what?" He's playing dumb, sipping his coffee and looking at me expectantly.

Can he not see how beat up Asher is?

I've gotten to know Asher better than I ever would have thought over the past three weeks. He's not the type to pick a fight. I have no doubt in my mind Clint did this to him. My face and neck burn with frustration. I've never wanted to hurt someone as bad as I want to take a tire iron to Clint's kneecaps. I'm far from violent, but that man needs someone to rough him up. That someone shouldn't be me though. "About Asher's piece of shit stepfather."

"Language," my mother warns, but I ignore her.

I'm pissed. My parents are acting like seeing an eighteen-year-old beat up by his father figure is no big deal. How can they be so ignorant? If Clint is doing this to Asher, chances are he's doing it to Mary Anne too. I hold my hand out in Asher's direction. "Look at him."

Asher's face falls. He takes a sip of the coffee my mother set in front of him and swallows it without a word. Either he doesn't care how it tastes, or she knows how he likes it. Either way, my curiosity is piqued.

"Go ahead," Asher says, his tone flat and devoid of all emotion. I'm sure he's thinking I pity him and his situation. I don't. I'm worried because Clint is violent and reckless. If only my parents knew that jerk had his hands around my neck. I bet they would act differently. Just as I'm about to let them in on that little secret, Asher mumbles, "She can know."

"Know what?"

Dad exhales then sets his mug on the counter. "Clint, the man you referred to as Asher's stepfather is under investigation."

"Good! He should be," I yell, excitedly. "If he's beating Asher like this, you know he's doing the same to his mom. When are you bringing him in? I'll testify. I've seen firsthand how horrible he is."

Dad's face pinches together. He doesn't ask what I know about Clint or why and I realize something about this conversation is off. "Not that kind of investigation."

"What do you mean?"

"We think he is running drugs across state lines for Giovanni Michlovich."

"Okay?" I look between Dad and Asher, unable to read between the lines. I don't know much about Giovanni Michlovich. All I know is that he's not a good guy, but I can't figure out what running drugs and physically abusing someone have in common, or why it affects Asher's safety. "What does that have to do with Asher?"

"It means the cops can't touch him." Asher turns to face me again. He looks exhausted. I would be too if I was locked in my room, trying not to get the crap kicked out of me. My fingers itch to touch the swollen parts of his face, my lips want to kiss away his pain, but that's not what friends do, so I dig my nails into my palms instead.

"The good ones don't want to screw up the case they're building against Gio and the bad ones are taking handouts to keep shit covered."

"This is bullshit." I clench my teeth and Dad shrugs, like there's nothing he can do. I don't believe it. It's his job to put the bad guys behind bars. Clint Whatever-the-hell-his-last-name-is is a bad guy. If Dad won't take that man away from Asher, he needs to take Asher and Mary Ann away from that man. "You can't keep living there, Asher. It's not safe."

I don't care what my parents have to say on this one. I will guilt them into letting Asher move in with us. Mary Ann may take some time;

battered women don't easily leave their abusers. I'm fired up, mentally preparing my argument when Asher says, "I'm not."

"Oh?" Mom asks, her curiosity peaked, like mine. She stops washing dishes and wipes her hands on a towel. "Where are you staying?"

"Some cop found me on the beach last night. He said he'd been in my shoes once and put me up at the Horizon Hotel. I didn't want him to, but his brother or something owns the place, so he got the rooms for free."

"Logan Harris." Dad smiles. "Good kid and one hell of a cop."

The adrenaline-filled bubble in my chest releases a little pressure. I still want to find someone to kick Clint's ass, but the mamma bird fight or flight complex eases up when I hear Asher isn't under the same roof as that monster anymore. "So, you're not sleeping in a cardboard box somewhere?"

Asher laughs. He stands and pulls me into his arms. I rest my head on his chest and let him hold me. I should be comforting him but here I am being pathetic. "No, Ellie. I'm good."

"Is that why you're here so early? To tell my dad about Clint?"

Asher's lips lift into a light-hearted grin. Busted lip and all, it's a beautiful sight. "No. I came to give you a ride to school."

"Oh." I pull back with the feeling that Asher is here this morning, unannounced, because he needs me but doesn't want to admit it. While the unexpected gesture is nice, it couldn't come at a worse possible time. "Um. That's sweet of you, but I have to leave school early today."

Asher's brow furrow and his lips tilt down into a frown. "That sucks. Is everything okay?"

I look to the kitchen, to Mom for support, but she and Dad seem to have disappeared. They probably went into his office to talk about Asher and his stepdad. I wish they'd do something to put that man behind bars, but at least Asher will be safe for a few days. "Everything is fine. I've got some stuff to do."

"Like what?"

"It's nothing." I bite my lip. From the look on Asher's face, that was a mistake. He can read me, plain as day, which makes me ridiculously excited inside.

"Ellie, you're a shitty liar. What's wrong?"

I swallow the lump in my throat and bite my tongue. I can't find the words to tell Asher where I'm going, let alone why.

"El?" he demands again when I refuse to answer the first time.

I look down at my hands, embarrassed Liam put me in this position, mortified Asher is about to find out my biggest fear. He takes my hands in his and holds them tight, waiting for me to be ready.

"I have an appointment at Planned Parenthood."

sher's face pales, which is a sight to see, considering how fair he is already. He takes my hand and pulls me down the hallway I came from earlier. He has no clue which room is mine, so he stops between my room and the bathroom. I point at the second door.

We walk in and I realize Asher Anderson is in my bedroom. All of the sudden those nervous needles are back. My room is clean, except for the clothes in a basket near my closet. A pastel pink comforter is folded neatly over my bed and my desk is orderly. My biggest fear is that Asher will notice all of the photos on my desk, specifically the ones of me and Liam. Most are from when we were little, but there's two of us since high school.

Asher opens his mouth to speak, but his words get caught in his throat. He looks past me to the bulletin board by my bed and smiles. "I like that picture."

I look over my shoulder and feel my cheeks flush. I was so worried about what Asher might say seeing Liam's face all over my desk, I didn't think about how he might feel about me printing the picture he took of us from my phone. I shrug and play it off as no big deal. "You're a good photographer."

"Will you send it to me?"

"Sure." I close my eyes and let out a slow breath as soon as my back is turned. I walk to my bed, where my phone lays on top of the comforter and open my photos app. I tap at the screen, finding the picture within a few seconds, and send it to him via text.

"Are you pregnant?" Asher whispers, his breath tickling my ear.

"What?" I jump, dropping my phone at my feet. I turn, not sure if I'm startled by the question or his proximity. "No! Why would you think that?" I look down at my stomach and second guess the pants I have on today. *Maybe I should change.* "Do I look pregnant?"

Asher's eyes widen as he shakes his head. "No! I just... That's what Fridays at Planned Parenthood are for." He looks down at his hands. "Abortions."

I chew on my lip. I've avoided the topic of Asher and his aborted baby since Liam brought it up in the cafeteria a few weeks ago. It never seemed right to openly ask, but now is as good of a time as ever. "Why do you know that?"

Asher exhales a heavy breath then lays back onto my bed. I don't know what to do. Sitting beside him seems too intimate, but standing, staring down at him, makes me seem like a jerk. "My neighbor, Marla, had one last year."

I sit beside him, one leg under me, my knee touching his side, the other hanging off the bed. "Was it... was it yours?"

Asher tucks one hand under his head. The other settles on my leg. "No. Marla's piece of shit step brother raped her and her mom wouldn't sign off on the procedure until she admitted who the *real* father was. I found Marla crying on her front steps and convinced her to tell me what was wrong. She's always been a good kid. Even though she was two years younger, we used to hang out when we were little. Anyway, I was sick to my stomach when she told me what happened."

My heart sinks for the girl. "I can't believe her mother didn't believe her."

"I can." He snorts. "That woman is a piece of shit. Anyway, I said the kid was mine."

I try to wrap my head around why Asher would claim a kid that wasn't his. He's set to go to college with Liam and me at UF on a football scholarship. Having a baby would throw a monkey wrench into that. There are diapers and late nights and cranky baby mammas and doctor's appointments. Things you can't do when you're training five days a week, playing on Saturday nights, and going to class. "Why would you do that?"

"Because Marla is a good kid with no one in her corner. It's not like the baby was actually mine. Nothing would have happened to me if she decided to keep it."

"Did she?"

"No." Asher turns to look at me, his amethyst eyes dark and sorrowful. "I drove her to Planned Parenthood a week later. It's kind of a scary place. Whatever you're doing there, you shouldn't have to go alone."

I squeeze the hand on my leg and Asher links his fingers with mine. "You're sweet."

Asher sits up and faces me. He mirrors my position and our knees touch. I shouldn't want to kiss him. We just talked about a girl being raped and I'm about to get an STD test. But the way Asher is looking at me makes my stomach drop and my heart flutter in a way I'm steadily becoming used to. He took the fall for some girl, probably paid for the procedure too, all so she didn't have to look at her child's face and be reminded of a monster. It's kind of a turn on.

"I'm serious," he insists. "Let me go with you."

"I'm good, I promise." I squeeze his shoulder because I need to touch him. A smile tugs at Asher's lips. I don't think he minds having my hands on his body. One of these days I'm going to feel every inch of him. Just maybe not today.

"Alright. What time are you leaving?" Asher pushes my hair behind my ear.

I think he feels the same pull I do. I close my eyes and lean into his hand. His thumb strokes my cheek, brushing against the corner of my mouth.

I open my eyes, wondering, *Is this an invitation to kiss him?* "Eleven forty-five. Right after lunch."

"If you change your mind, let me know," he whispers. He leans closer until the heat of his breath tickles my cheeks.

I lick my lips, aware I've drawn attention to them. We stay like this until it's obvious he isn't going to make a move. Until I get the all-clear from the doctor, I probably shouldn't either. The way Asher has me feeling, once we open that door, I doubt we'd be kissing long. Hands would be roaming and that orgasm he promised me wouldn't be too far off.

I pull back and walk over to my dresser, fishing a pair of earrings from my jewelry box. "I will. We should probably get going or we will be late."

～

THE MORNING FLOWS by faster than I would have hoped, and my appointment at Planned Parenthood is in less than an hour. I have to leave school in thirty minutes and I am freaking the F out. I hate needles, but more so, I'm terrified as to what my blood work will show. My opinion of Liam has changed in the past few weeks. I don't know how I was so ignorant.

"Oh, my gosh, Lainey!" Maggie squeals as she sets her tray down beside me. "I forgot to tell you! Mom and I finally found the perfect dress."

"Oh yeah?" I say with a forced smile at the same time Asher asks, "For what?"

Maggie rolls her eyes like she can't be bothered with Asher's ignorance. I'd laugh, but my mind is too cluttered with thoughts about this afternoon. "Do you live in a cave? Prom! It's next weekend."

"Oh!" Asher says, his eyes widening. They look to me with wonder, confusion, and a little bit of something I can't figure out.

I shift in my seat and stab at my salad with my fork. We've never talked about the dance. As Asher's fake girlfriend, it's implied that we go together. If he goes. Asher, however, hasn't made any indication that prom is something he's interested in. While I want to go to the dance, I can't if my fake boyfriend isn't at my side.

"Prom." Asher's brows knit together. "Huh. I forgot that was coming up."

"Forgot?" Maggie's face twists in disgust. "This is the last dance we will go to. Like, ever! How have you not asked Lainey to be your date yet?" Maggie doesn't wait for Asher to respond. She gasps as if he's said something horrible when really her mind is running away from her. "You cannot break up with Lainey before prom. I swear to god, Asher, I will castrate you!"

"Relax." Asher chuckles and throws his arm over me. "If I had my way, Ellie and I would grow old together, but that's not my call. It's hers."

I stare at Asher, not sure what to say. I know that things between us are fake but it's hard to know where the line is for him when he talks like that. I wish he meant it, because I like what we have. It's going to suck when school ends in a few weeks. I don't want to think about what college will be like. He's a great football player. It'll take no time for girls to notice him.

I roll my eyes and pretend that the string of faceless girls I'm imagining don't bother me. "Oh, please. You'll be sick of me before we hit our one-year anniversary."

"I doubt that." Asher rubs his fingers across my arm.

"Yeah, we'll see." I feel panicky. I don't want to think about the future. We graduate in six weeks. Asher will move on and I will be loser Lainey, the girl who lost the two boys she's ever cared about. Feelings suck. "Say we do make it to our first anniversary or even the second, sooner or later, you'll be drafted by some big-wig football team and be gone. Long distance relationships are hard. You talk a sweet talk, Asher, but we don't know where life will take us once we graduate."

"Who said anything about long distance?" He smirks. "I'm taking you with me."

"Really?" I ask in disbelief. I doubt he's thought about the seriousness of what he's implying. I'd have to put my career on hold to follow him around the country, possibly even the world. I push those thoughts aside and scold myself. This isn't real. Asher and I don't have a future. Not if I don't make us real, that is.

"Well, yeah." Asher leans over and kisses the side of my temple. I blush, loving the way his lips feel on my skin. It's been too long since I've had his mouth on mine. The alarm on my phone rings, signaling it's time to leave. I swallow hard and try to push the thoughts of needles and blood and possible STDs from my mind.

"Sweetie?" Maggie asks. "Are you okay?"

"I'm fine." I stand and blood rushes to my head making me sway. I press both hands on the table to steady myself. This is horrible. I can't do this. I think I'll stay at school. I'm not having sex anyway. I can live with whatever Liam may have given me.

Asher stands and takes my hand. "She's just nervous because I told her I had a surprise planned for after lunch. That alarm is our cue to go."

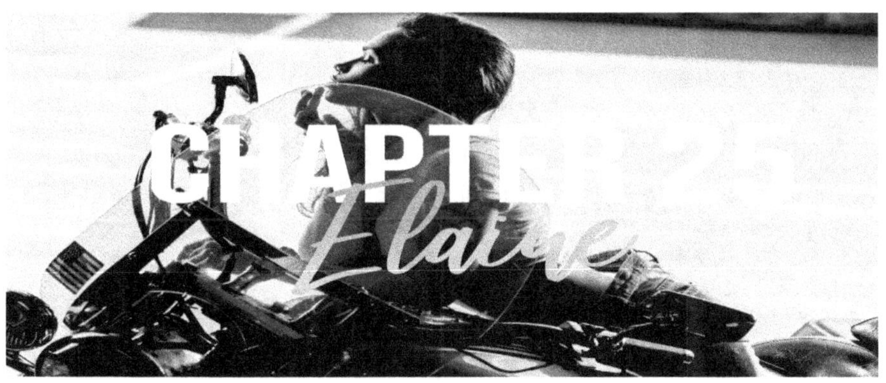

I stare out the window as we drive through town, twisting the hem of my shirt into a knot. Undoing it. Then twisting it again. Besides being nervous, I'm embarrassed. I didn't want Asher to be here with me. I didn't want him to see how pathetic I am when it comes to doctors. More importantly, I didn't want him to know that I may have an STD.

Asher reaches over and sets his hand on mine. There's no one around. This gesture, it isn't for show. It's to comfort me and again I'm left wondering where the line of our reality lies. "Want to tell me why we're going to Planned Parenthood?"

No. "We are going because you felt the need to save the day." I sneak a sideways glance and notice Asher smirking. God, that smile. How can it eat the bats wreaking havoc in me while letting loose a bunch of its own fluttering beasts?

"I am going because…" *Am I really going to say it out loud?* "Because…"

It was hard enough just to make an appointment. Mom thinks I'm going under the pretense of refilling my birth control subscription. She would have a fit if she knew the truth.

Asher squeezes my hand, once again reminding me that he's got my back. I smile and glance over at him. If the roles were switched, and Liam saw me having a mini freak out in the cafeteria, I'm not so sure he would have swooped in the way Asher did.

"I'm worried Liam might have given me…" *Gosh, this is so embarrassing.* "Something."

I watch Asher for a reaction. A stiffness to his jaw. A twitch of the eye. Anything to indicate that he is as disgusted with me as I am.

Instead, when the light turns red, he stops and looks me dead in the eye with nothing but concern. "Are you showing symptoms of something?"

Shoot me now. "No, but I didn't realize how many people Liam was sleeping with while we were together." I look down at my hands. "I feel stupid."

Asher reaches over and cups my cheek. I look up into his amethyst eyes, so clear and full of an emotion I know can't be real. "You're not stupid, Ellie. You can't help who you fall for. He's the idiot for not seeing how amazing you are."

~

"ELAINE WALKER?" a nurse calls after fifteen minutes of waiting in the waiting room.

Asher stands when the woman says my name. She raises an eyebrow behind her thick-rimmed glasses but doesn't comment. He holds both hands out to me. I take them, letting him pull me onto shaky legs. Despite my hesitations, I am glad Asher is here. I probably would have chickened out by now if I were alone.

"Sir," the nurse starts, "I'm sorry, but—"

"I want him with me," I interrupt, because I do. I never thought Asher would be the person I've come to rely on most, but here we are. My unexpected hero, once again saving me when I didn't know I needed to be rescued.

The nurse nods then leads us down a hallway. The walls are lined with posters warning wayward teens about drugs, tobacco, and pregnancy. I swallow the lump in my throat and wordlessly step on the scale when directed. The nurse jots the numbers on her clipboard, then directs us to the examination room. She takes my temperature, straps a blood pressure cuff to me, and even though it's probably written on her paper, she asks me why I'm here.

I'm okay with everything until that last question, where I have to explain the horror that is my sex life because the only person I've been with is a man-slut. "I...I..."

"We are here for an STD panel," Asher says. He squeezes my hand and I look up at him stunned.

"We?" the nurse inquires, vocalizing my thoughts. "I only have your…"

"Girlfriend," he inputs seamlessly. The way he says it makes my stomach flutter. For a moment, I forget where we are, and what the reality of our relationship is, and bask in the warmth of being Asher Anderson's first and only titled girlfriend. It's a great feeling.

"Let me check with the front desk and see if we can work you in." The nurse looks irritated as she collects her things, but keeps her tone flat. "Can I have your driver's license and insurance card, please?"

Asher pulls the cards out of his wallet and hands them over. The nurse leaves, closing the door behind her.

"You don't have to do this," I say, breaking the silence.

Asher shrugs and walks over to the counter. He lifts the lid on an apothecary jar and grabs a couple of condoms, then shoves them in his pocket. My cheeks flush both from embarrassment and nervousness. I know he hasn't been with anybody since we started our arrangement; he hasn't had the time. Still, the thought of him wanting to use those with me makes my body shake with excitement and then fear, because what if he's grabbing those for when this is over?

What if he's counting down the days until he can grab some chick at a party and take her to bed?

I frown, dread filling me at the thought of Asher with someone else.

"It's no big deal." He shrugs again then turns to face me, leaning against the counter. "It's been about a year since I've had one. I'm probably due anyway."

I stare at him wide-eyed. "You've…you've done this before?"

He nods. "I'm not some crazy philanderer. I don't sleep with a bunch of people, but you can catch shit from oral too. Some girls…" He pauses and shakes his head. "I don't trust 'em as far as I can throw 'em."

The nurse comes back in with a scowl on her face. "Fill these out." She hands Asher a clipboard then starts gathering his vials. My pulse races again. I watch the woman label a handful of tubes and set everything on two trays. One for me. The other for Asher.

Before I know it, she has my arm in her clutches and is wrapping a rubber tourniquet around me. She rubs her thumb over my veins then uncaps her needle.

"Wait!" I command, scooting an inch away.

"What?"

"I was going to go first." Asher sets his pen down and sits beside me. He winks as the nurse removes my tourniquet and wraps it around him.

Asher doesn't bat an eye when she sticks him with her needle and draws four vials of blood. When she's done, she presses a cotton ball to his arm and wraps it with some sticky tape.

The nurse opens a new needle and glares at me. She must be able to sense that I am not digging this. Asher wraps his arm around my waist as the woman ties the tourniquet over my arm again. I close my eyes and lean my head on Asher's shoulder. He takes my other hand in his and squeezes when the needle pricks my skin. Before I know it, the rubber around my arm is coming off and the nurse says she's done.

"You did it."

I open my eyes to the sound of Asher's voice. He's looking down at me with that gleam in his eye again. The one that hints that he might be feeling everything that I am. But there's a chance that I'm only seeing what I want.

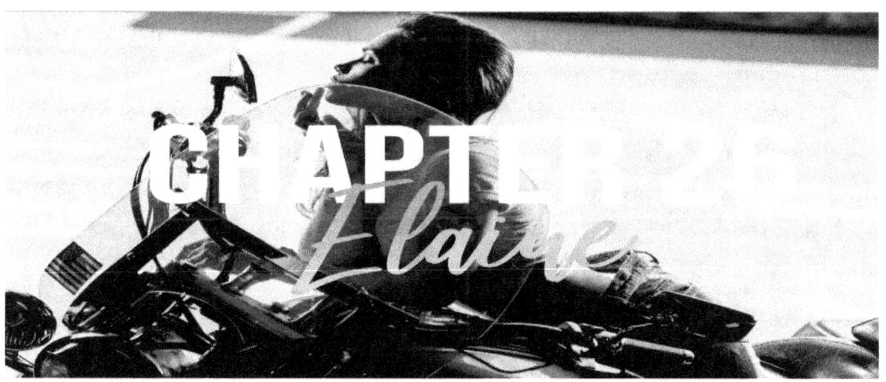

"We should probably go get your bike," I say, noticing Asher is driving us towards my house and not back to school. "I'm not worried."

I look at him curiously. How is he planning on getting home? Or back to school tomorrow? Am I supposed to pick him up? I can if that's what he wants. "But they'll lock the gate."

He chuckles and steals a glance at me before turning down Magnolia Street. "I can pick a lock, Ellie."

"Oh." I laugh nervously at the thought of Asher breaking into the school to reclaim his motorcycle in the middle of the night. I cross my legs, feeling myself getting turned on. *Who knew I was into bad boys?* "Of course you can."

"And what is that supposed to mean?" He sounds amused, not angry, which is a relief because that could have been taken the wrong way. Asher helped me through the most embarrassing and terrifying experience of my life. The last thing I want is to hurt his feelings.

"That even someone like you, who doesn't go to school or have friends over there, can still be corrupted."

Asher parks in my empty driveway. Dad is at the office, as usual, and while Mom works remotely, she is still required to go into the office one week per month. I purposely chose my appointment today because I knew she wouldn't be home. She'd take one look at me and know something was up.

Asher kills the engine and shifts in his seat. He stares at me, a worry wrinkle between his eyebrows. "I have friends, Ellie. I just don't talk about them."

It makes sense that Asher would hang out with people from his neighborhood. He's a handsome, social guy. We may not have been close the past few years, but he's never mentioned anyone from over there. Not even when we were kids. Marla is the first person he's been willing to talk about. "Why not?"

He sighs and runs a hand through his dark hair. "Because they've done bad things to get by. We all have." He pauses and mumbles shit under his breath. "I don't want you to know about that side of me. I'm not a good person."

I reach over and take Asher's hand in mine. My breath hitches because I feel it. The spark in my blood I used to get from being with Liam. The tingles I can't deny are anything other than desire. If there was any doubt left about having feelings for Asher, they're gone, because this is the side no one sees. The sweet, vulnerable side that is afraid of what I might think.

"Asher, I know things over there can be rough." I reach up and cup his cheek with my palm. He leans into my hand and closes his eyes. He's scared I'm going to push him away, but I'm not that easy to get rid of. "But nothing you've done can change what we have. It's safe to say you've weaseled your way into the best friend position." *And my heart.* "I promise, even after this fake dating thing is over, I'm not going anywhere."

Asher's gaze drops to my lips for a fraction of a second and I think, *He's going to kiss me.* I want him to kiss me. It's been so long, I've forgotten what he tastes like. But, Asher pulls back and says, "I should probably go."

"No!" My heartbeat thunders through my body. I'm scared I may have crossed that invisible line we dance on between reality and the fake world of dating. Asher might not view me as more than a friend, and I may have gone too far. "I mean... um... do you want to come in and watch a movie? Or something?"

Asher looks out the window, staring down the street. Liam lives four houses down, and he knows that. Even if he had forgotten, Liam's car is out front and it's hard to miss. "Sure, let's go inside."

Asher walks to the couch and grabs the TV remote while I head to the kitchen. I plop a bag of instant popcorn into the microwave and duck behind the fridge. My head drops against the cold metal and I take a deep breath. I have no idea what I'm doing. Asher gave me an escape and I should have used it. Instead, I invited him into my home, with no solid plan, and I'm freaking out. The microwave dings and I take the bag of popcorn out. I open the bag, shaking the steam out with a little toss and wonder, *One bowl or two*?

I bite my lip, internally chastising myself because if I were with Liam, we would have one bowl. No questions asked. I would curl up under his arm and watch a third of the movie before making out and then switching bases until the credits rolled. With Maggie, it would be two bowls on separate ends of the couch, critiquing the love interest in a sappy chick flick we've probably seen a million times.

Which leads me back to my original question: where do Asher and I fall?

I pick one bowl, rationalizing that he can decide how close we sit and head into the living room. He lounges on one end of the couch, TV remote in hand, scrolling through Netflix.

"Find something yet?" In a split-second decision, I sit in the middle of the cushions. It seemed like the best option considering we have one bowl. Not too obvious. I hope.

"Yeah, this one." Asher scrolls up to a movie called *Holidate*. He shows me the trailer. It looks funny, but I can't help but notice it's about two people who date but aren't actually together.

I nod as he presses play.

My mind runs as the movie starts, wondering if this is one of those movies where the couple ends up together. Is he trying to tell me something? Or am I overthinking this?

"Oh, my god!" I squeal when I realize what's happening on the screen. I zoned out the first few minutes, but now I cover my mouth with my hands as an Australian dude, who looks like he should be a Hemsworth brother, offers his date forty dollars in front of her parents for quote, "Coming in her mouth."

"He took the pants!" Asher laughs. He leans closer and puts one arm over my shoulders. His other hand reaches into the popcorn bowl that has somehow found its way into my lap. I thought I put it on the cushions, but at some point, the space between us was eliminated.

I swallow hard and shift to comfortably rest my head on Asher's shoulder. My pits are sweating to the point where I can feel the wetness on my shirt and I hope to god my deodorant works because if this stress sweat makes me smell bad, I might die from humiliation.

By the time the on-screen couple makes it to St. Patrick's day, our bowl of popcorn is empty. Asher moves it from my lap to the space beside him. I stare at the TV, unable to focus because his fingers are twisting a lock of my hair, giving me goosebumps.

"Ellie?"

I turn my head to look at Asher and he's close. So close I can feel his breath on my face. I look up into his eyes and bite the corner of my bottom lip, hardly able to breathe. This could be our moment, the one that takes us from fake to real. All the signs are there: the stupid movie, the closeness, how he's found a way to touch me nearly all afternoon.

"Yeah?" I whisper.

Asher leans closer until our lips are almost touching. "I..." He tilts his head and I suck in a breath, then close my eyes.

"Lainey!" Mom hollers as she unlocks the front door. Asher pulls back and scoots a few inches away. His arm leaves my shoulders and he clasps his hands in his lap. *Seriously, Mom?* I'm so frustrated I could scream.

"Can you...oh." Mom stops yelling and smiles. "Hi, Asher. Do you think you kids can help me with the groceries?"

"Sure thing, Mrs. Walker," Asher replies, rising to his feet. He holds his hand out for me. I used to think the gesture was him being kind, but now I wonder if it's another way to touch me. If he feels the same pull I do.

"Asher, hun," Mom states with a grin, "if you're going to keep seeing Lainey, we might as well get rid of the formalities. Call me Susan. "

"So, you approve?" he asks, one brow arched.

Mom giggles and opens the fridge to put the milk away. She ignores the question and reaches for another bag of things to put away. "Will you be staying for supper tonight?"

"Oh." Asher smiles politely and shakes his head. He hands over a tub of butter and says, "I don't want to impose."

"James and I have a date tonight, so it's no opposition." Mom tosses an empty shopping bag into the recycling bin, then smirks. "Just no hanky-panky. Clothes must be on at all times tonight."

My jaw drops. I'm mortified. I cover my face with my hands and mumble "Oh, god. Mom!"

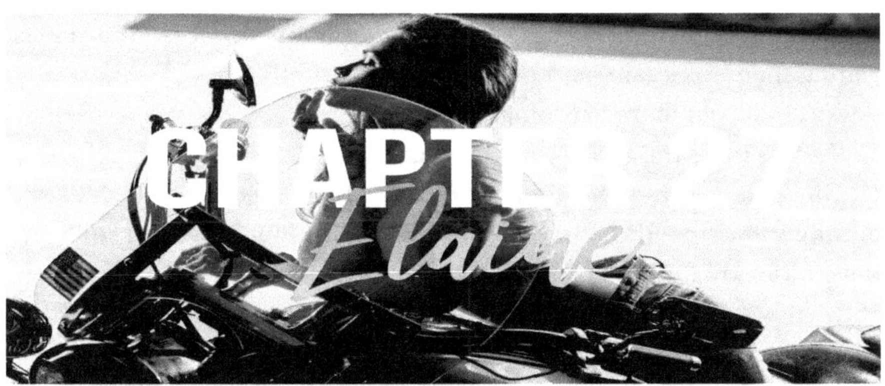

"I t's getting late," Mom whispers, rubbing her fingers across my scalp. When I was little, she used to wake me up for school that way, playing with my hair and singing a song. I smile at the memory and rub my eyes. "You should probably get to bed."

Asher and I ordered a pizza and watched both *Princess Switch* movies. They were cute and have the chick from *High School Musical*. Mom was obsessed with Zac Effron, so anything she could put on that was appropriate with him in it, she did. Asher and I must have watched those movies a million times when we were little. So, when we saw that chick was in the princess movies, there was no question what we'd watch.

Once I finished the first one, I had to know what happened next. I'm pretty sure I finished the last movie, but considering we fell asleep we might not have. Oh, well. The second one was predictable. Girl's evil cousin tricks guy. Guy leaves girl. Girl finds him just in time. The end.

"Okay." I yawn. "'I'll wake Asher."

Mom looks down at him, asleep on my lap. She's got that proud mother look in her eye, even though he's not her kid, and smiles. "No, he can stay, but you need to go to your room."

"Are you sure, Mom?" I ask, already knowing her answer. "Doesn't that break your sleep over rule?"

"Like that's stopped you before?" Mom arches her brows. "I know about you and Liam, Lane. He's been coming through your window for years."

I stare at her, jaw dropped. "You never said anything."

Mom shrugs and brushes her fingers over Asher's hair. She smiles, getting that look again, and says, "I'll tell your father about Asher so he doesn't freak out in the morning."

I guess that's the end of that. "Thanks, Mom."

She pats my shoulder then disappears down the dark hallway. I slip out from underneath Asher, careful not to wake him, my mind still spinning. Mom knew about Liam sleeping in my bed, which means she probably knows that we were doing more than sleeping. I swallow hard. Eventually, she's going to get the EOB from the insurance about today's visit at Planned Parenthood. I just hope when it comes, I'll be off at college and she can put two and two together. At least that way I won't have to explain anything.

I flip the light on in my room and choke back a scream. No one should be in my room, especially Liam, but there he is, sitting on my bed, looking like he's been to hell and back. "What the hell are you doing here?"

Liam stares at his hands and whispers, "I broke up with Corah."

"You did what?" I look behind me to Asher. He's still asleep. I don't want him knowing Liam is here, so I close the door. No matter how I look at this situation, it isn't good, but if I can keep Asher from waking, maybe I won't have to tell him about it. "Liam, you can't."

"She lied to me." He looks up at me, eyes red and puffy. "She was never pregnant. She used her cousin's ultrasound because she was scared I was going to leave her." He pauses and shakes his head. "She lied to me, Lainey."

"Holy crap." I sit on the bed and pull Liam into a hug. Big arms wrap around my waist, pulling me close, as his head rests against my chest. I thread my fingers through Liam's hair, waiting for the butterflies in my stomach to spring to life. They don't. The only thing I'm feeling is sorrow, because as happy as I am to hear that Liam won't be a father, I'm also heartbroken. No man should ever be put through something like this. "I'm so sorry. Are you okay?"

He shakes his head and looks up at me. "She only came clean because she knew I'd eventually leave her. For you."

"Liam..." I drop my arms to my slides and scoot back an inch. If he would have come to me a few weeks ago, before I found out about the almost baby and the need for an STD test, I might have felt differently. I cared for him so much, I thought I was in love. Now, I look at Liam and realize I do love him, but I'm not in love with him.

"I never would have stayed with Corah if it wasn't for the baby. I was going to take you to prom." He takes my hand. I look down at our intertwined fingers, still shocked there's no zing of electricity. I tuck my lips between my lips to fight a frown and meet Liam's gaze again. "It was always supposed to be you and me, Lainey. What happened to us?"

"You hurt me." I pull my hand back and hug myself. The wounds in my heart from every time I was pushed aside and forgotten for someone else burst open. All the pain I've locked away hits me at once, pooling tears behind my eyes. "You were sleeping with other people behind my back."

"We weren't exclusive. You knew I was with other girls."

I shake my head and wipe at my eyes before the flood gates break loose. "I knew you were doing stuff with those girls, but I didn't know you were doing that."

Liam snorts and leans back onto his hands. "What did you think I was doing with them? Cuddling and watching movies? I only did that kind of shit with you, Lainey."

"I don't know." I stand and pace across the room to my desk. That picture of Liam and I stares at me. I wish I could go back to that day, to when he was my moon and my sun, but now things are different. I'm different. "I never sat down and thought about it, but none of that matters." I turn to Liam and wonder, *Did he even think about the shit he was exposing me to?* Probably not. "We never used a condom, Liam. How many other girls did you do that with?"

"None," he insists, standing and crossing the room. He touches my elbow and looks me in the eye. "Only you."

I shake my head and step out of his grasp. Anger burns beneath my skin, scorching my insides. How dare he think I'm that naive. "Stop lying to me! That can't be true if you thought Corah was pregnant."

"Fine", Liam growls, his heartbroken, caring demeanor replaced with irritation. "Do you want the truth? All of them. I fucking hate condoms."

My face pinches together in disgust. Tomorrow's phone call with my results can't come fast enough. "Get out, Liam. You disgust me."

"Don't make me go," he begs, dropping down to his knees and holding my legs. "We can fix this. I can do better. I'll let everyone know we're together this time and I will only be with you. Please, Lainey."

My heart breaks because I did it. Liam finally sees me as someone worth having, but it's too late. I take his hands and pull him to his feet "I don't trust you. You've got to work on fixing our friendship before I'd even consider being with you like that again."

"Fine." He wraps his arms around me and nuzzles into my neck. " I'll do whatever you want."

"Thank you." I keep my arms at my sides until Liam realizes I'm not going to fall into his trap. There will be no cuddling that turns into kissing that makes its way into touching. He and I are starting over as friends. Nothing more.

Liam takes the hint and steps back, shoving his hands in his pockets. "So, that means you and Asher are over then. Right?"

Asher. I'd almost forgotten about him. I know things between us are fake, but it feels so real. I can't let what we have go until I know where he stands. I shake my head. "No. I'm not breaking up with him. Not until I know you're serious and feel like this is something I'm ready to do again. Asher has been the perfect boyfriend, Liam. You have a lot of work to do if you want to take his place."

"You're joking." He sneers. "You expect me to drop everything and everyone but you're still going to be with him? No. I'm not doing it."

I shrug not at all surprised. Or even disappointed. "You always know what to say to make me bend my will for you, Liam, but you fall short every time. Crawl back out the way you came and leave me alone."

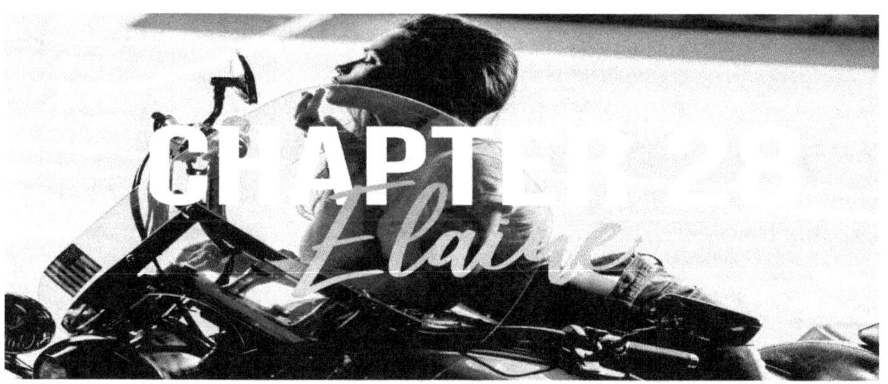

I lean against the hood of my car in the school parking lot and watch Asher talk to Russell and a few of the football guys. He hasn't noticed me yet, and for that I'm grateful. It's not often I have the chance to appreciate his beauty anymore. Asher throws his head back and laughs. His smile is boisterous and reaches his eyes. Even though I have no idea what they are talking about, I smile too. I tuck my hair behind my ears because just watching him makes me nervous.

Asher looks up, mid-conversation, as if he can feel my eyes on him, and turns his head towards me. Our gazes lock and heat climbs my neck. I feel stupid. We've been fake dating for weeks, but now that Liam and Corah have called it quits, our time is almost up. They've kept their breakup under wraps all week, probably because prom is Saturday and they don't want to risk losing the crown. I don't think Liam cares much about being prom king, but I know Corah does. Liam may have his faults, but he's got a good heart. He won't ruin Corah's dream just because she's a lying twat. Even if he should.

Asher and Russell do some bro shake and then he waves goodbye to the rest of their group. He walks over to me, hands in his pockets. My leg bounces as he crosses the blacktop. He smiles as he draws near and my heart flutters faster.

Asher sets one hand on either side of me, pinning me to the hood of my car, and leans in for a kiss, but it's too quick. It doesn't satisfy the ache in my stomach. "Hey, beautiful."

"Hey." My cheeks burn, releasing the heat down my neck and to my core. "How was your day?"

He chuckles and brushes his nose against my cheek until his lips reach my ear. I know this is for show, for everyone who may or may not be watching, but I love it. My chest tightens; need wraps a lasso around my heart. I toy with the idea of gripping Asher's shirt and pulling his lips against mine, parting his mouth with my tongue but we haven't kissed like that in weeks. Not since that party when we first started this mess.

"Better now that you're here." Asher pulls away and leans against the hood beside me. The breath I didn't realize I was holding burns my lungs. He looks at me funny when I exhale and asks, "Are you okay?"

"I'm fine!" I say, a little too loudly. I smirk and hope he can't see through my pathetic excuse for armor. "Are you working tonight?"

He chuckles, apparently used to my weirdness. "Nope. I'm off until Sunday."

"Really?" I rack my brain, trying to figure out what he could need this Thursday and Saturday for. I've got nothing. Prom is this weekend, but we haven't talked about going, so I don't think that's it.

"Yup. Why? Were you trying to get out of hanging tonight?"

For a fraction of a second, I think I see a glimmer of worry flash across Asher's face, but then he smiles. I must have imagined it.

I keep my gaze trained on the school and everyone who hasn't left yet. There aren't many people still on campus, most people bolted the moment the bell rang but there are still a few familiar faces lingering.

Liam shuffles down the steps and we lock eyes. He frowns and shakes his head. He hasn't made any effort to talk to me since crawling out my window last weekend. *So much for proving things can be different.* I look away and to the parking lot. I won't let him ruin this moment. "Actually, I thought I'd take you on a date."

Asher chuckles again and steps in front of me. I'm sure he noticed Liam and is putting on a show again. The thought hurts my heart. I want so badly for this to be real. I look up into his amethyst eyes. They're darker today, rich in color. "Isn't it supposed to be the other way around? Aren't I supposed to take you out?

"Yes." I wiggle out from underneath Asher. Being this close to him is too hard. Especially since there's a chance everything could end tonight. I need to get used to being without his touch, just in case things don't go as planned. "You've been so great the past few weeks, I wanted to do something nice."

Asher smiles and looks at me in a way I've only dreamed about. His eyes could be spilling the secrets of his soul, telling me how much he cares and how happy he is with me. Or, I could be over-analyzing things and setting myself up for heartbreak.

"Sounds like fun. What time should I pick you up?"

"Nuh-uh," I smirk and look over my shoulder at him. I lean against the driver's side door and cross my arms. "This is my date. Be at my house by seven, but then I'm driving."

Asher steps in front of me again. He dips his head, pressing those lips to mine for a tender, two-second kiss. "Whatever you say, beautiful."

"This place is nice," Asher states, staring out the window out our beach view from the table I reserved. The Ocean Side Cafe isn't the fanciest place in town, but the food is decent and the view is gorgeous. If you can snag one of the six window tables. Lucky for us, Alandra owed Maggie a favor and she cashed it in for me.

"It's alright." I hide behind my menu, pretending to decide what I want to eat. My head spins from nervousness. At some point tonight, we need to have the talk before Asher hears on Monday that Liam and Corah broke up. It needs to come from me, so I can control the conversation.

"El?" Asher asks. There's no denying the worry in his tone this time. He's onto me, and that makes my pulse race faster.

"Yeah?" I squeak, then clear my throat and ask again.

"What's wrong?"

Our waitress chooses that moment to reappear, giving me a few more minutes to get my bearings and figure out what I'm going to say. "Have you folks figured out what you want?"

She looks to Asher, batting her mascara covered lashes. I'm sure she's wondering what a guy like him is doing with a girl like me. Even in my best dress tonight, I feel too plain and boring to be his girlfriend. That's why the fake thing worked, I didn't have to worry about things like this. Asher looks at me and says, "Ladies first."

We order our entrees and, all too soon, the waitress is gone. Asher sets his hand on the table, palm up. I lace my fingers with his and force a smile. My lungs feel like they're trapped in a vice and I am freaking out inside. Maybe it's better to see how the cards fall on Monday. Maybe Asher will make the first move and ask me to be his forever. That could happen. Right?

"What's wrong, beautiful? You've been acting weird since lunch today."

"Liam and Corah broke up," I blurt.

Asher leans back into his chair, his hand sliding from mine. He looks out the window, at the waves crashing along the shore. The sun has just begun to set, painting the sky in wisps of red and orange. It's beautiful. Too beautiful for heartbreak. "I guess that means we're breaking up too then, huh?"

"Actually, I was thinking..." My leg bounces under the table with such fierceness I'm shaking. My stomach turns, bile climbing my throat. I grab a roll from the basket between us. I don't bother with the cinnamon butter. Just tear off a piece and shove it in my mouth. I need to soak up the acid boiling over inside me before it makes an embarrassing appearance. I swallow then ask my question in one rushed breath. "Would you want to do this for real?"

I shove another torn piece of bread into my mouth. I'm trying like hell to keep my composure but each passing millisecond feels like a lifetime in itself. I don't know how long it takes for Asher to turn his gaze to me.

When he does, he lifts his lips into a crooked smirk. "Elaine Melrose Walker, are you attracted to me?"

Our waitress returns with our orders in hand. She sets the plates in front of us then walks away without asking if we need anything else. Asher picks up his lobster sandwich, but waits to take a bite until he asks, "Well?"

I drop what's left of my roll in the basket and grab my fork. I twirl the spaghetti on my plate, refusing to meet Asher's gaze because my cheeks are bound to be red they're so hot. "Don't ruin the moment, Asher."

"Just answer the question." I hear the smile in his tone and give into temptation. I look into those eyes. The same pools of purple I loved as a child but dismissed as I grew up. Now, at eighteen, I've come full circle, falling into their depths and finding new slivers of color every chance I get. Today, the rich hues have trails of silver.

I stare into them until my own eyes burn. I blink twice, water covering my sclera, relieving the dryness. "What question?"

Asher smirks and folds his arms on the table, his sandwich forgotten. I huff out an exaggerated groan. *This is so embarrassing.* "Fine. Asher, will you go out with me and be my real boyfriend?"

He scoots his chair back. Stands. Then moves to the open seat next to me. I feel my heart everywhere. In my chest. My toes. Even my eyelids. Asher is grinning, so I think whatever he's about to say is good, but that doesn't soothe my nerves.

"Under one condition."

I swallow hard, expecting him to tell me I need to change the way I dress, or wear more makeup, or do something to my appearance to be worthy of the girlfriend title. Most days I wear my hair in a ponytail and put on a little eye makeup. Tonight, I straightened my hair, then curled the ends. To my amazement, it's holding. I've also put on a full face of makeup. Foundation. Eye shadow and liner. Lipstick. "What's that?"

"Go to prom with me." Asher reaches for my hand and I swear this must be what a real proposal feels like. "I've been wanting to ask you, but wasn't sure how you'd take it since things between us were supposed to be fake."

I don't have a dress, or shoes, or a hair appointment. I doubt I could get any of that at the last minute, but I don't care. I nod, my lips stretching wide across my face. "Yes!"

"Good." Asher reaches forward and threads his fingers through the hair at the base of my neck. He looks me dead in the eye and this time, there's no doubt in my mind that he's gonna kiss me. "Because none of this was fake for me, Ellie. I've wanted you since the sixth grade. Now that I've got you, I'm not letting you go."

Asher presses his mouth to mine before my brain can analyze what he said. He parts my lips with his tongue. I melt into him, scooting from my chair into his lap. I wrap my arms around his neck, and close my eyes, falling deeper into the kiss. Asher's mouth is dangerous, a hot sear of temptation and desire. It's better than I remembered, making it too easy to forget where we are. We feel right like this, but I need to remember we just started dating. As great as the last few weeks were, if we rush things, it could ruin them. But then this feeling of lust slithers through me and all thoughts of caution are forgotten.

Someone clears their throat and we're forced to break away. I fight the urge to yell at whoever interrupted us, but remember we are at a restaurant and look up at the person with a smile instead. It's our waitress, holding styrofoam containers. Her cheeks are red as she asks, "Do you want to finish everything here or take it to go?"

"Here," Asher says, applying a little pressure to my hip.

I slide back into my chair, the pang of disappointment slithering through me. He has an empty hotel room three blocks away. We could take our food there and get to know the parts of each other we've been dying to touch. But no.

I force a smile and return my napkin to my lap. Asher must be thinking the same thing I was a few minutes ago. We shouldn't rush things. Going from chaste kisses to sex on day one is a little much, but prom is in two days.

All bets are off on prom night.

My cheeks burn and I try to contain my smile. In two days, I'm going to sleep with Asher Anderson.

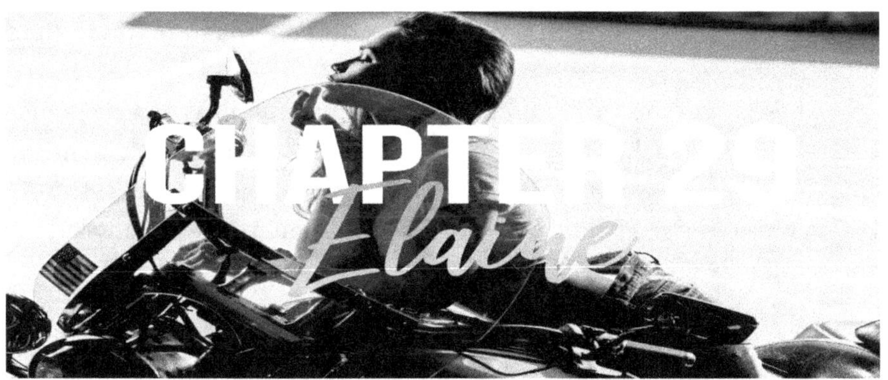

"**I** want to meet your mom," I say the next morning on the way to my locker.

Dinner was nice. We finished our meals and then, since Asher didn't suggest we do anything else, I drove us back to my house. I may be more anxious to ride him than a junkie looking for her next fix, but I don't want him to think I'm promiscuous.

Prom is different though. Everyone has sex on prom night. It's an unwritten rule. If you have a date, and you've never done it before, you're popping that cherry. My cheeks heat with excitement as I think about it. *Let's see if he can give me that orgasm he promised.*

"You've already met her," Asher states, pulling me back to the moment. We stop in the hallway and he leans against the locker beside mine. "You don't need to do it again."

"Meeting your mom when we were eight doesn't count." I twist the spinner on my lock and open the door. I grab my civics binder, since that's my first class after homeroom, then shut it again. I hold my binder in front of me, both hands on the edge, and wait for his reply.

It takes a solid three seconds to formulate a simple statement, but he says, "I'm pretty sure that if you've met her once, it lasts a lifetime."

I reach for Asher's hand. He laces his fingers with mine and smiles. It's not the grin I've gotten used to. There's no joy behind it, no playfulness in his eyes.

"Asher, what are you worried about?"

Is it his house? I've already been there, so he can't be worried I'll think he lives in a shithole. He does, but people can't help the environment they're born into. They can only strive to do better, and be more than their parents.

Asher is quiet for a minute, staring off into space. When he comes back to me, he reaches for his phone in his back pocket. Looking at the clock on his screen saver, he says, "If we leave now we can get there before Mom starts her shift at the diner. Clint should have already left for another job by now, so he shouldn't be a problem."

Now?

My breath hitches. I've never skipped class. I've always been that good girl that was more worried about the endgame. I needed the grades to get the scholarship. Even though my dad's a lawyer and we live in a nice house, we're not rolling in the dough. He put himself through school and accumulated a lot of debt in the process. We're not poor, but we're not St. Anastasia's rich, which is why I go to the school that's somewhere in the middle. "I guess we should get going then."

People skip school all the time. This is no big deal. Right?

Asher takes my hand and leads me out a door I never knew existed. We round the back of the athletics building and somehow end up in the senior parking lot. My car is four rows over and down a little ways, but Asher's bike is right here, waiting for us, as if he knew he'd be skipping class today.

"Here." He hands me his helmet.

"I don't wanna take the bike," I tell him, staring at the helmet. Asher chuckles and I drag my gaze up to his face. "It's loud and we could get caught."

Asher shakes his head, a lazy smile lifting his lips. "We won't get caught."

"But what if we do?" Will it go on my permanent record? Will I lose my scholarship? Panic snakes around my lungs, cutting off the flow of air.

"Breathe, baby. It's fine." Asher pulls me into a hug and rubs my back. I close my eyes and focus on the sound of his breathing. I can hear his heart racing inside his chest. It's beating almost as fast as mine.

"No one will know we're gone," he insists. "But if it makes you feel better, we can take your car."

Asher lets me go and puts the helmet back on his handlebars. if I were him, I'd worry someone might steal it, but most people around here don't mess with Asher for one reason or another.

"We'd better get going. Mom's shift starts at ten and it's a twenty-minute ride."

I let Asher drive my car across the tracks to the side of town my friends and I don't even joke about venturing into. He pulls into a trailer park that's a gravel road, so bumpy my head hits the side of the window as he tries to swerve to avoid a pothole. I don't remember the road being this bad the last time I was here.

"You okay?" Asher grimaces as I rub the sore spot with my palm.

My head throbs but overall I'm fine, and I tell him as much.

Asher follows a beaten path, pulling around to the back of his trailer park before stopping in front of a faded yellow mobile home. Nothing about this place looks familiar, but the feeling of dread that washes over me has crept into my dreams. I know without a doubt that this is the home of the monster who abuses Asher.

"Shit," Asher mumbles. He shifts the car into park and without saying anything rushes out, leaving my car door open as he runs up the doublewide's porch steps.

I've got this feeling tickling the back of my mind telling me to stay here, that something inside is wrong, but the fear of leaving Asher alone in a time of need outweighs my common sense.

I watch the door, anxiously waiting for Asher to reappear for about thirty seconds before unbuckling my seatbelt.

I run up the steps and freeze in the doorway. I recognize the woman lying on the carpet. Her hair has slivers of gray adding an elegant shine to the long honey colored strands splayed across the carpet. A hand reaches out to me, lifeless, like the eyes that beg for help. My whole body shakes as I take a step closer. I bend down and touch her fingertips. They're warm. She couldn't have passed long ago, but there's no denying that Mary Anne, Asher's mom, is dead.

My gaze shoots up at a gurgling sound. Clint kneels over Asher, both hands around his neck. Asher thrashes widely underneath him, but even I can tell it's useless. All he's doing is wasting his energy and killing himself faster.

I watch in horror for what feels like a lifetime, frozen beside Asher's dead mother. If I don't do something, Clint is going to kill Asher. But What can I do?

The gun is still in my glovebox.

I scramble to my feet and run down the front steps. My hands shake as I yank the passenger door of my car open. I've never fired a gun before. I don't even know how to tell if it's loaded, but I would think Asher wouldn't have pulled an empty pistol on his stepdad.

I find the black piece on top of a bunch of useless papers, where he left it, and pull the slide back. I run back up the steps and towards Clint shouting, "Stop!"

Asher is limp under his weight. My heart thrums faster, fearful I was too late.

Clint stands to full height and chuckles. "What are you gonna do with that, little girl?"

I tilt the end of the gun towards Asher then bring it back to Clint's face. "Is he dead?"

"What are you going to do if he is? Shoot me?" Clint steps over Asher, toward me and I instinctively take a step back.

"If you come any closer, I'll shoot."

"You don't have the guts." Clint takes another step towards me. I pull the trigger, but nothing happens. Clint laughs and continues his slow descent across the room. Panicking, I look at the gun to see what could have gone wrong. There's a tiny lever on the side, near my thumb, facing up. I flick it down and raise my arms again.

"Stop!" I demand.

Clint laughs again and takes another step. He's just over an arm's length away, close enough to hurt me if he lunged but far away enough that I can still defend myself. He lifts his foot to close the space between us and I try again.

I squeeze my trigger and lose my balance. The force of the gun topples me backward, to the floor. I land on my ass beside Mary Anne, unable to hear anything over the ringing in my ears.

I crawl to my feet and run past Clint. He gasps on the carpet as blood pools from the hole in his chest.

I fall to the ground beside Asher and press my fingertips to his neck. I can't find a pulse. I don't know how to do CPR, but I try anyway. It can't be that hard. Pinch the nose. Breathe into the mouth. Push like hell against the chest until he comes back to life. I can do that.

I pinch Asher's nose shut with one hand and open his mouth with the other. I press my lips to his, pushing my air into his lungs because I refuse to let him die. I blow one more breath then move to his chest. In the movies, people place their hands near the center, between the nipples. I link my fingers together and press with all my might. I'm not sure if it works, but I push two more times before trying to blow air into Asher's mouth again.

On my second breath, Asher gasps, then coughs. I fall onto my ass, struggling to breathe myself as tears pour down my cheeks. "Asher?"

He coughs again and rolls onto his side. "I think you broke my rib."

"Asher!" I yell and throw my arms around him. He pushes onto one arm and holds me tight. "I thought I lost you."

He comforts me for a few minutes before pulling back and rising to his feet. His eyes scan the room, taking everything in. He walks across the carpet, picks up the gun, and wipes the handle with his shirt.

"What are you doing?"

"Call 911, Ellie." Asher walks over to Clint's body and kicks his leg. Clint doesn't move, doesn't breathe. "Call your dad, too. I'm in serious shit."

"You?" I reach for Asher's hand but he pulls back. "I did this."

"No. You waited in the car until you heard the gun go off. Then you came inside and saw all of this."

I run my hands over my face and shake my head. "What are you talking about?"

"Ellie." Asher grabs my arm and looks me in the eye. "It's my fault you're in this mess. I knew better than to drag you into my life. I won't let you ruin your life for me. Call your dad. He'll help make this go away."

I rub my hand underneath my nose and nod. Asher is right. Dad can do just about anything. He'll see the holes in Asher's story and realize I shot Clint. He'll know that I had no choice and he'll make everything alright.

It takes thirty minutes for Dad to make it to Asher's house. I meet him outside and tell him everything before Asher can screw it up. Dad looks at me, tears welling in his eyes, and says, "It's okay, honey. You did the right thing."

He pulls me into a hug and we walk inside together. Asher kneels over his mother but stands when he sees us and wipes at his eyes. "Sir."

Dad nods, but frowns. "Want to tell me what happened?"

"Yes, sir, but can we go outside?"

"Of course."

I sit on the steps, hugging myself as they walk around the cul de sac. I wish I smoked. Maybe that would make the shaking go away. I rub my hands along the back of my neck and sigh. *Everything will be alright.*

Dad pulls his phone from his pocket and places it to his ear. This is it. The defining moment of my life. I'll be put in the back of a cop car and fingerprinted, but I'll be alright. I was defending myself and Asher. Any judge will see that. besides, the world is a better place without that scum on this earth.

The cops arrive in less than thirty minutes. They walk into the house. I take a breath, preparing myself for what's next. Yellow tape is strung around the exterior as one officer says, "Asher Anderson, you're under arrest."

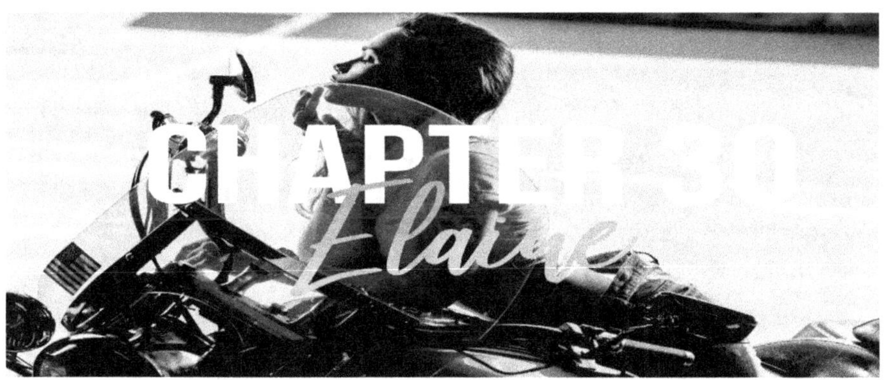

I don't know how I got home. Logic tells me I got into Mom's car sometime after the police carted Asher away and she drove. Logic also tells me that I walked inside. Changed out of my bloodied clothes. Took a shower. Fell onto my bed and possibly even went to sleep. I don't remember any of it.

All I remember is the blood seeping into the carpet under Clint's lifeless body. I remember Mary Anne's beautiful face, ashen and covered in bruises. The purple marks on her cheeks were nothing compared to the ones around her neck. Asher's step-dad choked his mom to death and then went after him.

Tears pool in my eyes and I shut them to push away the sting. I should be the one behind bars, not Asher. I shot Clint. I'm the murderer. And yet, I'm lying in my comfy bed while he lays on a metal slab. It's not fair. My life will go on as normal and he will lose everything. His scholarship to UF. His home. All of the belongings in that tattered house.

I should collect his mother's things and whatever is in his room before it's lost. With no one to pay the bills, someone is going to repossess everything they have. Or worse, someone from that neighborhood will ransack it.

I sit up with a start, terrified that Asher will literally lose everything he has. I never want to go back to that place, but I'll never forgive myself if something important to him is stolen. I wipe my eyes with the back of my hand and force myself out of bed. The sun has set, casting dark shadows throughout the house.

"Oh," Mom says, startled to see me when she turns around. "You're up. I didn't know if I'd see you tonight."

"I have to go." I don't sound like myself. My voice is husky and cracks from all the crying. My throat clenches, begging for a glass of water, but there's no time. I have to get boxes and pack up everything I can find then get to the school to move Asher's bike and... my thoughts trail off. I drove to Asher's house. I left my car there. Where is my car?

"Oh, no. You're not going anywhere." Mom sets the stirring spoon on the counter. She crosses the kitchen to where I'm standing, then guides me to a kitchen stool.

I collapse into the chair and rest my face in my hands. I thought I knew what heartbreak was. I thought the tightness in my chest and the whirlwind of insecurity and hate I felt when Liam ended things between us was the worst of it. I was wrong. Those emotions are minuscule compared to this. My heart feels like it's been put in a meat grinder. My chest is being squeezed in a tourniquet and my head feels like it's about to explode. All of that paired with the tears that rarely stop flowing and the blanket of darkness that's wrapped itself around me... yeah. Liam's breakup was nothing.

"What's going on, sweetie?" Mom's eyes are red-rimmed and puffy from her own tears. Her makeup, which is usually a thin layer of eyeliner and mascara, has washed away. She looks older. Tired. "Where do you want to go?"

"I have to go get Asher's stuff." I'm trying to talk, but the tears start flowing and without meaning to, I'm yelling at mom. I take a breath to try and calm down but the air doesn't fill my lungs. I take another and another, each one less effective than the last. Spots cloud my vision and, before I know it, I'm full on hyperventilating.

I don't know when Mom got up and left me but at some point there are two small pills in my hand and a glass of water in front of me. "Drink," she orders.

I toss the pills in my mouth and chase them with a sip. Within a few minutes, the pressure in my chest dissipates. My lungs fill with air and the brown spots clouding my vision disappear. Mom's eyebrows are pulled together, worry wrinkled nestled between them. "When did you start having panic attacks again?"

I shrug, feeling embarrassed. Asher is sitting in a cold jail cell, taking the blame for what I did, probably thinking about how he's become an orphan overnight, and I'm losing my shit. What is wrong with me? "I had one a few weeks ago before Asher started coming around. Besides that one, it's been at least a year."

Mom nods. It's been a crazy, unexpected few weeks. Never in my wildest dreams did I think Liam would turn his back on me or that Asher would become the person I turned to the most. "Your dad has already taken care of Asher's things. The house is a crime scene right now, but as soon as it's cleared, he has a company ready to go in and pack everything that's salvageable."

"His motorcycle is at school, Mom. We have to go get it before someone steals it."

"Sweetie." Mom wraps her arms around me and pulls me into a hug. "Your dad has already thought of that. It's safe in the garage."

I sniffle, tears of relief ready to pour out of me again. "He's thought of everything, hasn't he?"

Mom chuckles and smooths my hair. "He has, including who will represent Asher in court."

I pull back, feeling the color drain from my face. "Dad's not Asher's lawyer? No, he has to be." He's the only one who can save Asher.

"Sweetie, your dad is a prosecutor. He can't switch sides just because someone we know is in the hot seat."

"So Dad will be the one pressing charges?"

Mom nods. "But don't worry. Jeff Harris is the best defense attorney in the tri-county area. Between him and your dad, Asher will get a fair trial."

"A fair trial? Mom, what are you talking about? I shot Clint. It was self-defense. Ballistics will show that. Asher shouldn't even be on trial."

"Honey." Mom pulls me into a hug and presses her hand on my head. "Asher insists he pulled the trigger. Whether or not it's true, that's the story he's chosen to tell. He has chosen to let you go to college and live your life. You should be grateful he loves you enough to do this."

I don't feel grateful.

I feel guilty.

"**H**oly shit! Your door is open!"

The world is blurry as I peel my eyelids open. My head hurts from another night of crying. My back aches from sleeping on the floor. And the sun, it's bright. Too damn bright even with the shades drawn and the curtains pulled.

"Oh. My. Gosh. El, you look like shit."

I vaguely recognize Maggie's voice through the ringing in my ears. Fingers link themselves with mine and I'm pulled onto my unsteady feet. She brushes the hair from my face with her hand, her nose wrinkled in worry and probably disgust. I haven't showered in days, not since the cops laughed in my face when I insisted I murdered Clint, not Asher. I probably smell as bad as I feel.

"Enough of this self-pity," Maggie demands. "I know your mom thinks she's doing the right thing by giving you space, but I disagree. It's been ten days, Lainey."

Ten days? That's it? Funny how time moves. Sometimes a day lasts a lifetime, other times a week blurs into a few hours. I have no clue what day or time it is. I don't care. I just want to curl into a ball and go back to sleep. Guilt is a bitch, but depression is her mistress. I'd rather sleep than deal with the thoughts running through my head.

"We have to get you up and moving or you're not gonna make it," Maggie insists. She tugs at my arms and pulls me into the bathroom.

"I don't feel like going anywhere. Can't you leave me alone?"

Maggie unzips her pink makeup bag and sorts through the items inside. She pulls my mediocre bag from under my sink and finds my foundation, then sets all of the products she plans to use on the counter. "I don't care how you feel! Asher gets one day for visitors. How do you think he'll feel if you don't show up?"

"Asher can have visitors?" I ask through the fog. If he can have visitors, then I can convince him to tell the truth. It's not too late!

"Yes! Finally, I'm getting through to you! Now hurry up and jump in the shower. You smell horrible and I've got my work cut out for me with those dark circles.

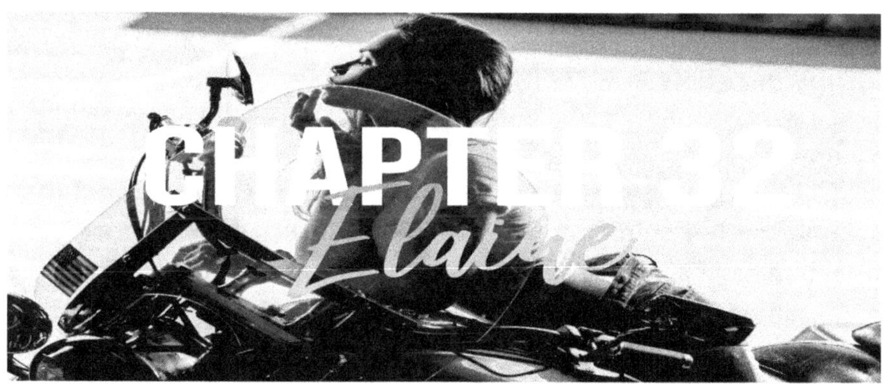

I run my hand down my dress for the umpteenth time, smoothing invisible wrinkles, as I wait for the guard to call my name. Nervous energy runs rampant through my veins. These past ten days have been hell. I can't begin to imagine what it must have been like for Asher.

Before today, the only thing I knew about jail was from the show *Orange Is the New Black*. Now, having binge-watched every incarceration documentary on Netflix I could find the last three hours, I realize that show portrayed the correctional system through rose-colored glasses.

I stand, unable to sit any longer, and chew on my thumbnail. The waiting room is tiny. White walls match the white tiles, plain and devoid of life. The only color to keep your brain from playing tricks is from the grey cushioned chairs. I pace the room, glancing at the watch on my wrist every few steps.

The door opens and I jump from excitement. A man, maybe my father's age, clad in his police uniform, holds a clipboard. "Elaine Walker?"

"That's me!" I don't bother to hide my excitement as I raise my hand and hustle across the room.

"I.D. please."

I reach for my phone from my back pocket and push my cards up from the holder on my case. I procure my driver's license then hand it over. The man places it beside my name on his clipboard. He checks it twice before handing the card back to me. "This way, Miss."

My heart ravages my ribcage with each step. The hallway I'm led down is wide but bare. Like the waiting room, it too is painted white, but the overhead fluorescent lights cast an eerie yellow veil upon them. We pass a series of doors, leading to what? I don't know. Until finally stopping in front of the one I've been waiting for.

The man gestures to a seat then says, "He'll be out in a moment."

I nod and sit in front of the plexiglass divider that separates civilians from inmates. I don't know what I expected, but I hoped we'd be in a big room, sitting across from each other, where I could get reprimanded for giving Asher the hug I so desperately need. I look around the room, impatiently waiting for the door on the other side to open. I'm the only visitor today and that breaks my heart. Not for Asher, but for everyone else.

A buzzing sound penetrates through the room. I sit up straighter, my body humming with anticipation. A door opens against the white wall. I hear the clanking of chains before I see him.

Asher, my Asher, doesn't look like the man I saw ten days ago. My Asher radiates confidence and brings light into a room. This shell of a man looks broken, beat down, and is sporting a black eye he didn't have before.

Asher holds up his hands for the guard, who uncuffs him and steps back against the wall. I pick up the corded phone on my side of our barrier and wait for him to do the same. Tired eyes reach mine. He reaches for his phone and I can't help but notice the wince he tries to hide.

"What happened?" I ask the moment the receiver is against his ear.

"Nothing. I'm fine," he grumbles.

The rubber band around my lungs snaps. Hearing Asher's voice, even as pained and tired as it sounds, is the medicine I needed. I wish I could hug him and kiss all of his pain away. I take a moment to study Asher, and he seems to be doing the same.

Asher rubs his hand over his face and sighs, what little resolve he had breaking in front of me. "You look like shit, El."

I shrug. I tried to make myself halfway presentable. Maggie straightened my hair then pulled it into a high ponytail, wrapping a braid around the tie. She even attempted to put on makeup on me this morning, but my physical appearance isn't what he's talking about. My dress hangs loosely from my lack of appetite. My eyes have sunk in a bit, and no matter how much concealer Maggie caked onto my face, she couldn't hide the dark circles that have tattooed themselves under my eyes.

"I miss you, Asher."

He smiles, but it looks pained. "El…"

Sensing whatever he's about to say won't be good, I cut him off. "Dad says your trial should start in a few weeks. June-B, from the diner, said she'd be a character witness. She's willing to go on trial and tell everyone how much of a monster Clint was. Dad thinks the prosecutor will offer a plea deal."

"El…"

"You're going to beat this Asher, I know you are." I insist because there's no other option. My conscience will eat me alive if Asher rots behind bars much longer.

"El…"

"And I'm going to be here for you every step of the way."

"Elaine!" Asher yells. "I don't want you here."

"What?" No. He doesn't mean that. He's doing what he did with my dad, saying what he thinks is necessary to keep me safe. I don't want safe. I want him. "What do you mean you don't want me here? Asher, I…I think I'm falling in love with you."

"You don't love me, El. You love the way I make you feel because you weren't treated right, but this isn't love. This is lust."

"You're wrong. I love you."

"Stop. Please."

"No! I won't stop. I will come here every day and tell you how much I love you. You need me, Asher. I won't abandon you."

"Goddamnit, El! Why can't you listen to me?" he booms. The guard looks at us but doesn't move to calm Asher down, which terrifies me. How often do they see this? How often are loving couples ripped apart in this room? "I was trying to be nice but, apparently, that's not working. I don't love you. I hooked up with you to piss Liam off."

"I don't believe you." He told me everything was real. He said so himself!

"Well, then, you're an idiot."

"I know what you're doing. You're trying to push me away."

"Of course I am! This isn't the life you're meant for. You can't waste your life on me. My trial could take years."

"It won't."

Dad won't let it. I won't let it. I'll barge into that courtroom and demand everyone listen to me. There's nothing they can do if I choose to tell the truth right then. Sure, it'll piss Dad off and screw up my first year of college, but Dad would do everything in his power to set me free. I know it.

"It could! People change in prison. What happens if you give up everything for me and when I get out we can't stand each other? Then what?"

"Asher, this is jail, not prison."

"I murdered my stepdad. You were there! I shot him in cold blood."

I slam my fist against the barrier between us. "No, you didn't! I did, Asher. Me. I shot Clint to defend myself and to save your life!"

"Keep telling yourself that, love. Facts are facts and the facts are: I don't love you. I don't want you here, and if you show up to any of my hearings I will have the police escort you out."

"You can't do that."

"Try me, El."

"I love you, Asher."

He shakes his head, disappointment etched across his face. I search his eyes for a glimmer of truth. Something to tell me that he's lying, but they're cold and empty. "Then figure out how to stop."

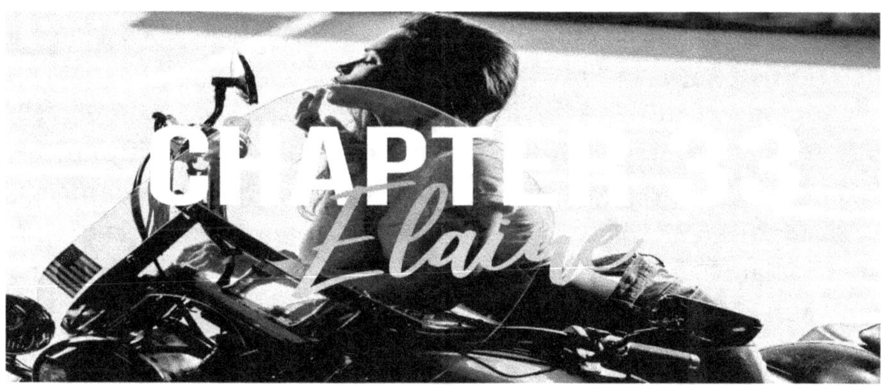

Dear Asher,

When we were eight, you left my house after our playdate and never came back. Something happened between our parents— yours, mine, and Liam's— and that was it. Everyone pretended like you didn't exist, and I couldn't understand why. We had known each other since diaper days. You gave me my favorite Ariel doll for my fifth birthday. You ripped her head off at the playground, and then, poof.

You were gone

I cried.

I cried every day for a solid week. That doesn't sound like long, but when you're eight years old with an attention span the size of a grain of rice, it's a big deal.

Now, imagine me today. Eighteen years old, mulling over our last conversation. You know, the one where you told me never to come back after I told you I was falling in love with you. How much do you think I've cried? How long do you think my tears will last now that you have my heart?

I'll tell you.

I'll never stop crying because I'll never stop loving you.

You can push me away, Asher, but I'm not going anywhere.

Forever yours,

El

. . .

I fold the paper into thirds and stuff it into an envelope. I lick it closed, half worried my dad will read it, half worried my letter will fall out and get lost somewhere. I lean back in my desk chair and stare up at the ceiling. To just look at it, the white looks smooth, flawless, but if you look, really look, there are waves and divots and imperfections. Just like life.

Before I know what's happening, tears fall down my cheeks. They aren't violent like they were last week, demanding the world understand their hurt. These are silent. Slow. The worst kind, because they represent the kind of hurt that goes unnoticed. I sniffle and rub them away with the palm of my hand. Feeling exposed and vulnerable, I move to my bed and hug my pillow. I close my eyes and try to picture Asher, the sweet boy who weaseled his way into my life and heart.

My eyelids feel heavy as I lift them. Darkness cloaks the room but I don't need light to know who's here. I'd recognize Liam's cologne from a mile away. I hug my knees closer to my chest, tears on the verge of spilling over again. I don't want him here. I don't want his condolences or pity or whatever words he's going to offer because, no matter what he says, nothing will bring Asher back to me. At least, not yet.

"Lainey?" Liam's hand leaves my back. His finger trails across my cheek, moving the hair veiling my face. "I'm worried about you. You weren't at school last week."

"I'm fine." My voice cracks, betraying me. I squeeze my eyes shut again, fighting the burn behind the lids. I don't want to cry, not in front of Liam. "I'll be there tomorrow."

Liam does the one thing I don't want him to do, he lays behind me and drapes his arm over my stomach. He holds me close. My body trembles against him, tremors of turmoil taking hold. Too tired, both physically and mentally, to fight, I let go. I cry until I fall asleep again, holding Liam's hand and wishing he was Asher.

My alarm goes off before the sun rises, but it's ringing isn't what wakes me. Liam shakes my shoulder until I peel my eyes open. I groan, not ready to deal with the day, but it has decided to take me by the horns.

Mom stands at the foot of my bed, arms crossed, jaw clenched tight. "You're lucky I came to check on you this morning, and not your dad."

"Shit. Mom," I say, sitting up and shoving Liam out of my bed. "It's not what it looks like."

"Oh, I know exactly what this looks like." She chuckles. "It looks like Liam trying to weasel his way back into your life."

"Mrs. Walker, I--"

Mom holds her hand up and cuts him off. "No. I don't want any explanations from you, Liam. You didn't just abandon Ellie the last six weeks, you cut us off, too. You were like a son to us." She sighs and shakes her head. "I never dreamed you would be just like your parents."

"Mrs. Walker, please. Let me explain."

Mom shakes her head again, her brows bunched together. "No. Your parents are nothing but poison to this world, and I can't let you infect my daughter with that kind of selfishness. Get out, Liam, and if I ever catch you in my daughter's bed again, it'll be my husband you deal with. I promise he won't be this calm."

Liam's head falls as he climbs out of my bed. "See you at school, Lainey."

hisper.

That's all anyone is doing. Whispering. I guess that's what happens when your boyfriend is a murderer, or so they think, and you avoid life for almost two weeks. I wish I could go back to my room, curl back into a ball, and avoid everyone.

Mom won't let me.

She says this kind of depression isn't healthy and that if I don't get my shit together we're going to see someone about it. So, I forced myself out of bed today. I made myself smile when I said hello. Shoveled a bowl of Frosted Mini Wheats into my stomach and prayed it didn't come back up. I don't feel good, but at least my breakfast is staying put.

"What are you all looking at?" Maggie scolds a group of people who stare as they walk by. Their hushed tones stop for all of three seconds as they pass us in the hallway, then start again.

I draw my gaze away from my open locker to the people who passed us. I have no idea how long I've been standing here. I look around and notice a lot of eyes darting away from me.

"You okay, sweetie?" Maggie asks, rubbing my back. She showed up at my doorstep today, ready to carry me to her car if she had to.

Apparently, no one believed I would show up to school if allowed to drive myself. They're right. I wouldn't have. I would have gone straight to the Horizon Hotel, booked a night in room three-oh-three, Asher's room, and hugged the pillows tightly. I want to be where Asher was and find some lingering piece of him.

I force another smile, the second of what I'm assuming will be one of the hundreds I'm going to wear today. I don't know how to answer Maggie's question. I hurt in ways I can't explain. I thought the pain of Asher getting arrested and it being my fault was the worst of it all.

If I hadn't insisted on meeting his mom that day, we would have never stumbled upon Clint mid murder. Asher would have come home to find his mom dead, which still would have sucked, but at least the outcome would have been different. He would have called the cops. Testified to the abuse his mom went through at the hands of that monster. And that's it. Clint would have been arrested and we would still be together.

So am I okay, knowing I could have prevented everything? Am I okay letting Asher take the blame for what should have been self-defense? No. No, I am not. "I just want to get through today."

Maggie squeezes my arm and she smiles. "If we hurry, we can get a table in the back of Ms. Honey's class."

I close my locker without taking anything out of it. I don't feel like being here, and I doubt anything anyone will try and teach me this week will stick. Why bother with my books or anything like that? I'm merely here, going through the motions.

Ms. Honey smiles as we approach her door, but her eyes are sad. She, and most everyone in the school, probably feels bad for Asher and me and I hate it. I don't want anyone's pity. I want to be left alone. "Welcome back, Miss Walker."

I stretch my lips into a grin, so fake it hurts.

"You're wanted first thing in the guidance counselor's office." Ms Honey switches her attention to Maggie. "Miss Mills. Would you mind escorting Miss. Walker there?"

"Of course." Maggie links her arm with mine.

I've sat in this office a total of two times over the past four years and it hasn't changed. Brightly colored posters adorn the white walls, telling teens not to bully one another, or that sexual assault is not your fault.

There's even one that preaches how smoking is bad for you. These kinds of rooms, they don't change.

Mr. Fitzpatrick, our school's pathetic excuse for a guidance counselor, takes a seat on the other side of his desk. The side that says, *This is my office, but you're safe here. Tell me your problems.*

I don't have any problems to tell, so he's going to be disappointed.

"I think this is the first time I've seen you this year, Miss Walker. How are you holding up?"

I shrug. One thing I learned over the years, I'm not required to answer anything because he doesn't have any power.

I came to Mr. Fitzpatrick freshman year when a few jealous girls set their sights on me. They viewed me as a threat when I wouldn't be their wingman and sing their praises to Liam. And so the bullying started. It was simple enough, at first. A few snickers behind my back. Poorly worded notes dropped on my desk or in my locker calling me a slut.

All of which I could handle, until Hunter Braun. The first boy to ask me on a date. Not just any date, homecoming.

Liam hated the idea of Hunter and I going together, but he had a date of his own, so I ignored him. Hunter showed up at my door in a limo. He introduced himself like a gentleman. He took me to a restaurant where we were to eat with his friends.

And then his real date showed up.

The one he abandoned me for to screw in the bathrooms. The one everyone knew existed but me. I was humiliated but I kept a smile on my face until Nola purposely spilled her drink down the back of my dress. My night ended there. Hunter and his date left in the limo he rented for her. His friends and bitch of a sister left a few moments later, probably to the dance. As for me, I hid in the bathroom.

Too embarrassed to call Mom.

Unable to get a hold of Liam or Maggie.

So who came to my rescue?

Asher.

I swallowed my pride as I climbed into what was probably a stolen car. We weren't old enough to drive and yet there he was, picking me up after I begged him and insisted there was no one else. He took me to

Maggie's house, where I crawled through her window until she got home some hours later, and we never talked about that night again.

When I brought my problem to Mr. Fitzpatrick, requesting to be switched out of the English class I shared with Nola, he handed me a pamphlet on bullying and, in more or less words, told me to suck it up.

"I'm glad to see you're back, Miss Walker," he says, with faux excitement. We both know he could care less if I was in school or not. James Fitzpatrick is a fifty-something-year-old man who actively counts down until his retirement.

How do I know?

He has DUR and the number two hundred and thirty-seven written in the bottom left-hand corner of his white board. "I've talked to all of your teachers. Given the unfortunate circumstances around your absences, they were all more than willing to let you make up any missed work."

"Thank you." I wasn't worried. My grades are high enough that even if my teachers were to give me a zero, I'd be fine. Even if my grades dropped, we still have two weeks until final exams and those tests have more weight than the rest.

Mr. Fitzpatrick clicks the end of his pen and flips a notebook open. "We should probably talk about what happened between you and Mr. Anderson."

I suck in a breath, holding the air in my lungs until the pressure is nearly unbearable. I've known all morning that Asher would be a hot topic. That people would poke and prod about how he is and our current relationship status. Or lack thereof. I was prepared to ignore all requests and have Maggie shoo away anybody who couldn't take the hint. I was not prepared for this.

"I'd rather not."

"Elaine." Mr. Fitzpatrick frowns. "You have been through a traumatic event. It's important to open up and not hold onto any negative feelings you may have."

"What negative feelings do you think I'm harboring?" Because the only ones on the forefront right now are annoyance and impatience.

"Depression for being dumped," he implies.

"I was not dumped!" It's hard not to yell at Mr. Fitzpatrick. For one, my relationship statuses none of his concern. But also, being dumped, as he so eloquently put it, is only the tip of my iceberg. I grab my backpack and stand. "I'm done here."

"Sit down, Miss Walker," he demands. "You're not excused."

"What are you going to do? Send me home?" I wait for a witty response, but Mr. Fitzpatrick doesn't say anything. I knew he wouldn't. Like I said, he's useless.

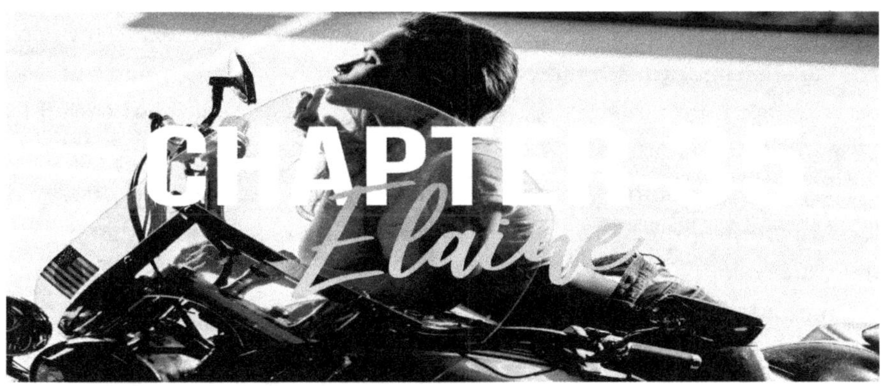

"You're here!" Liam jumps off of the table he's sitting on in the cafeteria and pulls me into his arms. My body stiffens under his touch. We have never hugged in public and he is holding onto me like I was the one who died. The past four years, all I wanted was for Liam to look at me like he is, with adoration in his eyes. To greet me in public like I mean something to him. To make me an important part of his world, not just the girl he grew up with.

Liam just did all of those things.

The plan with Asher worked better than I could have hoped, but I don't feel the same way anymore. Being with Asher tilted my world on its axis, and now all I want is for things with Liam to go back to how they used to be. Minus the secret hookups.

He drops one arm but keeps the other around my shoulder as we walk to what used to be my table. "I didn't see your car out front."

It feels wrong to be so close to Liam when my mind is on Asher. I know that I am not doing anything wrong, but it feels like cheating. "Maggie drove me."

"Oh." Liam laughs at himself. Why? I'm not sure because I haven't done anything funny. "How about I give you a ride home then?"

I wiggle out of Liam's hold and sit at the edge of the table in the cafeteria I never planned to eat at today, let alone come into this damn room. I would rather curl into a ball and hide, but Maggie knows how to make me feel better. Besides, the only place to disappear to this time of day is in the girl's bathroom, and that sounds worse than braving the masses.

Liam hops on the tabletop beside me, his feet resting next to my legs. He talks excitedly, his hands moving with each word I've tuned out. My gaze drifts to the table across the cafeteria, the one Asher and I used to sit at.

My stomach churns, not from hunger but from a memory. I have no food in front of me. The thought of eating anything more today makes me want to puke, but Asher would have noticed. Even if he didn't have the money to spare, he would have bought me something. He did buy me something. He made it a point to put me first, even knowing that piece of shit stepfather of his would give him hell for it later.

I glance up at Liam. He's smiling, excited about whatever he's rambling about. I force my lips to tilt up and return the gesture, but I'm dying inside. Liam either doesn't notice that I'm not eating or doesn't care. I realize he's never paid attention to me the way Asher did, and that makes me sad for completely different reasons.

"What do you say?" Liam asks.

"About what?"

A wrinkle of frustration appears between Liam's brows, but then he hides it with another over the top smile. "After school. You. Me. Mini golf then ice cream at the place by the beach you like so much." He laughs and runs a hand through his hair. He cut it, reshaping the style I learned to love. "You're so cute when you're lost in thought."

"I..." This sounds like a date and that is literally the last thing I want right now.

"Move," Maggie demands, her hands on her hips. Her timing couldn't be better. My heart is broken. Shattered into a million pieces that are crushed into oblivion with each day Asher is behind bars. Even if I were still into Liam, there would be nothing left for me to love him with.

Liam's smile falls. "Piss off, Magdalen. I was here first."

Maggie smirks then looks at me. "Ellie."

She uses Asher's nickname for me and tears pool behind my lashes. No one has called me Ellie in almost two weeks. I miss the way my name sounds rolling off his lips. I miss how he always smelled like the beach, even if I never knew why. I miss how he found innocent ways to touch me throughout the day.

I.

Miss.

Asher.

"Is this jerk bothering you?" Maggie asks me. I laugh because she is one hundred percent serious about Liam being a jerk and he thinks she's joking.

"Her name is Lainey," Liam growls. "Why the hell are you still letting people call you that? Asher is gone. It's time for things to go back to how they were before he fucked everything up."

"See." Maggie arches her eyebrows. "Jerk."

I shake my head, too numb to buy into their banter, but the fact that Liam is willing to throw Asher away doesn't sit right with me. For the first time since losing him, I feel something. A fire that should scare Liam and everyone around us because I'm not sure I can control it. "He's not gone, Liam. He's just...away."

Liam huffs out a hearty laugh. "He's in jail, Lainey, and he's probably going to stay there. For life. The sooner you get that through your head, the better off we'll be."

I ball my fist at my sides and fight the inferno building inside me. I try my hardest to keep my voice stoic, but it has an edge that makes Maggie smirk. "You don't know what's going to happen to him. You weren't there when his mom died."

"And you shouldn't have been either!" Liam hops off the table and stands over me. He's asserting dominance. When I cared about keeping him happy, this move would have swung the conversation into a fit of apologies and graveling. Too bad for him, I don't care what he thinks anymore.

"Why?" I raise my voice a little louder. "Why shouldn't I have been there?"

"He's not who you think he is, Lainey."

"He's exactly who I think he is!" I stand. Liam may still be a head taller than me, but we are equal in this conversation. I won't be railroaded into thinking Asher is anything less than the great man he is.

"Yeah? And who is that?"

"He's the man who took your place in my heart. My other best friend.

And..." I pause, chewing on my cheek as I debate whether or not to spill the secret that isn't mine. Fuck it. Asher pushed me away. Liam is being a dick. What does it matter if they get hurt? "And your half-brother."

"Come again?" Maggie asks in disbelief. I fight a smirk because I remember how I felt when Asher told me for the first time. Shocked. In disbelief. And eventually, I accepted it.

"Of course he would tell you. That asshole never could control himself when you were involved." Liam turns and kicks a nearby trash can.

"Hey!" one of the cafeteria monitors yell, but we both know she isn't going to do anything.

"What the hell does that mean?"

"You, Lainey. It was always you." Liam guffaws and runs a hand through his hair. "I can't tell you how many fights Asher and I got into because of you. Because he didn't like our relationship."

"I thought you said we never had one," I mumble, my arms crossing over my chest.

"Whatever, semantics."

"Not semantics," Maggie shouts. "You are such a jerk, Liam." She stands and shoves him in the chest. "Ellie put everything on the back burner for you, including her pride." She shoves him again; this time he takes a step back. "She has always been there." She pushes him again and they take another step. "She waited years for you to notice her." Shove. "And it wasn't until Asher stepped in that she was finally happy." Maggie pushes Liam again but he has nowhere to go. She's backed him into a pillar and it feels like everyone is watching. "You don't get to downplay how much you hurt my best friend because it makes you feel better."

"Maggie." Russell puts his hand on his girlfriend's arm. She looks at Liam one more time, shakes her head, then lets Russell hold her. I knew she didn't like the unorthodox relationship Liam and I had, but I never knew it bothered her this much.

"What Lainey and I do isn't anyone's business but hers and mine!" Liam yells, and I'm certain people are watching us now. "You got that?"

I take a breath and hold it in my lungs. *One. Two. Three.* Then let it out. I thought I would feel better telling his secret. I thought the fire inside me would ignite and spring more emotions back to life. In a way, it did. More sorrow. My anger is gone and now I just feel bad for everyone.

"Liam." I step closer to him and he looks at me, his guard up, like he thinks I'll attack. I extend my arms out and his lips twitch with a sad smile. I hold him, resting my cheek against his chest, and shut out the world around us. It's nice to be in someone's arms again, but it's not the same. With Asher, my whole body tingles, and I never want to leave. With Liam, it's just a hug.

"I missed this, Lainey," he says, his voice raw with emotion.

My heart sinks into my chest because I miss us, but not this per se. "Liam." I look up into his green eyes, wondering how I ever thought they were better than Asher's. "I don't need a boyfriend or a secret lover, or anything with strings. I need a friend because I am hurt. Everything hurts and I don't know why."

I pause to gauge his reaction. His brows knit together as he processes my words and then he frowns. "Physical hurt or heart hurt?"

"Heart hurt, but it's so strong even the littlest things are hard to do." I close my eyes and press my forehead into his chest. My middle school therapist would probably call this depression. My mom would call these dramatics. Me? I call it a broken heart. A pain that one day I know I'll get over, logic tells me so, but right now it's excruciating. "I need you to be my friend again. Can you do that?"

I look up at Liam and he smiles, but his eyes are sad. He dips his head, pressing a kiss to my forehead. "Yeah, Lainey. I'm sorry. Whatever you need."

Dear Asher,

I don't know how I've managed, but I've gone three weeks without hearing your voice. Three weeks without your touch. I wish you'd write me back. I know you're getting my letters. Dad hand delivers them. At least, he says he does. Just to be sure, I mailed this one. I hope you don't get too much grief for the pink paper. I thought it might stand out. I even added blank paper for you to write me back. I wanted to include a pencil but Maggie said it could be considered a weapon.

I miss you.

Graduation was lame. I didn't walk, but I went to support Maggie. I couldn't handle the thought of everyone staring at me. People did that enough the last few weeks.

Can you tell me what things are like in jail? (Never thought I'd be asking that question lol.) Do you have your own cell?

I have to leave in a few weeks for college. It kills me. I don't want to go. Dad says your trial will start soon. I hope it's while I'm still here. I know I won't be able to hold or kiss you, but I don't care. Being in the room with you will be enough.

Please write back to me.

Forever yours,

Ellie

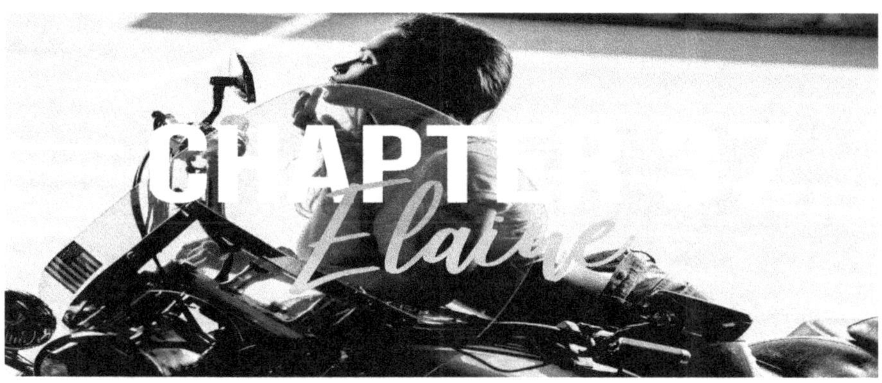

Dear Elaine,

Stop writing to me.

I do not love you.

I never loved you.

If you show up at my hearing, I'll have your dad escort you out of the building.

Leave me the fuck alone,

Asher

"You're going to be fine, kid," Jeffery Harris, my lawyer, claps his hand on my shoulder.

It's an open and shut case, or so he said ten weeks ago when this mess started. If that was true, why am I still here? Why is Mr. Walker, Ellie's dad and the state appointed prosecution, dragging this out? I never meant to kill Clint. Did I want him dead? Abso-fucking-lutely. But I never wanted to be the one to kill him. Yet, here I am because of a sick twist of fate. Story of my life, nothing ever goes the way it should.

I hold my wrists out and the guard sticks a key into my cuffs. He unlocks them and puts the aluminum shackles into a pocket on his belt. I rub the bruised skin with my wrists. I'm only cuffed for transport, but it's enough to drive me crazy. Long enough that with every twitch of my arm, they tighten. I don't mean to move, to make things harder, but I can't stop shaking.

I'm nervous.

I don't want to spend my life behind bars, away from Ellie, but it's a possibility. A scary as fuck possibility. Mr. Harris says my emotions are a good thing. They make me relatable and show a side of me that's vulnerable. Juries like that, to see that murderers have a heart.

"It's time," Mr. Harris says. He stands and leads us down the same hallway I've walked at least once a week. We've had so many hearings, my head spins trying to remember what happened when. Hearings to record my plea. Hearings to set bail. Hearings to discuss placement after the attack on me in the courtyard that first week. Hearings to discuss my psych eval. And of course the actual trial, which has lasted three days. To me, this is the opposite of an open and shut case. This is an open and never ending story.

My cellmate, Killian, says I'm lucky. His charges took over a year to work through and he's been sentenced to twelve years. Even if my mess wasn't about to end with the possibility of freedom, he'd be leaving me. County jails won't keep you if you've been sentenced to more than a year. His transport is set for Tuesday. As much as I want to be out of my cell, I don't want to leave before him. Before getting the chance to say goodbye.

Killian has been a godsend. An unexpected protector from my side of the tracks. Mr. Harris explicitly warned me not to get in any fights, which put me in a shitty situation on more than one occasion. If not for Killian, I'd probably be dead or someone's prison bitch.

Killian says I won't owe anything for the protection. I remind him of his son, so he says. Besides being my guardian angel behind bars, he was a distraction. Listening to his stories helped keep my mind off of Ellie.

I hate myself for breaking her heart, but I know Ellie. She's the type of girl to put her own needs aside to be there for the people she cares about. I don't want Ellie throwing her life away, waiting for me. There's still a chance I'll be found guilty. A terrifying possibility that I'll spend my entire life, or close to it, behind bars.

I can't risk it.

I have to do what is best for Ellie, even though it kills me.

Mr. Harris and I walk down the hallway to meet my fate. Our shoes squeak against the linoleum. His, fancy Dockers. Mine, state issued loafers. White walls only make the fluorescent lights brighter. And then there's the air, so cold it makes you shiver. Thank fuck the cuffs are off, or I'd have lost circulation.

Today's bailiff opens an oak door and guides Mr. Harris and I to our side of the courtroom. There's no crowd anxiously awaiting the verdict. No news crew here to report the story they once spun as tragic and heartbreaking. Most importantly, there is no El. She hasn't been to one day of trial hearings. It's what I wanted, for her to go to college and forget about me, but that doesn't mean I don't hold on to a sliver of hope that she'll show up. Especially today.

"Please rise," the bailiff announces.

Judge Parker has presided over my case since day one. Mr. Harris says he's fair and understanding, and that we were lucky. From what I can't tell, he's expressionless.

"Mr. Anderson," Judge Parker says, his voice commanding the room. "You have found yourself in an unfortunate position. To come home and interrupt the murder of your mother is..." Judge Parker shakes his head. "Nothing shy of tragic."

I refrain from looking down at my hands. I don't like thinking about Mom and how I should have been there. If I had come home sooner, like I originally planned before Officer Harris got me that hotel room, I could have stopped this. I knew Clint was an unstable prick, and I still left. Killing Clint may have been an accident, but it's my fault Mom is dead.

The judge folds his hands over his podium and says, "I'm very happy to announce that you, Asher Anderson, are hereby found not guilty."

"Asher," Mr. Walker says with a grin. He holds his hand out for me to shake it, then changes his mind and pulls me into a hug.

"I didn't think we'd get self-defense."

Mr. Walker chuckles and rests his hands on my shoulders. He pulls back and looks me dead in the eye, still smiling. "What can I say, kid? I'm that good. Besides, Jeff and I agreed that no one could argue reasonable doubt for this one."

He runs a hand through my hair, like I'm six years old again. The sentiment is nice, but then I remember I'm essentially an orphan. My mom is dead and my dad wants nothing to do with me. My house has probably been ransacked, or worse foreclosed on, because I doubt our slum lord will be understanding. The realization that I have nothing and no one hits me like a sledgehammer to the nuts.

"Asher?" Mr. Walker sounds worried and I wonder if I've got a look or something. "You've got to go back with the bailiff for processing, but I'll be there to pick you up."

"Thank you. I appreciate it." I don't know how long the exit process takes. I hadn't even begun to think about it or how I'd get home, let alone where my bike is. Knowing Ellie, she probably moved it from the school grounds but the question is, where? I can't call her; I doubt she'd even talk to me.

Had I known I was only going to be in here a few weeks, I wouldn't have pushed Ellie away. I want to get her back, but I don't know if that's possible. Hell, I don't even know where I'll live after this.

"For a kid who's just got his life back," Mr. Harris says with a grin, "I thought you'd be happier."

I look over to him but can't bring myself to smile. "I am. I'm just worried."

"About what?"

"About what happens next. I have no home, no money. Nothing. I can't even go to college because classes have already started and I'm pretty sure I've lost my scholarship."

"Your scholarship is intact," Derek Heiter says from behind me. He holds his hand out to Mr. Harris and shakes it. "Thanks, Jeff. I owe you one."

"I didn't do this for free, asshole." Mr. Harris scoffs.

All three men laugh and I feel like an outsider trapped in an inside joke. "What are you doing here?"

"Kid." Mr. Walker claps me on the back. "You two have some catching up to do." He turns to Mr. Harris and says, "Want to grab a drink, Jeff?"

"Can't. Hunter's first birthday dinner is tonight." Mr. Harris smiles proudly.

"I can't believe Logan's kid is that big already," Mr. Walker says as they leave the courtroom together.

"We need to talk, son," Derek says.

"You're my sperm donor, not my father. Don't call me son." The bailiff walks over to us. "I've got to go."

CHAPTER 39

"Here," Mr. Walker says, handing me a plastic bag with a new set of clothes in it. "I figured you might not want to wear those."

I left the jail with what I came in with. A dead cellphone that's been shut off. A brown wallet with thirty-six dollars in it. Black lace up boots. And blood-splattered clothes. My pants aren't bad, only a speck here and there, but my button-down has seen better days. I reach into the plastic bag and grab the black t-shirt. "Thanks."

Mr. Harris claps his hand on my back and squeezes my shoulder. "You're gonna be alright, kid."

I force a smile, wishing I could believe him. I have no job. No money. Nowhere to live. School started a few days ago, which means I missed registration and everything required to secure the scholarship I busted my ass for. Basically, I'm fucked. "If you say so."

He chuckles and unlocks his Mercedes CLS with his key fob. I climb inside, and silently gawk at the car's beauty. I haven't been in a fancy vehicle like this since I was a kid. On my side of the tracks, the cars are old because that's what we can afford. Shit that has no payments and something wrong. Unless you're one of Micklovich Romanov's low-life dealers; they drive the black Nissan 350Zs that loiter on our side of town.

The drive to the Walker house passes quickly. I look out the window with new eyes, watching in awe how freely people move about. The ability to go where you want, when you want is a privilege everyone takes for granted. You don't realize how much freedom you have until it's taken away. We pull into the Walkers' driveway and there's a car in front of the garage I don't recognize.

My stomach churns with excitement and worry. I hope it's Ellie, that she got a new car for graduation and has come home to meet me. Surly her dad would have told her I'm free. Once I get some money, I'm going to see her and apologize. That conversation needs to happen in person, rather than over the phone, but at the moment I don't have a pot to piss in. However, her being here means I have a chance and haven't screwed everything up.

I climb out of Mr. Walker's car, purposely slowing my movements so as not to seem too anxious. When we walk into the house, my heart drops. Ellie isn't here.

Derek is.

Susan, Ellie's mom, blows on a party horn. The kind people have when they ring in the new year. Her other hand shoots into the air and draws my attention to a Welcome Home banner. This isn't my home, but I appreciate the gesture. I doubt party stores make *You're Out of Jail* decorations.

Derek stands, one hand in his pocket, the other holding a glass of what looks to be scotch or whiskey in the other. "Asher."

"Come on, kid." Mr. Walker walks in front of me, towards the display of food Susan has set out on the counter. "We have some things to discuss."

I follow because I'm grateful for everything Mr. Walker has done for me, but inform them, "I have nothing to say to him."

"Don't be like that," Derek states, hurt seeping into his tone.

"You can cut the act, Dad," I reply, and he chuckles at the name. "Just because Mom died doesn't mean you have to jump into the caring parent role. I've gone eighteen years without you. I don't need you now."

"Asher," Susan says empathetically.

Derek holds up a hand, silencing her. Susan's lips stretch into a tight smile and she nods. "I get it. I wasn't there physically when it counted, but I did everything your mother asked me to. I even went to all of your football games."

"Because Liam was there," I interject.

Derek huffs through his nose, knowing I'm right. He can't claim to have been at those games for my benefit. "I made sure you had a good education. I paid the child support every month."

That makes my blood boil. Mom and I lived in poverty, both having to work to pay the bills. Even going as far as paying Clint his bullshit rent. I paid for the electricity and the water because Mom's salary barely covered the rent. As for food, we had to fend for ourselves. "Bullshit. You never gave us a dime."

Derek holds a manila folder out for me. I snatch it from his hands. The papers inside are gibberish. They look like bank statements, in an account with my name on it, but I don't have a bank account. What's even more confusing, the balance in the account is over a hundred thousand dollars. "What the fuck is this?"

"Your graduation present from your mother," Derek says with a smile. "I gave Mary Anne five hundred dollars a month since the day you were born."

"You what?" It's hard to wrap my brain around this kind of money. Mom should have used it to fix up the house, not hide it in a secret bank account.

"Mary Anne had a bad feeling about Clint from day one. She was worried he'd find out about the money and piss it away." Derek pauses to make sure I'm following. I am, but not at the same time. "We decided to make a joint account, one with my name on it and yours, so that Clint wouldn't see the bank statements."

"Asher." Susan beams. "This means you can go to college and not have to worry about anything."

I look from Derek to Susan, mouth slack, still processing. Derek chortles and claps his hand on my shoulder. "I wasn't there like I should have been and I'm sorry, but that was what Rayna and Mary Anne agreed to."

I shake free of his hold, pissed that he's trying to pull the apologetic parent card. "How could you let Mom hide this kind of cash? We needed it!"

"No." Derek's tone hardens. "I told Mary Anne if she needed anything I was a phone call away. I may be married to Rayna, but I loved your mother. She chose to refuse my help, no matter how often I offered."

"You're lying! You never cared about Mom. If you did, you wouldn't have abandoned her or me!"

"Asher," Mr. Walker says, sternly. "I have the custody agreement if you want to see it. Derek's involvement in your life was spelled out to the T. As long as you and Liam were under that age of eighteen, Derek could not reach out to you."

"I don't want your money." I toss the file folder onto the counter.

"Want it or not, you need it. And me," Derek insists. "I am the only family you have, son, and the reason you can still go to college this semester. I enrolled you in online classes and have been turning in your assignments so they wouldn't drop you. As for your football training, the coach and I are friends. He expects you bright and early in his office Monday morning. Without me, you'd have nothing. I don't expect us to be buddy buddy, but I'd like a chance to redeem myself. What do you say?"

I want to tell him no, but he's right. I need this money. "Fine, but I'm not staying at your house tonight."

Derek chuckles and smirks. "I didn't think you would."

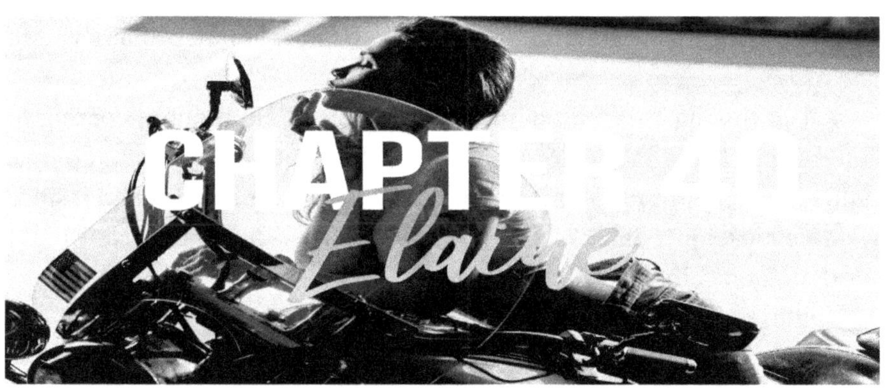

I see him leaning against an oak tree across campus. Long, denim clad legs crossed at the ankles. Hands tucked partway into his pockets. I blink twice, wondering why is my mind still doing this to me? I thought I was over seeing Asher everywhere. His face plagues my dreams, a constant reminder of how he's rotting behind bars because of me.

I thought the ghosts of Asher's memory had finally moved on and was letting me have peace, if only while awake. I hadn't seen Asher in weeks. Not that I ever actually saw him. Usually, my heart raced at the sight of fair skin or dark hair, torturing me with hope. Occasionally, my mind would even show me a flicker of a broken memory, making me question my sanity.

I never told anyone I was hallucinating, drawing conclusions, and essentially driving myself crazy. Mom would have freaked and sent me back to my childhood shrink. Maggie would have scolded me that my feelings were irrational. She still thinks you can't fall in love in six weeks. I want to agree with her. The logical part of me says she's right, but my stupid heart doesn't listen to reason. It still aches for Asher, even with Liam by my side again.

The apparition lifts his head and looks straight at me, a frown tugging at his lips. I shudder. It's too real this time. The man, who is now moving towards us, looks too good to be true. I bite my lip and train my gaze to my feet. My mind is a cruel mistress. Today she teases me. Tonight she'll taunt me. And tomorrow, she'll do it all over again.

Liam wraps his arm around me and rubs my shoulder. "Lainey? Are you okay"

All of this has been an adjustment for Liam. He thought coming to college, and living in the dorms, would pull me out of my funk. It didn't. Asher has a part of me I can't find again. In truth, I think he's had it since we were kids. I just never realized that something was missing. Now that I do, there's no going back to who I was before.

"Ellie?"

I bite my lip, tears filling my eyes. This is a new form of torture. I've never imagined Asher's voice before, but it seems like my mind hasn't forgotten. It's so beautiful it hurts.

"I..." I shift out from underneath Liam's hold. I can't do this, break down in public again. I'm ruining Liam's college experience. He's too focused on me and making sure I'm alright to party or date or do anything besides go to class. It's been nice, considering Maggie got that last-minute acceptance letter to Berkley, but sometimes I want to be alone. "I've got to go."

I quicken my pace but stop in my tracks when I hear, "Ellie, wait!"

A cold hand touches my wrist and I shudder. Liam doesn't call me Ellie. He doesn't feel like this. My hallucinations don't feel like this, so real. I turn towards the hand touching me and my head spins.

"Asher," I whisper, not sure if I said the words aloud or in my head.

He smiles, those perfect lips lifting in the corners. I remember what they felt like against mine, the blaze that engulfed me from the inside out. That same fire spreads through my veins, starting at my wrist until it consumes every inch of me. I look at the amethyst eyes before me, in shock.

He's here.

Asher is here.

I thought the day I'd see Asher again I'd be filled with emotions. If I love him, like I think I do, I should be throwing myself into his arms, crying tears of joy, running my hands over every inch of his body while kissing him into oblivion. I should have butterflies or fireworks or something resembling excitement.

I have crickets.

And the only thing I feel is fear.

"Ellie," he says hesitantly, "it's me. Asher."

"What…"

Asher is here, and he's real, and he wants to talk. Why does he want to talk? He said enough the last time I saw him at the jail, and he put the nail in the coffin with that letter. I don't think I can handle it if this is some weird *I forgive you* bullshit like alcoholics do when they're in recovery.

"What do you want?"

"Can we talk?" He looks at Liam, anger, confusion, and disappointment spreading across his face. Believe me, no one was more surprised than I was at Liam's one-eighty in behavior. He dropped the asshole act and became the friend he was before high school ruined us. "In private?"

I shake my head and pull my hand out of Asher's grasp. I clutch my wrist to my chest, still feeling the burn under my skin from his touch.

Asher sighs, shoulders falling forward as his gaze meets the ground. A fraction of a second later, he looks me in the eye again. "I'm sorry. I pushed you away, but I didn't know what was going to happen to me. I didn't know how long I'd be in there and it wasn't fair for you to wait, because I knew you would. I knew that you wouldn't move on if you didn't one hundred percent believe that I didn't love you, but I do. Oh god, I do. I thought about you every minute of every day. And if I'm too late, I understand. If all I get with you are those six weeks with you back in high school, then so be it. I wouldn't trade them for the world because it wasn't fake. None of it was fake to me, Ellie."

It wasn't… he didn't…Oh my God!

"Asher…I…"

"It's okay." Asher cuts me off. He takes my hand and brings my palm to his lips. Everything hits me at once, the butterflies, the uncontrollable need to touch him, and most importantly the unexpected feeling of being whole again. The heavy blanket that had wrapped itself around my soul lifts and I can take a full breath for the first time in months.

Asher's mouth leaves my skin, but I can't stop staring at my palm. I didn't know there were so many neurons in such a tiny space. Each one is firing off, sending jolts of electricity up my arm. "I just needed you to know that I love you. I couldn't live another day knowing you thought I used you." He pauses and looks behind me. "Does he make you happy?"

I snap back to the moment with almost painful volition. I blink twice, trying to figure out how Asher could think I've moved on. You don't just move on from how I feel. These kinds of emotions wrap around your soul. They either make you a better version of yourself or they break you. There's no in-between. Until now, they've broken me. "Who?"

"Liam." Asher tilts his chin up. "Does he make you happy?"

The thought of Liam and I together is comical. The things I felt for him senior year pales in comparison to how I feel for Asher. I think I clung to Liam because he was my first everything. What he and I had wasn't love, it was lust dipped in unrealistic expectations and an unwillingness to let go. Asher opened my eyes and I'll never close them again. "Liam and I aren't together"

"You're not?"

"No." I laugh. I don't know what's funnier, the relief on Asher's face or that he thought I'd run back into Liam's arms. For better or for worse, I'm not the same girl I was senior year. "We're friends. Just friends. No benefits. No secrets. Real, platonic friends."

Asher smiles and my heart soars. I never thought I'd see it again. "Are you…" He runs a hand through his hair. Tapered on the sides and long on top. It's different, but a good difference. "Are you dating anyone else?"

I shake my head.

"So…would you…um." Seeing Asher nervous makes my heart spin. He was always so confident. Collected. But this is nice too. "Would you like to do dinner with me tonight?"

"Yeah. I'd like that."

I sit at the edge of my couch, the tip of my black peep-toe wedges tap, tap, tapping. My thumbnail has found its way into my mouth, a chip of nail polish bitter against my tongue. I spit it out and reach for my phone again.

6:59.

Asher is supposed to be here in one—

Knock. Knock. Knock.

I suck in a deep breath and struggle to release the air. My hand shakes as it reaches for the doorknob. I don't know if any of this is real. Seeing Asher at school. Agreeing to dinner, which may or may not be a date. There is a chance I imagined the whole conversation and Liam is on his way over for a movie. If that's the case, I'm severely overdressed.

"Wow," Asher whispers when I open the door, his eyes trailing down to my feet then up again. "You look stunning."

I smile, my checks heating at the relief he's actually here, and say, "Thanks, so do you."

Asher looks good enough to eat in his navy blue slacks and white button down shirt. Jail hasn't altered his appearance at all, which makes me happy. I don't know what I expected him to look like when he got out, but I'm glad he's the same, handsome Asher I fell for in high school. He extends a bouquet of white daisies and I thank him again.

"Are you ready?"

"Just a sec." I run back into my dorm room and set the flowers on my desk, then grab my purse. I was lucky to get a single room this year. Liam is bunked with two other guys, but he doesn't seem to mind it too much. "Okay, I'm ready. Where are we going?"

Asher takes my hand and that familiar tingle I've longed to feel springs to life. He lifts my palm to his lips, pressing his mouth to my skin and my heart skips a beat. "It's a surprise."

Twenty minutes later we're pulling into a hotel parking lot. We took my car because riding on the back of Asher's motorcycle in a dress—with my legs spread, hugged tight against his body—it feels too intimate.

I frown and look down at my hands, remembering the night that was stolen from me and the things we never got to do.

My door opens. I look up at Asher, forcing a smile, but he can see right through me. "What's wrong?"

"Nothing." I take his outstretched hand and allow him to help me to my feet. "Just remembering."

Asher's lips turn down and a small line appears between his brows. He brushes a lock of hair—that was already in place—behind my ear and I lean into his hand. "I'm too late. Aren't I?"

I look down at his lips, trying to remember what they felt like against mine. I know they were the best I'd ever kissed, but why? Why did they keep me up at night, haunting my dreams with empty promises of pleasure?

I tried to replace Asher in my heart at a summer party with a guy I barely knew once. It sounds silly, now, but at the time it seemed like a good idea. I wanted to feel something, anything besides numb, but it was like kissing a fish. Adding insult to injury, I dreamed of Asher that night, feeling more in the sleeping world than I did in the waking.

Right now, though, I feel more emotions than I have in weeks.

Nervous needles trail down my spine, twisting my stomach into knots. Asher glances at my mouth, then meets my gaze again. I freeze, caught between wanting to answer him and needing to know what his mouth feels like again.

I lean back against my car when Asher steps closer. The cold metal against the open back of my dress makes me gasp.

Asher reaches for my hand and threads his fingers with mine. He lifts my palm to his mouth again, and I snap. I grab him by the back of the neck and pull him to me. Our mouths crash together, lips parting with such fierceness, our teeth clack. His tongue sweeps into my mouth and every feeling I'd longed to find again comes rushing back.

Asher's hands grip my thighs, lifting me, and I wrap my legs around him. He breaks away from our kiss and moves his lips to my neck. I arch my back and groan, "Asher," when he sinks his teeth into my shoulder.

He pulls back again to look into my eyes. I'm panting, shocked at how close I was to climaxing from a simple kiss.

"I missed you so much it hurts, Ellie." Asher's head falls, forehead meeting mine. He closes his eyes and takes a slow, steady breath.

I cradle his cheeks with my hands, feeling my pulse everywhere and say, "I dreamt of you, every night, Asher. I would wake up just as heartbroken as the day they took you away, desperate to fall asleep again because there I could hold you." I press my mouth to his for a fraction of a second. "Kiss you." My legs squeeze him tighter. "Feel you."

His hands dig into my thighs and that burning pressure builds inside me again. I bite the corner of my lip and he chuckles.

"I dreamed of you too."

A new emotion hits me, relief, and it's so strong it brings tears to my eyes. I sniffle, refusing to let a single tear fall, and ask, "What's the plan tonight? I know you better than to think you brought me to a hotel for sex without buying me dinner first."

That last bit was a joke. Although, If I'm being completely honest with myself, I wouldn't mind. A lifetime ago, he promised me an orgasm and has yet to deliver. My cheeks heat at the thought and he smiles, seeming to be thinking the same thing.

Asher lets my legs go and I stand, leaning against the car again. He takes my hand and we stroll across the parking lot towards the entrance of the hotel. "I rented the ballroom, thought I could make up for prom." He stops walking, a frown falling across his face. "I never thought to ask. Did you go?"

I shake my head. "No. I could barely stand to look in the mirror, let alone face the senior class at that point."

He smiles again, only this time it looks sad. He takes my other hand, facing me. "I couldn't let you go to jail, Ellie. I know I didn't handle that mess the best, but I was trying to protect you."

"I know," I say, tears welling in my eyes. I wipe them away with my thumb before they can ruin my makeup. *Damn it. I said I wouldn't cry.*

"Aw, shit." Asher pulls me into a hug. His strong arms wrap around me and I've never felt more at home. I love the way he kisses, but this... I missed this more than I can describe. "I'm fucking this up, aren't I?"

I shake my head and look up into those perfect, purple eyes. "No. This is perfect." I rise on my toes and press a chaste kiss to his lips. "We should go. I had big plans for tonight, and someone owes me a mind-blowing orgasm."

Asher chuckles and takes my hand again. "Then I guess we'd better get started."

Eight months later

"Jesus, woman." Asher huffs, moving the last of my boxes into his two-bedroom condo. "How much stuff did you cram into your dorm room?"

I roll my eyes, ignoring his faux irritation, and rip the tape off a box labeled *bedroom.* Things between Asher and I have been like a dream. We picked up right where we left off, like jail and heartbreak never happened.

I grab the stack of books in the box and walk them over to my nightstand. "I thought I'd be in that room for four years. How was I supposed to know you'd come back into my life and make my wildest dreams come true?"

"Really?" Asher arches his eyebrows and shakes his head. He sneaks up behind me and wraps his arm around my waist, pulling us onto the bed. I squeal, falling on top of him, and then roll onto my side. Asher pushes the hair out of my face and smiles. "Is that all you dreamed about? Crappy take-out and mind-blowing sex?"

I bite my lip and shrug. "I'm nineteen. What else should I be thinking about?"

Asher looks at me with an intensity that makes me shiver. That worry line appears between his brows again and my stomach twists. I push up onto my elbow and ask, "What's wrong?"

He blows out a breath then climbs out of bed. He walks out of the room, without a word, leaving me to wonder, *What the hell just happened?*

I sit there, my heart ravaging my rib cage. My brain is racing a million miles a minute, asking questions I don't want the answer to. Are we moving too fast? Is he having second thoughts?

Asher comes back into the room a few minutes later, hands in his pockets. He stops at the edge of the bed and stares at me. I sit up fully, waiting for the ax to fall and for him to say he's changed his mind. But he just stares.

"Asher, you're scaring me," I manage to whisper. "What's wrong?"

He sits on the bed beside me and takes my hand. He's shaking. I put my other hand on top of his and wait. Finally, he says, "Marry me, El."

I blink, too stunned to speak for a second. Marry him? He wants me to marry him? I let out a laugh, relieved. "I thought you were going to tell me you weren't ready to live together."

He shakes his head and pulls a small, velvet box from his pants pocket. The air in my lungs vanishes, my chest tightening as he lifts the lid. A white gold, solitaire diamond stares at me. Waiting for an answer.

"Not right now," he insists. "But after we graduate."

"Asher," I say, breathlessly. I look up at him, happy tears welling in my eyes. "Yes."

I throw my arms around his neck and kiss him. Asher doesn't linger on my lips long before he's pulling back to slip the ring on my finger. I lean into him, resting my head on his chest. I stare at my hand, at the beautiful ring that means I'm his.

"A thousand times yes."

Also By Bailey B

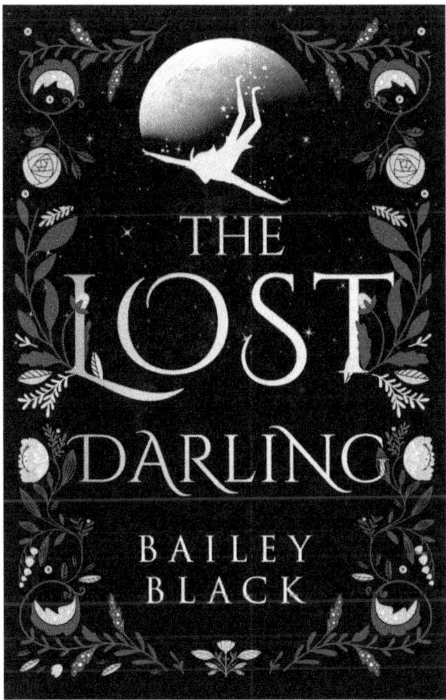

S econd star to the left and continue until morning.

I got that line tattooed on my wrist the day I turned twenty-one. So much symbolism in such a simple sentence. At the time, it was a nod to the future and the infinite possibilities to come, while reminding me to remember the past and to look for magic in the world.

Growing up, nothing was ever what it seemed. The shift of leaves on a tree was a faery skipping by. Shooting stars were a chance to make wishes. Shadows were souls stuck between this world and the next, mirroring a life they once had.

My imagination was limitless, the world a wonderful adventure waiting to unfold.

It's easy to lose that sense of wonder with the weight of life on your shoulders and I wanted a reminder to get me through the hard days.

Most importantly, it was an ode to the boy who earned the title of my first crush, even if he was animated. Peter Pan wasn't a *save the damsel* kind of prince. He was daring, and selfless, and took care of the ones he loved. He was a friend to all but never afraid to fight the Pirates when their moral compass broke. Wendy was an idiot for leaving him. She rushed home to a heartless world full of men willing to lie through their teeth to get down her pants.

But that's the beauty of a book, the characters are perfectly flawed. Damaged just enough that we still love them. Whereas reality is nothing but empty promises and baggage the size of mountains.

The day I got my tattoo I would have given anything to be whisked away into a fairytale. My world was crumbling and all I wanted was to go back to when life was simpler. I didn't realize I had sealed my fate in ink.

Branded myself as one of the Lost.

Neverland was everything the stories made it out to be. Beautiful. Full of magic. Filled with handsome men and debonair pirates. But the author of my favorite tale left out one crucial detail.

In order to get there, you have to die.

A note to the reader: this is an ADULT retelling of Peter Pan. There is sex, drinking, foul language, kidnapping, and more.

Read for Free with Kindle Unlimited

Josh

I met the girl of my dreams in a church parking lot while my best friend was having sex in my truck. Her name was Layla and she was trying her hardest to ignore me, and them, from two parking spaces over. I swear, I've never seen someone so beautiful in my life. I've also never struggled to get the girl, but for some reason my foot and my mouth became friends that night in the worst of ways. Cheesy pick up line, that failed? Check. Inability to form coherent sentences? Check. Ego crushing let down? Yup. That happened too. I can't put my finger on it, but there's something about Layla that sucks me in. I need to get to know her. Spend time with her. Make her mine. Who knows, maybe she will be the one to finally settle me down. That is, if I can convince her to give me the time of day.

Layla

Everything about Joshua Thomas screams, run away. His sharp jaw.

Those vibrant eyes. Lush lips that have probably tasted every girl in this tiny town. I know better than to give him a chance, but knowing what I should do and listening are two different things. He makes my heart flutter in ways I thought only possible in Hallmark movies. He makes my legs shake from one look. I resisted him once. I don't know if I can do it again.

R ead the Ebook free with Kindle Unlimited

I've sworn off men forever!

Okay, not forever but for a few months. After my last hook up, my vag needs a reset because the last man to touch me broke it in the worst of ways. Not a problem, until my new dance partner comes into the picture. He's turning into my forbidden fruit, tempting me in ways I didn't know possible.

I have three months of celibacy ahead of me and eight weeks to whip my new dance partner into shape.

Someone save me.

Who knows. Maybe I can win Harlow over. Maybe she will finally see me.

Being in love with your best friend sucks

Read the Ebook free with Kindle Unlimited

Piper

Most people don't think about the day they'll die. They coast through life, blissfully unaware of how their time is ticking away. I wasn't like most people. I welcomed death, wanted her to take me away from the prison I called life, but she refused. I tried twice only to survive. And then, when I thought I had nothing left it came.

A reason to live.

Rex was a small, unexpected ray of light my world of darkness that blossomed into a beam of sunshine. I thought, maybe this was why Death didn't take me. Maybe she knew that if I held on a little longer things would turn around. But the third time Death came to my door wasn't by choice. Someone else brought her, and I fear this time she might take me.

Rex

Being the son of a country star sucks. My parents are never around, I move every year or so, and I have no real friends. Everyone around me has an agenda.

Everyone except Piper Lovelace. I can't get that girl to notice me. Trust me I've tried.

Thankfully, fate stepped in and gave me the break I needed. I've got her attention, now I need her to give me a chance.

Read the Ebook free with Kindle Unlimited

I Hate You, I Love You Part 1

They say when you meet the person you're supposed to be with, time stops. Your brain takes in every micro-detail, committing it all to memory, and you're hit with this unexplainable need. A need to get to know that person, talk to that person, simply be beside that person. And then there's the kiss. A fire spreading, earth-shattering, kiss that wipes all others from your memory. I've felt that pull towards someone once, and it consumed me. But it wasn't for love, it was hate. I absolutely, without a doubt, HATE Logan Harris.

Read for Free with Kindle Unlimited

I fell in love with my next door neighbor when I was eighteen. It was fast and crazy and the best experience of my life, until I got pregnant. Logan, he pushed me away when I needed him most. Without his support, I made the hardest decision of my life and then I left. I ran away to start over with no plans of looking back. Only now I have to go back. My dad is about to marry his mom and it's just a matter of time until my secret comes out. When it does, everyone is going to hate me.

I Love You I hate you is the second book in the Duology. If you have not read Part I, please do so first.

Read both parts for Free with Kindle Unlimited

ABOUT THE AUTHOR

Bailey B is an up and coming New Adult author. She lives in Lehigh Acres Florida with her husband, twin girls, and two fur babies. She enjoys (but doesn't get to take part in because of her crazy daughters) the simple things like Disney+ binge watching, Netflix romcoms, reading and sleeping. She reads two to three books a week and thinks if narwhal's are real animals then unicorns might be too.